Kilchii

J W Throgmorton

Gunsmoke Publishing · Bradenton, Florida

ISBN 13: 978 - 0615825090
ISBN 10: 0615825095

DISCLAIMER

This novel is a work of fiction. Names, characters, places, and incidents either are the product of the author's imagination, or are used fictitiously. Any resemblance to actual persons, living or dead, events, or locales is entirely coincidental.

DEDICATION

Without the blessing, and patience of my bride, DJ, this book would never have happened. Big thanks to my son Jade. Without his artwork, you might not have looked at much less decided to purchase this book. Then, there is Deb Myers, fan, and beta reader.

Other Books by this author:

Duncan at Green River

Talon's Debt

Visit the author's webpage:

www.jwthrogmorton.com

Chapter 1

In the shade of the tall pines that grow along the river banks above four-thousand-feet in the White Rock Mountains, rode two-Mescalero Apache warriors. The spring morning was warm. They wore only long deerskin breech-cloths and high moccasins tied below their knees. A gentle breeze ruffled through their shoulder-length black manes tied in place with strips of leather. Except for the occasional white scar, which testified to youthful misadventures, their sinewy torsos were the color of oiled leather.

The warriors sought a location for their clan to live during the hot Arizona summer. Before long, their band would move higher up in the mountains, where the days would be cooler, and the game plentiful.

"Brother, look there," said Bidzil, brother of Mosi, who is the wife to Sani, their clan's leader.

Sani, the smaller of the two men, looked in the direction Bidzil pointed. In the distance, he saw black dots—too many to count. He recognized them as vultures as they glided in spiral circles up and down the thermals rising from the desert.

Bidzil asked, "Have you ever seen so many at one time, Brother?

"I have not," said Sani, "truly a large beast has died to attract such a number."

"Is it near where we hope to make our summer camp?"

"We will soon know," said Sani.

Skillful heels to their horse's flanks; they urged them onward. They followed the sinuous river northward. Finally, a horrific, nearly palpable odor told them they were close. Around a bend, they came upon the carnage that beckoned the vultures. Three wagons, the kind used by white settlers, formed a semicircle against the river. Their canvas covers peeled back to reveal wooden bows that resembled the exposed ribs of a great buffalo.

Livestock was gone; clothes and broken furniture strewn about as if erupted from the wagons. A dozen bodies lay where they fell on the ground. Vultures landed and like sentries, they formed a loose line around the gore. Impatiently, their fuzzy blood-red heads bobbed. They hissed and grunted as they fixated on the coyotes' feasting and waited for their turn. The dead were not Apache, so Sani and Bidzil saw no need to prevent nature's consumption of the dead.

A late arriving prairie wolf[1] rushed to an unclaimed corpse of a woman and began to gnaw at her flesh. Teeth deep, it tugged to tear a hunk of meat from the body—a baby cried.

Instinct influenced Sani. He vaulted from his pony, waved his arms, and hollered as he ran to the body. Startled, the coyotes retreated to the outskirts of the camp, and the vultures took flight. Kneeling by the corpse, he turned the near naked woman over. To her breast, she clutched in her right arm a young child, who began to squall. In her left arm, she clutched a decorative wooden box.

He gently lifted the child from the dead woman's bosom, and cradled it in the crook of his arm. From a gourd-canteen hung from a leather strap around his neck, he dribbled water on to the baby's parched lips. It ceased to cry and thirstily smacked its lips at the stream of water. Sani carried the child to his horse.

---

[1] Coyote.

From a fringed saddlebag decorated with bone and colored beads, he removed a piece of agave[2] cake. He took a bite of the sweet concoction and began to chew. When it reduced to a soft paste, he removed the chaw from his mouth, and with his finger fed it to the baby. With the first morsel of food, the infant seized Sani's finger, and while the child ate, it looked at Sani with trusting eyes. "You are strong," said Sani, "that is good."

With water and food in its belly, the exhausted child drifted off to sleep. Bidzil held the infant while Sani returned to its mother's body. The box she held must also have been important to her to protect its contents even in death. He retrieved the box. Inside, aside from a square of tin painted with the likeness of the dead woman, a man, and a child, he saw no items of value. However, it was the child's heritage, so he closed the lid and placed it in his saddlebags. Then, he fashioned a carry sling for the infant and mounted his pony. Bidzil passed him the child, and they walked their ponies through the camp. They paused here and there to read sign and examine the bodies.

Sani pointed to the many imprints on the ground. "All the horses have the white man's metal on their hoofs."

"Most died from bullet wounds—none of the people[3] own guns," said Bidzil, "and all their scalps remain. The few arrows present are from the Comanche[4]."

"Comancheros," said Sani. His words ended the conversation. He turned his pony south back toward their clan and let the coyotes and vultures perform their tasks as nature designed.

****

---

[2] The hearts of the Agave or mescal plant were roasted in cooking pits and made into cakes for later consumption.

[3] The name the Apache use to refer to themselves.

[4] Indian people native to the Texas plains. Texas Rangers originally formed to fight against the Comanche.

The people turned to look at them as they rode into the camp. They seemed surprised to see them return so soon. Sani and Bidzil smiled and nodded or waved, and the Nde[5] returned their salutations. In front of his wickiup[6], Sani swung his leg over the horse's neck and slid to the ground. The jolt on landing woke the child, and it began to cry. The people quickly gathered around Sani and his noisy bundle. Mosi, his wife, pushed through the crowd, when she saw Sani, she asked, "What have you brought, husband?"

Sani passed the clamorous bundle to his wife, who wrinkled her nose. "It is not only noisy, but it is wet and smelly." Mosi laid the child on the ground and removed it from the sling. The child wore a badly soiled off-white gown. She picked the baby up. "We will talk later," she said. Followed by the other women, she carried the baby off for a bath and a change of clothes.

The men from the clan asked, "Tell us, Brothers, where did you find the white child?

"Along the Salt River," said Sani. "Comancheros killed three families of white settlers—if not for the baby's mother it would also be dead."

Another asked, "Is it near where we will have our summer camp

"No—less than a long day's ride from here. We go out again tomorrow to search for a place for our summer camp. I will make sure to keep far to the north."

"That will be good." Agreed one and others nodded.

Mosi returned with the child and interrupted their talk. "Husband, I would speak with you about your son."

Sani's jaw dropped, and his eyes glazed with confusion. He turned to Mosi and asked, "Son?"

The other men began to laugh and slapped Sani on the back and shoulders.

---

[5] The formal name the Apache use when referring to themselves.

[6] Domed structure built of wood and covered with grass or hides.

"I am now an uncle, that is good," said Bidzil. "You and my sister have waited too long for children. The boy is a gift from Ussen[7]—be thankful."

Sani followed Mosi into their wickiup. Freshly bathed, the boy's long fine hair cast a hue of red, a sharp contrast to the other Apache children's raven-black hair from birth. Dressed in fresh clothes and moccasins, the child laid on a blanket sound asleep. "I have decided that we shall raise the boy," she said. "He is of the age, and it is spring. You shall send for the Di-yin[8] to cut his hair." She did not allow him to respond. She changed the subject, and asked, "Have you selected our summer camp?"

Sani smiled, no longer surprised by her decision. They'd been married for nearly ten-seasons and remained child-less. He recognized that the boy filled the hole in Mosi's heart and would cease the desire that shown in her eyes as she watched the children of the clan play. The boy may not be of her womb, but he knew she could not be more proud.

"Not yet, Wife, the boy interrupted our trip. I shall set out again tomorrow and will return in four days—if all goes well."

---

[7] The Apache word for God.

[8] Spiritual leader.

Chapter 2

Twenty-years later ....

It was a peaceful spot to camp. Off the trail among boulders next to a rapid stream that carried cold clear water from somewhere high above, the redheaded young man napped. His eyes snapped opened flashed an emerald green, as he instinctively sensed danger. He leapt to his feet, grabbed his Henry on the way up, and levered a round. Too late—the blackness swallowed him—then slowly the darkness lightened and became a shadowy void, and his mind floated back to when he lived with the Mescalero Apache.

****

Stars sparkled brightly against the moonless blue-black of the cloudless night sky. To warm themselves against the cool mountain air, the clan sat around campfires in front of their hide covered wickiups. Seasoned with sage and other wild herbs, the smell of venison and elk, roasted over the open flames permeated throughout the village. Seated at Sani and Mosi's fire, were their extended families there for celebration. He sat between Sani, his father, and Bidzil, his mother's brother. Tonight's ceremony marked his passage into young adulthood.

Sani, the clan's leader, stood and faced his son. The campfire flickered to make his serious expression appear solemn, but when he spoke, his voice held elation. "My Son, it has been nine-seasons since Ussen[9] sent you to our wick-iup. You have learned well the way of the people. Your mother takes great pride in the obedience and respect you give to your elders. You are ten-summers now, and it is time to take a name."

The boy glanced at his mother then back to his father; his mind filled with anticipation.

Sani continued. "Your hair is the color of rusted iron; your skin is spotted like a bobcat, and turns red when licked by the sun, so you will be called—Kilchii—Red Boy. Guard your name well, as it is sacred."

Bidzil, the hulk of the clan, placed his huge right hand on Kilchii's head. He playfully mussed his hair, and said, "The name fits you well—Kilchii."

He looked up at his uncle's dark eyes and toothy grin and laughed. "Likewise your name, 'The Strong One,' suits you, Uncle."

Kilchii rose as did his mother, and she embraced her son. She then held him at arm's length, and he saw a single tear spill from her eye as she looked at him and pronounced his name, "Kilchii."

When she released him, he walked around the fire. He made eye contact with each guest. His chest swollen with self-importance, he made his voice deeper, and said, "It is a good name, Father, and I will guard it well.

---

[9] Apache name for God.

The celebration continued, and Kilchii, for the first time, sat with the men. Mosi and the other women served them sweet cakes, meat, and a tea made from herbs. When the hour grew late, Kilchii began to yawn and rubbed his eyes to ward off sleep. Sani saw that his son tired, so he also yawned and turned to Kilchii. "It is late and we should rest for tomorrow.

They rose early for a hunting trip with the men of the clan. Ready to leave their wickiup[10], Sani paused next to his son and squeezed his shoulder. "Come. We join the others and will see what Ussen offers for our hunt."

At the edge of the village, the men of his clan grouped to discuss their final plans for the hunt. Each man spoke in turn. Their breaths were visible in the cold mountain air, like exhaled smoke from clay tobacco pipes. Kilchii listened intently—he didn't want to miss a single detail that might cause him to make a mistake and bring disgrace on his first hunt. With duties assigned, they set out in groups to replenish their clan's meat stores. Kilchii accompanied Sani and Bidzil.

The sun burned through the mist that hung among the tall pines; Bidzil led the trio, each vigil for signs of game, as they stalked through the trees. Bidzil halted and signaled to Kilchii. He came and knelt by his uncle. "Yes, Uncle?"

"Tell me, what do you see?" Bidzil swept his arm in front of them to indicate that is where Kilchii should investigate.

Kilchii immediately saw the animal's hoof print. "I see the track of a deer."

"Is it a buck or a doe?"

"It is a doe, Uncle—I think. Yes, it is a doe. Here are the tracks of its fawn."

"That is good. What else do you see?"

"Uncle?"

---

[10] Domed structure built of wood and covered with grass or hides.

Bidzil stood and again gestured. "Look about, Nephew. What more can you learn—look closely."

Sani moved up behind Kilchii and pointed over his shoulder. "Look there."

Kilchii moved to the matted grass. "This is where they slept."

"Good, Nephew. How long have they been gone?"

The boy's brow pinched with concentration, then he understood, and he dropped to the ground and felt the earth inside the bed and then outside. "The grass is still warm—they are near."

Kilchii grinned at his father's show of pride. Sani's shoulders pulled back and his chest pushed out, and he said, "You do honor to your uncle, My Son. Your skills have grown." He slapped Bidzil on his shoulder. "It is good he learns quickly, Brother, as soon you will be too old to teach the ways of the hunter."

Bidzil returned a slap across Sani's back, and said, "You are the one named, 'The Old One', and your tooth grows longer each day as well." They all laughed at the good-natured bantering.

★★★★

The priest's sleep wasn't as guarded as the young man's and the shot, which took down his companion at the stream, startled him awake—men were on him. They pinned him before he was fully aware. Adrenalin surged, and he momentarily shook them off. As he tried to rise, a third man stomped his chest, which forced him back to the ground. Breathless, he was too weak to resist.

They dragged him, tightly bound, to the ring of rocks that contained the dying embers of the campfire. The priest renewed his struggle against the ropes, but he stopped when he saw the young man's lifeless body face down in a pool of blood. His eyes welled, and tears streaked his cheeks. Limp, they dropped him to the ground. In a voice that conveyed his anguish, he decried, "Why did you shoot the boy? We would have given you our supplies without resistance."

"Maybe you would, Priest," said their leader. "The boy had other ideas."

One of his men, an Indian, whispered to him. The leader turned to the priest. "The boy isn't Indian," said their leader. "How'd he come to act like one?"

"He lived with the Apache until he was sixteen," said the priest.

Herberto squeezed his eyes closed. Memories hurled to the forefront of his mind ... he could see the day they first rode to the mission ....

★★★★

Outside the mission's gate, a stocky man strong from years of physical toils, who dressed very much as a Mexican peasant might, tended his garden. As a youth, he discovered that the cultivation of plants provided him with great gratification. Since then, he's spent a portion of each day in his garden.

He straightened and placed his hands on his back, and stretched to relieve the ache he felt in his muscles. Relief came and he sighed, *next year I will plant a smaller garden one that requires much less work.* He removed his straw sombrero and held it high to shade his eyes. Father Herberto saw movement in the distance. Still far, three riders approached. Like mirages, they faded in and out of the heat waves that rose from the hot desert floor. They rode slowly and in the open, a sign that they were friendly.

Father Herberto's years at the mission were many. When he came to Xavier[11] twenty-plus years ago to assist the senior priest, he was still relatively young. After Father Juan's death, fifteen years later, the Santa Fe diocese made him responsible for the mission's operations. He has enjoyed the assignment, and the years have passed quickly.

Nearly thirty-minutes passed before the travelers reached the mission gate. Father Herberto, who had changed to his garments, stepped through the man-door, cut into the heavy timber and iron constructed gate, to meet his visitors. "Bienvenido," he called a welcomed in Spanish.

"¡Gracias." Sani thanked him, also in Spanish.

The priest studied the Apache's face. "It has been many seasons, but it is good to see you again, Sani."

Sani smiled. "Your memory still remains. That is good, Padre."

Herberto glanced at Sani's two companions—his eyes stopped on the boy. "What brings you to the mission after so many seasons my friend?"

"This is my wife's brother Bidzil, and this is my son Kilchii."

A direct response never came from an Apache, but Herberto was prepared to be patient. "I'm happy to meet you. Would you come into the mission where it is cooler and share our food and drink?"

They dismounted, tied their ponies under a tree near the mission's gate where there was water. Sani removed the wrapped box from Kilchii's saddlebags, and they followed the priest into the mission courtyard beyond the gate. Herberto saw that Kilchii and Sani lag behind. He smiled when he understood the gist of their conversation. The boy ask, "Father, how is it that you so freely give our true names to this man?"

---

[11] San Xavier Mission founded 1692 south of what is today Tucson, Arizona.

"Your concern is correct, My Son," said Sani, "but these men of black robes can be trusted with our names."

At the door in the gate, Kilchii halted and peered inside before he entered. Bidzil and Sani watched Kilchii exercise caution as he dealt with a new and unaccustomed place. "He does not let his curiosity blindly lead him into possible trouble," said Bidzil. "He has learned well, brother."

Kilchii placed the palm of his hand on the smooth white surface of the stuccoed adobe walls. Through the gate, the boy studied every minute detail of the inner courtyard. His gaze paused on the friars as they moved about engaged with their chores. At length, his shoulders dropped and his posture relaxed. The action reminded Herberto of the jungle cats he saw at his first posting in South America.

****

"—I wondered about his red hair," said the bandit-leader. His words returned Herberto attention to the present.

While the leader questioned the priest, his men ransacked their supplies, and discovered the priest's bible with hand written papers stashed between the pages. They brought the book and papers to their leader, who sorted through them. He found a letter, which he opened and read. He halted when he got to, 'Father Herberto, your awaited donation of silver and gold will greatly help our order's work.' The leader raised his face from the letter to look at the priest. "Father Herberto, may I introduce myself? I'm Cain, and you have something that I want—where is the silver and gold?"

Herberto looked away; he thought of the day that Rory answered his summons ....

****

There was a quick knock and then his office door opened. The priest's office was dim, and heavy drapes adorned the walls to stay the evening's chill present in the desert. Herberto sat behind an ornately carved desk and wrote in his journal. Rory stuck his head into the room. "You sent for me, Padre?"

"Yes I did. We have much to discuss, come in, and take a seat."

Herberto put aside his journal and spread out a map of the territory on his desk. "The trip to Santa Fe is over 500 miles. If everything goes as planned it should be less than twenty days travel."

"When do we leave?"

"Monday next, but that isn't why I called you to my office." The priest rose and stepped to the closet door behind his desk. "Look in here, Rory. I wish for you to know why we travel to the Santa Fe Diocese." Herberto opened the door and moved back for Rory to see.

Rory leaned forward and peered over the desk into the tiny room. His eyes widened. Slacked jawed, he slowly rose from his chair. Opened on the closet floor, was a strongbox constructed from mesquite and reinforced with heavy iron straps. A padlock lay on the floor. The box contained ingots of silver and gold, and jewelry fashioned with blue turquoise gemstones.

"Padre, where did all of that come from?"

"Gifts from our parishioners—the silver and gold came to us as nuggets and over time, we melted them into ingots. We help the Navajo with their farming, and they in turn are generous with their jewelry."

"That is a great deal of treasure, Padre. Why do you show it to me?"

"It's the reason for our trip to Santa Fe. This treasure will be added to their coffers, which in time will go to Rome."

Rory's brow furrowed. "Where are the guards to protect such a treasure?"

The priest smiled. "It will be just you and me."

"But—" Rory tried to protest.

"We'll use guile, My Son. Hidden among the supplies of two pack horses, who would suspect that an old priest and a young man transported such a treasure?"

"I'm not sure this is a good idea, Padre. You understand that to reach Santa Fe, we'll have to travel through Comanchero country."

Again, he smiled at Rory's worried expression, he said, "Yes, My Son, I understand there may be danger for us, but I'm also confident that God will protect us."

Rory's shoulders relaxed and his pinched expression softened. "As you wish, Padre, but I would feel better if we had a war party along to help God with our protection." The priest shook his head at Rory's comment and put his arm across the young man's shoulder. They walked out of his office and closed the door behind them.

****

"Priest—Priest, do you hear me? Asked Cain.

Herberto's eyes blinked as his mind returned to the present. "We carry no silver or gold." He nodded toward the letter in Cain's hand, he added, "It was sent to the dioceses weeks ago under a heavy guard. It would be stupid to transport a treasure any other way."

"Why don't I believe you, Priest?" Cain's face grew sinister. "Build up the fire" he commanded. Two of his men gathered wood and stoked the embers. Soon, they had a raging fire. "You will tell me where it is hidden," said Cain

One of the vaqueros stepped in front of Cain, his hand on his pistol. "You will not harm the priest."

Without a word, Cain drew his revolver and shot the man. Hammer cocked, he turned to the rest of his men. "Anyone else want to dispute my orders?"

Herberto muttered a prayer, "Father, give me strength to endure and damn them to hell."

Chapter 3

E.B. Parker lifted his hat to better shade his eyes; he scanned the westward sky where buzzards circled. Something is dead, or soon would be, and they waited for the coyotes to find the carcasses. He spurred the gray's flanks, and the horse loped off toward the foothills the direction of the circling vultures.

The foul odor of burnt hair and flesh assaulted his nostrils he coughed and breathed shallowly through his mouth to keep from retching. At the ready, his Lang[12], from his cavalry days, rested across the front of his saddle as he slowly rode in.

Near the fire lay the body of a man tortured to death with coals from the fire. Based on the number of scorched places on his skin, he must have held on for quite a spell. Wisps of smoke drifted from the campfire; he thought, *whoever did this hasn't been gone long.* Parker's guess, based on the clothing lying nearby, was that the man must have been a priest or a monk. "I hope you've found peace with your God, Padre." He said aloud.

---

[12] Lang was an early manufacturer of the double barrel shotguns.

Near the edge of camp, he saw the crumpled body of a vaquero. He dismounted to inspect the body, it weapons had been stripped, and the marks on his boots indicated they took his spurs as well. *Silver,* he guessed. He knelt for a look at the man's face, and as he turned the body, he heard a quiet moan come from the stream behind him. Parker looked over his shoulder; someone still lived. As he rose to investigate, he looked around suspiciously. *It pays to remain on guard against an ambush.* Knelt by the body and felt for a pulse; it was weak but steady. This one would survive.

A practiced glance took in a lot of information; moccasins instead of boots, white-man's trousers and shirt, but a leather band held his red hair in place. *He's lived with Indians. The padre must have helped him get away or traded for his release, which is more likely the case.*

He turned the boy over to examine his wound. A slug had glanced off his skull, torn his scalp, and plowed an inch-long furrow in the bone. It bled a lot, but not enough to be life threatening. Parker went to his horse and returned with his medical supplies. He flushed the wound with water, pulled the skin flap into place, and stitched it closed. As he bandaged his head, the young man's eyes opened. He moaned and tried to put his hand to his head, but Parker gently pushed it away. "You're hurt bad, Son. Just lie still and let me get this dressing in place." The young man slipped back into unconsciousness.

****

Six years had passed since his first hunt with the men of his clan. Kilchii sat next to Mosi and Bidzil around their campfire. Sani stepped from the wickiup. In his hands, he carried something wrapped in an oiled cloth. He approached the group and seated himself next to his son. The boy glanced at the package. Mosi's eyes began to well, and Bidzil sat stiffer than usual. His large square shoulders pulled back, his face tilted, and he looked at nothing in the evening sky.

"Kilchii, the clan has accepted you as a warrior—an adult," said Sani. "You can live as you will subject only to clan law and their traditions."

Sani passed the package to his son and waited. Kilchii peeled back the oiled cloth to expose a wooden box with the image of a thorny rose garland wound around a cross finely carved into its lid. The box contained a black leather pouch of sorts and on its cover, a golden cross. He removed the pouch and examined it closely. The layers of the cloth like material bound between the covers were thin and fragile; almost transparent; each layer covered with symbols.

Beneath the pouch, he found folded pieces of cloth, heavier than those bound by the leather, and they also bore symbols, but these were lines of squiggles. Lastly, there were metal plates with images of a man, woman, and child.

The man clothed in tight fitting restrictive apparel appeared solemn and the woman wore a flowing dress, a hat, and chain necklace with a decorative bauble. In her arms, she held a baby dressed in a gown its head covered with a cowling of sorts. The baby seemed occupied with an ornately decorated metal disc that hung from a chain held by the man.

Kilchii held up the leather pouch, and looked to his father. "Father, I'm sorry, but I don't know what to make of this."

"Nor I, My Son," said Sani. "When I found you, your white mother's body protected you and that box. It must be important, to her at least."

Bidzil nodded. "It was as your father says."

Kilchii studied the enlarged image of the woman. She didn't smile, but she looked to be a pleasant person. The leaf-shaped bauble on her necklace was metal and held three jewels. "These images, they are of my white parents?"

Sani nodded. "It is time for you to learn of your white family. Tomorrow, your uncle and I will go south to find a suitable place for our winter camp. You will ride with us, and we'll escort you to the Spanish mission. The men who live there are good men and can tell you what those symbols mean and teach you about your white family."

****

Parker returned the young man to his bedroll near the campfire. After making him comfortable, Parker set about burying the priest and the vaquero, and then, he salvaged what was left of the looted supplies. When he finished, he moved back to the fire. The young man was awake and watched him intently. "You've been out cold for several hours. I've made some jerky broth. Do you feel well enough to eat something?"

The young man nodded and pushed himself up to lean against a nearby boulder. "My name is Rory McLeod. Father Herberto and the friars call me Rory."

"Please to meet you, Son. My name's E.B. Parker, but most folks call me Parker. My friends call me E.B."

Rory looked about the camp. "If you search for your friend," said Parker. "I buried him yonder under that scrub oak."

His eyes welled, but Rory didn't cry. "His name was Herberto Mendoza, and he was much more than my friend. Since I left the Apache—he's been like a father."

Parker glanced at Rory's moccasins. "I wondered about those. With your red hair, freckles and green eyes there was no way you could have been an Indian."

E.B. sat quietly for a spell and let Rory drink some broth, but finally, he asked, "What happened here?"

Rory took another sip from his cup before he answered, "We were on our way to Santa Fe when the Comancheros attacked us—at least I think it was them. They shot me first thing; they clearly thought I was dead."

"Why would they want to torture a priest?"

Parker noted that the young man didn't answer and decided that there was more to the story than what he understood. However, he saw no reason to force the issue, so he let it drop.

Rory sat contemplatively. At length, he asked, "Why are you here, Mr. Parker?"

"I hunt outlaws for the bounty posted on their heads. Presently, I search for a man named Robert William Cain. He leads a band of Comancheros—most likely the ones that shot you and killed your friend."

"By yourself?" asked Rory.

E.B. smiled at the boy's incredulous tone. "I'm not after the whole gang—just Cain."

"But still. Isn't that a large chore?"

"He's wanted dead or alive—alive isn't under consideration. I've got a .50 caliber Sharps that will take him out of the saddle at a safe distance. Should any of his men want to make an issue of it, I'll give them the same.

"How will you know which one is Cain?"

Again, Parker smiled and pulled from his pocket a folded piece of paper. "Aside from him leading the gang, I've got this." He unfolded it and passed it to Rory. The poster contained a crude sketch depicting the wanted man and a detailed description of his features, which included a scar on the left side of his upper chest in the shape of the number seven. E.B. closely watched Rory as he studied the poster for several minutes. He was sure Rory had committed its information to his memory.

"$5,000, dead or alive?" asked Rory.

"Like I said, I plan to collect it with him dead."

"Parker—"

"Call me E.B. I think we're likely to be friends."

"Alright, E.B., Cain is getting away while you stay here to nurse me. You head out at sunup—I'll be fine."

"I appreciate your grit, Son, but you've got a pretty bad head injury. I've seen men in the war that had them. One minute they seemed fine and the next they were dead. Cain will be in my sights again—I'll get him one day. In the meantime, I have to decide what to do about you."

****

Rory studied E.B. Parker. Parker appeared nothing like the Apache or the Spanish. He was a tall man, taller than any he had met—even Bidzil. His square jaw, rugged features, and cerulean blue eyes intrigued Rory. His dress was different too—high top black leather boots that reached his knees with his wool pant legs tucked inside. His pullover cotton shirt left unbuttoned and a bandana loosely knotted about his neck. He wore a wool lined short leather coat that left his revolver handily exposed. A Stetson stained with years of wear sat prominently on his head.

"You could take me with you," said Rory.

"Like I said, Son, you've got grit, but you'd be more problem than help." Parker scratched his stubbly chin while he considered. "I think it best if I took you to Santa Fe."

That wasn't what Rory wanted to hear. "If you won't take me with you, I'll go after Cain on foot."

"Son, grit's one thing, but bein' stupid is another. If you like, I'll just shoot you now—it'd be a lot easier on you, and I won't have to worry none about what happened to you."

Rory smiled. "Alright, you've made your point. I'll go with you to Santa Fe."

"Now that makes more sense. We'll stay here a day or two so you can mend and then head for Santa Fe."

That would do for now. In a couple of days, he'd be on his feet and then there wouldn't be a need for him to go to Santa Fe. He planned to use the time henceforth to convince E.B. Parker that taking him along to kill Cain was a good idea.

At daybreak, Rory rose before E.B. and made breakfast. E.B. awoke to the noises Rory made, but the smell of fresh coffee brought him out of his bedroll. "Hope that grub tastes as good as it smells, Son."

"I'd prefer you call me Rory. I'm not your son."

"Fair enough, Rory. I got into the habit durin' the war. I call my trooper's son—hell toward the end most of 'em weren't more than boys anyway. Anyhow, it saved me from havin' to learn their names."

"Which side?"

He paused a long time before he answered, "I spent four bloody years in the cavalry fighting for the South." E.B. Parker's eyes glazed over, and he stared off at nothing.

He's remembering the past. Rory decided to change the topic. "Do you have a family?"

E.B. looked back toward Rory and returned to the conversation. "Yes, I have a daughter—I expect she's about your age." His enthusiasm for the subject showed. "She lives in St Louis—goes to a girl's school there."

"What about her mother?"

Rory saw sadness cloud the bounty hunter's eyes. "She died near the end of the war. A fever—I expect it was cholera. Lucy got sick too, but she recovered."

Again, Rory changed the subject. "How long have you been a bounty hunter?"

"Since the war ended," said E.B. He scratched the stubble on his chin as he recalled the years. "Everythin' was lost, and I needed money quick." He chuckled. "Short of turnin' outlaw, this profession was the only way of earnin' it fast.

E.B. stopped talking and stared suspiciously at Rory. "I can't remember the last time I told this much about me to someone—let alone a stranger?"

Smiling at his comment, Rory said, "I learned to be a good listener from Father Herberto." Rory's expression grew somber with thoughts of the padre. He had come to love the priest, and he now felt the emptiness his passing left.

"Enough about me," said E.B., "you, seem like a well-educated young man. How'd you come to be out here?"

"That's a very long story."

"We've plenty of time. I'm truly curious."

Rory collected his thoughts and began at the beginning. "My white parents traveled to—" More than an hour past while Rory told his tale. "—and you found me by the stream."

"Whew. That's one hell of a story, Son—I mean, Rory."

He had left out a few details that E.B. didn't need to know, including about the treasure hidden among the rocks in the stream. Rory glanced to the rocks to confirm they remained undisturbed. It wouldn't be soon, but he planned to honor Herberto's wish and see that the wealth found its way to the Diocese in Santa Fe.

Tired, after, he'd recounted the details of his life, Rory laid back to rest. He grieved for the priest, and his thoughts returned to his early days at the mission.

****

Silent, his expression stoic, Kilchii sat cross-legged on the straight-backed chair, its purpose lost to him. He listened as the priest spoke in Apache. "Good." He placed the box and its contents in front of him. "White family—Kilchii to learn."

Kilchii sorted through the contents. He held up a portrait and studied it. Herberto leaned over and pointed to the baby's image and then at him, he said, "Kilchii."

Kilchii turned to Sani, who nodded confirmation. The boy picked up each item and carefully placed them back into the box. He left the portraits until last, he returned the lid, placed the box in his lap, and sat quietly.

Sani reverted to Spanish, so the priest and he could speak more fluently together, he asked, "The things in the box—do they say what his white parents called him?"

"His given name is Rory, and his surname is McLeod. He's the son of John and Rose McLeod."

"What does his white name mean?" asked Bidzil.

Herberto looked questioningly at Bidzil. Bidzil placed the palm of his hand to his chest and said, "Bidzil is Nde[13] for He is Strong. Sani means The Old One and Kilchii is Red Boy."

"Oh. The whites name their children differently than the Apache. Their names are given at birth and don't reflect features or personalities. The name Rory may not mean anything, but I will try to find out. How long will you stay?"

"We have been away from the clan for fifteen days and must start back tomorrow."

"Of course you will be our guests for tonight. I will have rooms made ready for you."

Sani raised his hand to halt the priest. "The nights are pleasant. We'd rather sleep under the stars than inside your caves, but we thank you for your hospitality."

Herberto smiled and said, "As you wish." He added, "The church is much changed since you were here last. Would you care to see the inside?"

Sani translated the invitation. Kilchii's eyes sparkled with eager curiosity, but outwardly, he remained composed, as was the Apache way. Sani smiled and gave a slight nod to acknowledge his approval of his son's behavior.

Being polite, Sani said, "I'm sure there is much to see and we'd be honored to visit your place of worship."

---

[13] The Apache word for Apache.

Herberto and Bidzil led the way from the courtyard through the living and administrative areas of the mission to the chapel. At the chapel doors, Herberto entered first and then stepped aside to allow his guests to follow. It was obvious to all that the priest was proud of the chapel's distinctive architectural features, the detailed carvings, the colorful frescoes, the life-size statues, and the domed roof.

Kilchii stood transfixed with visual overload. Sani and Bidzil followed and they too seemed equally mesmerized. He walked to the center of the nave[14] and slowly rotated several times to take in all that he could with each turn. After many minutes, Kilchii said, "This is the most wondrous place I have ever seen." Sani didn't translate, but Kilchii knew from the priest's smile that he understood his sentiment.

A friar came into the chapel and spoke to the priest. "My friends, food, and drink have been prepared. We can return to the chapel later if you wish, but in the meantime, please join me for a meal."

Back on the veranda, Herberto led them to a table sat for four. The repast consisted of chicken, bread, cheese, fruits and all manner of vegetables; mint tea or water to drink. Bidzil selected the chair closest to the chicken and sat. He tore off a leg from the chicken and then a chunk of bread, and began to eat before the others sat. Sani and Kilchii were not so forward and waited for the priest to take his place before they sat.

---

[14] The central area of a church.

Herberto bowed his head and prayed. Only after he finished did Sani and Kilchii take portions of the food. No wish to embarrass his guest, the priest also ate with his hands. He used a knife to cut off slices of the cheese but for no other purpose. "Please have some cheese. We make it from goat's milk." He passed pieces to his guest. He seemed amused as he watched them first smell, then nibbled the cheese.

Bidzil smiled and shoved a large bite into his mouth and mumbled, "This is good."

Sani and Kilchii didn't seem as impressed with it, but they politely consumed their pieces. Except for an apple eaten by Kilchii, Herberto's guest didn't sample further any of the additional offered unknown fare.

After their meal, Herberto, Sani, and Bidzil rested in the shade of the veranda. Herberto sent for brother Fidel to escort Kilchii and gave him permission to tour the mission and take as much time as he wished. Kilchii led off at an eager pace, he headed in the direction of the chapel.

Later, Father Herberto told him of their conversation. "Sani, tell me what is it that you desire for the boy?"

"This isn't a simple question for me to answer, my old friend." Sani sat quietly for several moments and then asked, "Did you know that there is much trouble between the Apache and the whites?" Herberto nodded, but he didn't interrupt. "There will be war. Cochise has called for the clans to come together. When Bidzil and I return, we'll lead our clan into the mountains and join Cochise."

"And you don't want Kilchii to be involved?"

"It is more than that, Padre. Yes, it is true—I do not wish for him to fight against his white parent's people. But, he is not known to the other clans, his red hair and pale speckled skin standout, and when we join with Cochise, there could be trouble." Sani paused and Herberto waited patiently for him to finish.

"Padre, I don't think the fight will go well for the Apache. I would see Kilchii learn the ways of the whites, and that he live among them as an equal. Will you be his teacher, become his uncle?"

"Has Kilchii agreed to stay with me as my student, and does he understand that it will be for a long time?"

"He has agreed to stay as long as it takes to learn the white man's ways. We haven't talked about how long that would be. Tell him many moons—there are many moons in several seasons, no?" Sani smiled, and his eyes twinkled with the humor of his joke.

The priest nodded, he understood Sani's intent. "I will do as you ask."

Kilchii, Sani, and Bidzil camped outside the mission under the tree where they'd tied their horses. He talked with his father and uncle late into the night, so the dawn, when it came, felt like it arrived too early. They joined the priest on the veranda for a breakfast of cheese, bread, and fruits. While they ate and conversed, the friars placed Kilchii's belongings in a private bedroom and took his horse to the mission stable. The priest spoke to Kilchii's father in Spanish, he explained about the boy's horse. He also explained to Sani about the historical research he'd completed on origin of Kilchii's Christian name.

Sani translated the priest's words for Kilchii, and it pleased him to know that in the far away land of the McLeod's, Rory meant Red King. Awkwardly, Sani pronounced his son's white name. "Ro—Roar—Rory." Herberto nodded.

Sani slapped his son's shoulder. "That is a good name for you, My Son; its meaning is strong medicine. You shall walk free among the Nde, the whites and the Spanish."

The courtyard grew brighter as the sun rose above the eastern horizon. Sani stared at his son with watery eyes. He rose and said, "It is time. Bidzil and I must return to the clan and begin the move to a new camp ... walk with us to our ponies."

Outside the courtyard, Kilchii locked forearms first with his uncle and then his father. Kilchii held his grip, and said, "I will study hard to learn all that you wish me to know and will return to the clan as soon as I can."

****

E.B. had unpacked his gear and had it spread out on a ground cloth[15] for inspection and maintenance. He owned a sizeable arsenal. His activity brought Rory back to the present. Rory asked, "How'd you come to possess so many weapons?"

"It's a bonus of the trade," said the bounty hunter. "When I capture a fugitive if he has a weapon, I keep it for myself, or I sell it and add the proceeds to my coffers."

"May I examine them? I've only ever used a rifle, and the Comancheros took that along with everything else."

"Before you do, let me tell you the rules of handling firearms," said E.B., and then, he went into a fifteen-minute lecture on gun safety and protocols of use.

Patiently, Rory listened as he did when Herberto or the friars were instructing him. Eventually, after explaining its operation, E.B. passed Rory a Colt revolver. "Most of them are .45 calibers. It's simpler that way—less ammunition to deal with. The exceptions are the Sharps .50 caliber rifle and the Lang—he patted the shotgun. I carry number 00 buckshot for men, and I ride with number 8 for small game. I have fresh meat to eat most days."

Rory eased a short-barreled Colt revolver and a lever action Henry lever-action rifle, like the one he'd lost, close to where he sat. "These are .44 calibers. How much would you sell these for?"

"I'd sell those for a hundred dollars—gold and I'd throw in what little ammunition I got that goes with them."

"If I worked for you until it was paid for how long would that take?"

---

[15] A piece of oiled canvas to retard moisture.

E.B. laughed. "What makes you think I want to hire you in the first place?"

Rory had to think about that. At length, he said, "I can hunt. Take care of the animals, cook, and keep the camp. Most importantly, I can scout and track man or beast. With my help you would collect your bounties sooner."

E.B. shook his head and smiled at Rory. "You're persistent—let me think about it, but in the meantime, you can go ahead and use them. There is a holster and shells in the pack."

Rory's excitement overcame his condition, and he scurried over to the canvas packs and searched for the cartridges and the leather holster. The belt was too large, so he slung it over his head and wore it bandolier style. He loaded the Henry and the Colt. Hefting the rifle an ominous expression clouded his face. In a dark voice, that conveyed deep conviction, he said, "Cain will pay for killing Father Herberto."

****

Over the next two days, Rory impressed E.B. with his talents as a cook and camp manager. E.B. didn't have to expend ammunition for game as Rory snared rabbits and birds. The bounty hunter was in his mid forties now, and the aches and pains from the last fifteen years had started to haunt him. *I like the boy. If he's serious about learning the business, then I will teach him.* "I think your health is no longer a concern," said E.B. "So tomorrow we'll light out for El Paso."

"El Paso?" Rory asked, more than a little surprised. "Why there? Cain and his men are headed west."

"If you're going to work for me then you do what I say without out argument."

"You're going to let me work with you?" E.B. nodded. "Then I have to ask questions if you expect me to learn." Again, E.B. nodded. "Then why to El Paso instead of after Cain?"

A smile slowly developed on the bounty hunter's face. "Okay, you got me there. The reason we're goin' to El Paso is that you're not ready to hunt down dangerous men. You need a horse and some decent clothes. Aw—that's enough for now." He walked over to his bedroll and stretched out for a nap.

The next morning they started east for El Paso. From the mountains, they came down onto the high desert, where the cactus and scrub became more prevalent. Rory walked along side E.B., he led the packhorse. "There is a way station up ahead we'll find you a horse there." Later in the day, they glimpsed the stagecoach way station; a white adobe structure built against a large outcropping with a corral and lean-to that provided shelter for the livestock. An hour passed, and they stood outside the front door. The station was closed up tight.

"Higgins," E.B. called. "Higgins, are you in there?"

"Is that you Parker?" A gravelly voice sounded from behind the door.

"You know it is, Higgins. Now open the damn door."

"Hold your water, I'm comin'." The sound of a heavy timber dragged across iron vibrated through the door, and then finally, the door swung open and there stood a bent old man who had neither shaved nor bathed for a long time. His toothless grin and the twinkle of his bright blue eyes conveyed his friendliness as he stuck out his hand to E.B., and asked, "How've you been?" While he still shook his hand, Higgins glanced at Rory and then back to E.B. with a question in his eyes.

"Higgins, this is Rory McLeod. He's had some difficulties with Comancheros and needs a horse and tack if you have it."

"Must've been the group that attacked here a few days back," said the old timer.

E.B. scanned the station. "You've still got your livestock and the building's no worse for the wear."

"Yeah—there were a couple of miners laid over here. They was headin' back east to find a new grubstake when the Comancheros attacked. Two of us manned the front, and one covered the horses. Once they figured out we wasn't goin' to be an easy target, they moved on. So did the miners—I've kept the place locked up just in case."

"Can you spare a horse?" E.B. asked again.

"For you, E.B., sure I can—I got tack too. Give you the whole lot for $100."

"$50—you old reprobate. You're goin' to claim the Comancheros got the horse and two-to-one the saddles didn't cost you anythin' either."

The old timer stroked his beard. "Well seein' how you're a friend and all—$50 it is." He spat in his hand and presented it to E.B., who did the same, and they shook on it.

"E.B., come on in here and I'll get you a drink."

"Son, you can go on out to the corral and pick out your horse." The old man snickered, "Mind—they ain't used to the saddle."

****

Rory, who hadn't yet said a word, nodded and left the two men while he went to inspect the horses. He climbed up, and sat on a rail to observe the animals. After several minutes, he settled on a large black gelding. The horse had a white blaze shaped like a lightning bolt and three of his four legs socked. After a short walk to the feed shed, Rory returned with a small bag of oats.

He stepped between the rails and stood quietly, as the animals, gathered at the opposite side of the corral, watched him. Patiently, Rory stared at the black until they made eye contact. He began to chant softly, held out a hand full of feed, and waited. Its head lifted nostrils flared the black trotted over to where Rory stood. The black reminded him of the beautiful horses the rancho patronos rode when they visited the mission. The horse put his muzzle into Rory's hand and ate the oats. Rory rolled down the bag and let him feed.

While the horse finished the oats, Rory spoke softly to him. When the feed was gone, Rory stroked the horse's neck moved slowly to its side. In a single motion, seemingly without effort, Rory pulled himself to the black's back. Its nostrils flare, and its eyes opened wide, but he didn't move. Rory continued to speak to the horse and stroked its neck. "Easy—it'll be fine. Settle now—settle."

The horse shivered once as if it shook off its fear and relaxed. Rory, with a fist full of it mane urged the animal with his heels, and they rode around the corral. After a few minutes, Rory halted near the lean-to and examined the tack. He selected the best of the gear, saddled, and unsaddled the horse several times, and then he mounted again. Rory waited; the animal sidestepped and turned, but soon the horse calmed and accepted the saddle and Rory on his back.

Rory rode to the gate, where E.B. and the old man stood and watched him with the horse. Rory said, "Open the gate, I want to take him out for a ride."

****

E.B. swung the gate ajar to let them out and watched them gallop away. The old timer said, "Has a way with horses, he treats 'em like the Indians do—gentle like."

The bounty hunter nodded. "He ought to, he was raised by Apache."

The old man led E.B. back into the stationhouse and began to prepare food for the three of them. While he cooked, they talked. "What are you plannin' to do with the boy?"

"I know he looks young, but he's over twenty and not a boy. He wants to learn the bounty trade. So I plan to teach him what I can."

"Does he understand it's a lonely business and there'll be some folks that'll want to put him in the ground for his trouble?"

"I've explained all that—but does Rory fully understand? That's another question."

Rory stepped through the door. "What's another question?"

Higgins, who doesn't have visitors often, spoke for E.B., "E.B. tells me you're goin' to be a bounty hunter—is that so?"

"Just until we get Cain," said Rory with a glance to E.B. for verification. E.B. nodded.

"He the one they call seven-scar?" Higgins asked with interest aglow in his eyes. "I heard of him. Suppose to have killed his brother and maybe his parents too. He's a bad one."

Now it was Rory's turn to be interested. "What can you tell us about Cain, the one you call seven-scar?"

Higgins poured another drink for himself and E.B. Holding out the bottle, he offered some to Rory, who shook his head. "What about Cain."

The old man liked the attention and warmed to the subject. "Well—the way I heard it was that he lived on a farm somewhere back east. He had an older brother, and there was this girl— Cain and he got into a fight over her, and the elder brother swung a choppin' hoe at him. It missed his head, but cut deep into his chest leavin' an ugly scar in the shape of a seven. Cain took the hoe away from his brother and damn near chopped his head off—least ways no one could recognize his face. When his pa came upon the scene, he tried to kill Cain. I've heard different accounts about how it ended. Anyway, he ran away and got into more and more trouble. He joined up with the Comancheros some years back, and now he leads a band of twenty or so."

"The number is closer to sixteen," said Rory.

"We must've got a few of them after all," said the old man. He winked at E.B. "I can still shoot straight."

Chapter 4

Higgins and E.B. settled down with their bottle of whiskey and began to reminisce about younger times. Rory smiled to himself, *I suppose I will too ... one day.* Usually, he enjoyed listening to the old men's stories, but tonight he felt restless. He looked around the room, saw a writing desk, and asked, "Mister Higgins, can I mail a letter from here?"

Higgins stared at Rory with a quizzical expression. "Yes. The stage carries the mail—who you goin' to write a letter to?"

Rory looked to E.B. "Don't pay Higgins any mind," said E.B. "He doesn't get many visitors, so his manners aren't what they should be. You write your letter, and he'll make sure it gets in the mail bag."

"Mister Higgins, do you have pen and paper?"

"Yonder in the drawer of that table; the area manager uses it for his reports when he comes through." Higgins paused, and then said, "You know, you talk just like that dude manager that comes through here. How'd you manage schoolin' bein' raised by Apache?"

Rory smiled. "The friars were rigid school masters, so I learned proper English, as well as Spanish and Latin."

"Whew," said Higgins. "That sounds like a powerful lot of work." He walked him to the desk, where Rory rummaged through the drawers.

"It kept me occupied." Finally, Rory found the supplies he needed. He removed the box from the drawer, and could smell the lingering odor of the sodium sulfite use to produce the paper. The cap was tight, but he finally opened the inkbottle, and took pen in hand to write a letter. Higgins stood over his shoulder and watched expectantly. Rory looked up at the station manager, and said, "Mr. Higgins, some privacy please."

Higgins chuckled. "I can't read nor write a lick, Son. It's just that I enjoy watchin' the process, but if it bothers you, I'll leave you alone."

"Thank you, Mister Higgins."

The table sat next to a window where nature's light could cast brightly on its surface. It was a formal piece and didn't match the crudely made furniture of the station, and Rory casually wondered how it came to be there. Had the area manager brought it, or was it standard issue for the stage line?

Rory found himself examining the many scratches and pits that scarred the surface. He stalled ... he didn't know where to start the letter, or how to share his terrible news. Finally, he decided to write it how he would say it if he spoke to the Archbishop in person.

'Dear Archbishop Vega,

I have the saddest of news to report. While en route to the dioceses, Comancheros attacked us and Father Herberto killed. Wounded, they left me for dead. A Mr. E.B. Parker, a Good Samaritan, found me and has since nursed me back to health.

Mr. Parker buried Father Herberto while I was still unconscious, but he provided me with the details of his death. I am sorry to report that he was tortured to death. Most likely, it was in an attempt to make him tell of the treasure. He did not reveal where it's location. The treasure is still intact and remains hidden were Herberto hid it before the attack.

Please know that after I have brought justice to those who murder my dearest friend and mentor, I will retrieve the treasure and bring it to Santa Fe as Father Herberto desired.

Your servant,

Rory McLeod'

He stared at the words; they seemed woefully lacking. Father Herberto, as a person, was so much more than what words could ever convey. He was been every bit the parent to him as Sani and Mosi. Herberto mentored and taught him with the same pride and understanding as his uncle Bidzil. Tears streamed down his cheeks. As he wiped them away, he realized, he hadn't yet fully grieved for his friend.

After a deep breath to calm his hand, he took another piece of stationery and held the pen at the ready.

'Dear Brother Fidel,

I have grave news to share with you and the other friars at the mission. Father Herberto is dead. He was murdered by Comanchero bandits while en route to Santa Fe. The bandits shot me as well and left me for dead, but I was found and nursed back to health by a man named E.B. Parker.

Archbishop Vega has been informed of the Herberto's death. I travel with Mr. Parker with the intent of finding the men who murdered him. Please keep me in your prayers.

Your friend,

Rory'

He folded the letters and stuffed them into their respective envelopes. Turning to Higgins, he asked, "How much is the charge to have these delivered?"

"Mail ain't cheap, Son. That'll be one U. S. dollar for each one—still want to mail 'em?"

Rory nodded approval and then stood with the letter, which he handed to Higgins. He looked at E.B. and gave him a half-hearted smile, and said, "I will spend the night in the hills and will return before morning."

E.B. seemed to recognize his solemn manner and nodded, but not Higgins, he was obtuse to Rory's melancholy mood, and asked, "Where you goin', Son?" Without waiting for a response, he added, "You know it's dangerous out there at night. There's Indians and wild critters that'll kill you if you lets 'em get too close."

Rory smiled politely at Mister Higgins. E.B. said, "Higgins, he's safer out there than we are in here—he'll be all right. Quit botherin' him."

Outside in the corral, Rory saddled his horse, mounted up, and rode west toward where Father Herberto died. Atop a hill a few miles from the station, he made camp and started a fire.

As darkness settled around him, Kilchii stared at the hypnotic flicker of the flames and it brought remembrances' of his time at the mission.

****

"Rory, you speak English and Spanish better than I do. Today you shall start to learn Latin."

"Padre, I understand why I should learn English, and Spanish is also useful, but why Latin?"

"You shall also begin classes on the sciences and ancient history. If you are to learn, then Latin is necessary." The priest looked down at the book Rory held under his arm. "What's that you're reading now?"

"Voltaire's, 'Letters on the English.' "

"Why did you choose that book?"

"Brother Fidel selected it for me from the library."

"Don't you find it difficult to understand?"

Rory grimaced. "I have made great use of Webster's Lexicon," said Rory and they both laughed.

"When you have finished Voltaire come see me. I have a book by Alexandre Dumas titled 'The Count of Monte Cristo'. It is a tale of betrayal, revenge, and high adventure that I'm sure you'll enjoy. Now off with you—Brother Fidel and your Latin studies are waiting."

Rory learned that Cochise continued to raid United States and Mexican settlements. More importantly, he learned that the great civil strife between the northern and southern states had ended. With the war concluded, the American Army had the resources to take the fight to Cochise and his Apache warriors.

"Rory, wake up," said Herberto. There is someone here to see you."

"It is very late, Padre. Who is it?"

"Your uncle brings word. He isn't well, and I'm afraid he has bad news regarding your parents."

He rolled from his bed, quickly dressed, and followed the priest to the infirmary. The candles placed along the corridor wall produced an eerie orange light that distorted their shadows.

Herberto opened the door for him. He halted at the sight of four friars as they tended to an emaciated figure lying on a bed. One held an oil lamp high; another cradled the body while the third tried to spoon a clear broth past his lips. The fourth friar bathed his bruised and scraped torso. The Apache looked somehow familiar, but he couldn't place the tortured creature in his memories. Then he moved closer and peered into his eyes. "Uncle—Uncle, is that truly you?"

"Kilchii," he replied in a weak voice, and his hand trembled when he reached out to his nephew.

Rory moved to Bidzil's side, and clasped his forearm in the fashion of their clan, and he greeted him. "Uncle, what has happened?"

The friar who cleaned his wounds said, "Not now, Rory. He's very weak—I don't know how he managed to reach us."

Herberto stood behind the young man and put his hands on his shoulders. "Come. We'll go to the chapel and pray for his recovery. The friars will send for you when he can talk." The priest led him away.

Soon after arriving at the mission, Rory had concluded that the white man's God and Ussen were the same, but he had doubts about Jesus. He didn't share his questions with his friend. It was important to the Padre, so he let Herberto assume that he accepted Christ and allowed the priest to baptize him. In the chapel, Father Herberto sat on a pew and began to pray. Seated next to him, Rory asked, "Padre, what happened to my family?"

"The details are unknown to me. But, before he left, your father told me that your clan would join Cochise's fight against the U.S. Army. He wasn't confident that Cochise could win, and he feared that your clan would suffer."

"You should have told me, Padre, I would have joined the clan and protected my parents."

"Sani didn't desire that, which is why he brought you to me. He hoped you would avail yourself of the opportunities your white heritage offers. If it turns out to be the worst, you mustn't become angry and do something reckless."

Fidel came into the chapel and approached the priest and Rory. "Rory, your uncle asks to speak with you."

Together, they returned to the infirmary. Although his uncle still appeared unwell, his eyes were clear, and he raised himself to one elbow upon seeing Rory. "Uncle, you seem better," said Rory as he rushed to his uncle's bedside. "How do you feel?"

"I'm stronger. The water and broth have helped. A few days of rest and food and I will be 'He is Strong' again."

"What of my parents?"

Bidzil lay back, but kept his eyes on Rory. "Kilchii, my news is filled with sorrow."

Father Herberto stepped near Rory and laid his arm across his shoulder.

His uncle continued, "Sani and your mother are dead."

Rory's eyes welled, but otherwise he didn't react to his uncle's words. "How did they die?"

"The war against the bluecoats has not gone well. They kept us trapped in the mountains, and we were unable to feed our families—many died from starvation." Bidzil closed his eyes and didn't speak for several seconds. The friar who nursed Bidzil raised his head and gave him water. At length, Bidzil resumed his woeful tale. "Your father decided to take those of the clan that still lived and surrender to the bluecoats. He could no longer stand by and watch his clan die from hunger.

"With Cochise's blessing, we left the mountains—many too weak to walk. The warriors walked, and the women and children rode the few horses that remained—many we'd already eaten. As we approached the bluecoats with our women and children, they began to fire their rifles." Again, he had to rest before he could continue. Rory waited. He hadn't moved a muscle while Bidzil's told the story of what happened to his parents.

Bidzil at last came to the finish. "Sani and Mosi led the clan and surely the first to die. Sani's body covered Mosi—it looked as if he tried to protect her—even in death. I trailed the clan to make sure no one fell behind. By the time I reached them, everyone was dead." Bidzil closed his eyes, and tears streamed down his face. "I'm the last of my clan."

Herberto said, "Your uncle shall remain with us until he's fully recovered, and he decides where he wants to go."

Rory didn't respond; he turned and ran from the room. He wanted to be alone to think, but he couldn't—not at the mission. So he gathered the things from his room, he went to the stables for his pony, and he rode out into the desert's night air. The conflict he felt pulled strong in both directions. The way of the warrior demanded that he revenge his parent's death, but Herberto's council was to forgive and move on with life.

After hours of riding and thinking, he halted and greeted the sunrise. The sight and beauty of the dawn reminded him of his youth when just he and his mother were up early, and they too watched the sun peek over the eastern horizon. He could still hear her voice as she told him the legend of the two wolves. 'Inside of every man,' said his mother, 'two hungry wolves fight for control, one benevolent and the other malevolent.' When he asked her, which one would win? She replied, 'Whichever one you feed.'

His instinct—no—his desire was to avenge, but his intellect told him nothing would be gained. Which wolf would he decide to feed?

It was late morning on the second day after he learned of his parent's deaths when he returned. Rory went directly to the infirmary to check on his uncle's convalescence. He was pleased to see him eating solid foods, and that color replaced the pallor he displayed on his arrival. Bidzil chewed a piece of meat, and he paused to look at Rory as he approached. "Kilchii, I feel your sorrow. My sister and your father were all the family I had left. My wife and daughter were among those who died from hunger in Cochise's camp."

"Uncle, I'm sorry to hear of your loss. We shall help one another to become whole again."

Bidzil nodded and then laid down his leg of lamb to stare at Rory. "You have grown, My Nephew. What have they been feeding you?"

"Food—the same as you eat now. They've also fed me knowledge and educated me on the ways of the Europeans and Mexicans, who inhabit our lands. I now understand that the whites far outnumber the Nde and that their greed for land, gold, and silver know no limit. I believe the war is lost, and the Apache should no longer fight."

Bidzil studied his nephew's face for a long time. "You speak as your father did—you have become wise."

Rory stepped close to his uncle's bed and placed a hand on his shoulder. "I have had many good teachers." He squeezed Bidzil's flesh. Herberto came into the infirmary, so Rory changed the subject. In Spanish, he asked, "What are your plans once you recover?"

"I have not decided."

Overhearing the question, Herberto said, "Your uncle is free to stay here and make a life with us if he wishes."

Bidzil looked to Herberto, and said, "We shall see what time brings, Padre."

****

When the stars seemed their brightest, Rory began to chant to Ussen. He asked him to help Father Herberto find his Anna Mari and their son. When dawn came, he was at peace.

At the station, E.B. and Higgins waited before they started to cook their breakfast. When Rory returned, E.B. asked, "You seem different—what happened?"

Rory could see the concern in his friend's eyes. "I said good-bye to Father Herberto. He's with his God."

"That's good," said E.B., and added, "We'll head out after breakfast."

Higgins hollered, "Come and get it while it's hot, you two."

Chapter 5

Once they cleared the pass, Rory could see El Paso. Closer to town, he noted that the newer section of El Paso, the downtown area, had been constructed with lumber and brick. Many of the recently built structures displayed em-bellishments; applied architectural features to make them appear more stylish than the other buildings.

The bounty hunter, not a stranger to El Paso, explained that trouble brewed in the community. The Mexicans re-sented the Europeans who came to search for gold, and the Europeans disliked the Mexicans for being in their way. The soldiers at Fort Bliss, north of town, kept the peace.

E.B. led him down El Paso Street. Rory's attention jumped from one novelty to the next. At first, he was amazed by the colorful merchant's signs, then he stared at the people and their fancy attire, the saloons, and finally, at the grandeur of the El Paso International Hotel. E.B. reined up and dismounted. He pulled his saddlebags and bedroll off his horse, and then he grabbed his rifle. "This is where we're goin' to stay, Rory. Gather your personals and let's get signed in."

"What about the packhorse and the gear?"

"We'll board him and the gear at the livery after we get settled. I know the owner, so everythin' will be safe."

Rory recalled the grandness at the Xavier Chapel, but it was greatly different from what he now saw. The hotel lobby filled with ornate woodwork, artwork, and gilded framed mirrors hung from the decoratively papered and freshly painted walls. Generous sized colorful woven wool rugs covered the polished hardwood floors and carved wood and fabric-covered furniture sat strategically located within the room.

At the reception desk, a pinched-face man in a dark suit waited. His thin hair parted in the middle and pasted to his skull with perfumed oil that Rory smelled from the entrance to the hotel. Parker stepped to the counter and turned the register around to sign in. "Mr. Parker, it is good to see you again," said the pinched-face man. "I hope your trip was successful?" He glanced suspiciously at Rory.

"I guess it depends on how you view the situation. My quarry eluded me, but I gained an associate. Haley, meet Rory McLeod."

Haley offered a slight bow. "An associate of Mr. Parker's is always welcome here at the El Paso International Hotel." His smile was disingenuous; Rory didn't know what to make of him, but he instinctively knew that he didn't like or trust the man.

"We'll take two rooms—connected if you have them, Haley."

"Yes, Sir, Mr. Parker—front or rear?"

"Front, I think, so my associate can get acquainted with El Paso."

Haley showed them to their rooms and stood expectantly until E.B. gave the clerk a quarter. After Haley left, Rory asked, "Why did you pay him to show us where our rooms are located? I'm sure we could have found them on our own."

E.B. smiled. "It's called a gratuity. Haley provides small services and he receives a payment."

"Why?"

At this question, E.B. chuckled. "In my—our profession it's important that we have additional eyes and ears to watch and listen. If Haley sees or hears anything, he thinks we should know, he'd tell me. Understand?"

"No."

E.B. sighed. "Sit down, this might take a while." Rory sat down on the floor and waited. "Use the chair would you? It makes me uncomfortable seein' you sittin' on the floor when there is a perfectly good chair beside you." Rory shrugged, rose, and sat on the chair.

"Rory, don't let the niceties of El Paso fool you—it's a border town. They may not all be wanted by the law, but there are some pretty bad men who pass through El Paso. For the most part, they avoid trouble because the law is strict here, but like I said, 'for the most part.' Do you follow?"

Rory nodded. "We're in enemy territory and we should be cautious."

"That's a little oversimplified, but you've got the idea. There are two reasons that we need to be aware of who is in town. There could be someone with a bounty that we're searching for and two; they could be on the lookout for us. I have a reputation and wanted men assume I'm hunting them, whether I am or not, so they shoot on sight—usually from ambush."

Rory considered the bounty hunter's words. "It is like being on the cougar's mountain. Even if you are not hunting him, he may still be hunting you. You should be aware, and if you are warned where the cougar is located before he finds you, then you can decide your actions—is that correct?"

"Exactly."

"So Haley is a paid to lookout for the cougars that might be in town?"

"Precisely."

"How do we know he isn't being paid by the cougar as well?"

E.B. laughed aloud. "You perceive the situation quickly," he said. "Haley may very well be getting paid by the—cougar, but he will still tell us who is in town and where to find them. I'm here often and if I collect a bounty from one of his warnings I give him a sizeable gratuity."

"But he isn't a friend, and we should not trust him."

"You have it, Rory." E.B. winked.

E.B. scratched his bearded face, and said, "Let's find you some decent clothes, and then a bath. A haircut and shave wouldn't hurt either."

As they prepared to leave their rooms, E.B. checked his revolver's load and made sure the keeper loop was free. "Bring along your Colt. We'll see what can be done about the holster and get more ammunition so you can practice."

Downstairs, Rory asked, "What about the pack horse?"

E.B. motioned to Haley, who scurried over. "Would you have our pack horse and gear taken to the livery? Tell Griffith it belongs to me and I'll see him later."

"I'll handle it personally, Mr. Parker." He waited. E.B. retrieved coins from his pocket and tipped the clerk.

At the mercantile, Rory selected a holster that fit his Colt snugly. He chose a cross-draw rig similar to that Parker wore. E.B. explained that he could reach his revolver while standing or seated, and it was readily accessible to his weak-side[16].

His next order of business was clothing. E.B. bought him a pair of dark wool pants and two poplin shirts. When E.B. started looking at boots, Rory said, "Father Herberto and I had a long discussion regarding boots versus my moccasins. He relented and agreed that for me, moccasins were better."

"Suit yourself. They're your feet."

---

[16] The left hand is the weak-side to a right-handed person.

Although Rory bathed often, he had never seen a formal bathroom with a tub. The ornate apparatus reminded him of a horse trough—but made of copper. The bathhouse was a long building with partitions, which reminded him of horse stalls. There was a bench to sit on, and it held a clean towel. On the wall were attached hooks for your clothes and gun belt. A small table stood beside the tub with an ashtray for your cigar and drink. He imagined E.B. placed his Colt there as well to keep it handy.

Once in the tub, he eased back, closed his eyes, and let the hot water soak away the trail dust and his muscle aches. Aloud he said, "Aah, this is nice."

The curtain pulled back and the old man who ran the place asked, "Do you need more hot water? It'll just take a second to drain some off."

"I'm fine, thank you—maybe later."

Dressed in his store-bought clothes, Rory followed E.B. into the barbershop. There he followed his friend's example and stepped up onto a barber's chair. To have his hair cut wasn't anything new, but this would be his first time shaved by anyone other than himself. The hot, moist towel and the soft lather soothed his face, but the idea of someone else with a sharp edge to his neck gave him pause. Rory's eyes grew larger with each strop of the blade across the leather strap. So when the barber approached him brandishing a razor, Rory involuntarily started to climb backwards out of the chair.

E.B. watched; he chuckled, then he said, "Sit down, I've got him covered. If he makes a wrong move, I'll plug him." The barber scowled when he saw E.B. place his hand on his forty-five.

Cleaned up, they returned to the hotel's restaurant for dinner. The dining room's elegance out matched those of the hotel's lobby. Seated at a white cloth-covered table with two lighted candles, Rory considered the menu. In addition to its standard fare, they offered several French dishes that piqued his interest. In the end, he ordered steak, potatoes, and vegetables.

Despite all his education and reading at San Xavier, table etiquette wasn't among the subject matter. He looked at the utensils and then to E.B. "Follow my example," said E.B., his voice low and casual. "Most of those you won't use tonight. Remind me later and I'll explain what's to be used when." They brought a sharp knife when they served his steak, so a fork was all he needed.

More so than he first thought, Rory wanted to fit in. He observed the people inside the restaurant, and they watched him. Their eyes consistently dropped to stare at his moccasins and then back to his red hair. E.B. seemed oblivious to the other diners, yet on guard against all of them. Rory concealed his feet back under the table. He leaned forward and spoke quietly to E.B., "If the offer's still open, I'd like to purchase a pair of boots. I'll wear the moccasins on the trial."

E.B. looked up from his plate and glanced around the room. "The offer's still open. We'll get them tomorrow."

****

Their routine for the next two weeks was the same. Up early, breakfast, and then out to the countryside, so Rory could practice with his .44 Colt, and his long-distance marksmanship with the .50 Sharps. The Colt would take continued practice, but Rory had a knack for the big bore Sharps. Windage, distance, and elevation seem to come to him naturally. E.B. wondered if years of relying on a bow and arrow for survival had any influence on his abilities.

When they returned to El Paso, they stopped by the Sheriff's office and checked the wanted posters to see if they had posted anyone new. Today, there was a fresh poster,

'$2,000.00
WELLS FARGO REWARD
(DEAD OR ALIVE)
John Flynt
5'-10"
160 lbs.
Blue eyes
Robbed the WELLS FARGO westbound stage near San Angela[17], Texas and killed the guard.'

E.B. pulled down the poster. "We'll head out tomorrow. Meantime, we need to get our gear ready." They left the Sheriff's and went to the livery where their animals and Parker's gear was stored.

At the livery, Griffith showed them to the bundles he stored away for E.B. "Here ya go, E.B. You can use the tack room to sort your gear."

"Obliged, Grif," said E.B. "Get my bill ready and I'll settle up today. We'll want to leave early tomorrow."

"Sure thang, E.B., I'll have your horses watered and fed—ready to go."

"Good man," said E.B. They picked up the bundles and carried them to the tack room, and began to clean and inspect their armament and other implements E.B. would bring along on the trail.

When they finished they headed for the hotel and a late meal. Over coffee, Rory asked. "What's our plan?"

"How so?"

---

[17] Later renamed San Angelo in 1883.

"Well. How do we know where to start looking for Flynt?"

E.B. said, "Huntin' a man is no different than goin' after a cougar—except a man is more dangerous." He paused to give Rory a minute to think about that, and then he asked, "How would you go about it?"

Rory thought about the question. It was like being with his uncle; E.B. had begun teaching him the skills needed to hunt men. "I suppose I would go to where they were known to have been and start tracking."

"Correct," said E.B. "We'll start in San Angela. There's bound to people there who know Flynt and what he looks like. How much money did he steal? Has he got family close by that might help him? Where has the local law searched for him and how thorough? Just like when you're trackin' a cougar—you can't rush it if you want to be successful."

It was a ten-day ride to San Angela. As before, Rory practiced every day, except it was from horseback. E.B. gathered an assortment of debris every morning and during the day, as they rode, he would toss pieces up into the air at different angles and call for Rory to draw and shoot. By the end of their trip, Rory was hitting eight out of ten targets. He couldn't tell for sure, but he guessed that when Rory missed, it was only by fractions of an inch. During the early evenings, while there was still light, E.B. would select targets and they would draw and shoot at them in competition. Rory was now faster than E.B.

"Tomorrow we'll reach San Angela. I'll do all the talkin' even if someone asks you a question—I'll do the talkin'. Understood?"

"Yes, but why?"

E.B. chuckled and shook his head. "Should've known you wouldn't just do as I say."

"How else am I to learn, if I don't ask questions?"

"Don't take this the wrong way, Rory, but you're more than a little naïve when it comes to dealin' with people. Folks just aren't as straightforward as the Apache and the monks at Xavier. Without meanin' to, you could give away information that I would just as soon people didn't know, so I'll do the talkin'. Okay?"

"I'll do as you say, but I do understand guile and when to use it." Rory's feelings were hurt, but he understood that E.B. was just being cautious, so he let it pass.

****

People have inhabited the point where the north and south Concho Rivers converge for thousands of years. Only after the United States Government erected Fort Concho did it become a town. San Angela's adobe and wood buildings were hurriedly constructed and seemed temporary. The Cactus Hotel was its only two-story structure; if you didn't include the fieldstone buildings at the fort across the river.

The town's start was rooted in satisfying the needs and desires of the fort's soldiers. Like any camp town, there were numerous saloons and cantinas to compete for the soldiers pay.

It was early afternoon when they rode into San Angela. E.B. stopped in front of the Cactus Hotel. "Remember. I do the talkin'." Rory nodded. As E.B. dismounted to enter the hotel, he said, "Stay with the horses." Again, Rory nodded.

Still mounted, Rory casually appraised the town. El Paso was a metropolis in comparison. Off-duty soldiers walked the street and frequented businesses to spend their pay. He studied their movements and picked up on their routine. First, they went to the general store to buy a few necessities, then to the saloon for whiskey, and finally to the prostitutes for sex. Rory concluded that the life of a soldier was lonely.

E.B. returned. "We've got rooms here. Let's unload our gear and then find the livery and take care of the animals."

As they left the stables, Rory asked, "Do we go to see the sheriff now?"

"No. We don't want people to know what we're about—we'll see him last."

Rory looked at E.B. from the corner of his eye, and said, "Guile." E.B. slowly nodded.

At the hotel, E.B. spoke to the clerk. Rory waited by the stairs, and he noted the clerk nodded his head and pointed toward the east end of town. When E.B. joined him, he asked, "Does he know anything about Flynt?"

"I don't know yet—I didn't ask."

"Then what was that all about"

"Our dirty clothes and a place to get cleaned up—come on, let's get our things."

With their personals under their arms, E.B. led Rory down the street. The sign over the door read 'KATE'S'. E.B. smiled and nudged Rory, he said, "It's been a long ride. We need to get our clothes, and ourselves washed."

Inside, Rory was surprised to see that the owner had made an effort to enhance the establishment's appearance. A portly woman greeted them, "I'm Kate. What can I do for you gentlemen?"

"We've been ten days on the trail and we and our clothes need cleaning," said E.B., and then he winked.

"That'll be five dollars—each. The whiskey is extra."

E.B. displayed a twenty-dollar gold piece, and said, "On account."

Kate took the coin and examined closely, then smiled and said, "This way if you please." She led them down a close corridor where several small rooms lined each side. At the end of the hall was the wash area. Unlike the El Paso bathhouse, it was a single large space with three copper tubs separated by curtains that pulled for privacy. The tubs, already full waited for hot water and a new occupant.

E.B. pointed to one of the women. Her sagging and tired face made her appear older than she probably was. He stepped to one of the tubs, and laid his bundled dirty clothes on a nearby bench and began to undress. The woman lugged in two buckets of steaming hot water from outside and poured them into the tub. She pulled the curtain closed, and Rory heard the sound of water splash followed by a contented sigh from his friend. The woman stepped back through the curtains and handed his clothes to a young Mexican boy who scurried out the rear door.

The two women who remained looked at him expectantly, he pointed to the younger of the two. Modesty wasn't an issue with the Apache, so Rory had no qualms as he followed his friend's example. Nevertheless, once in the tub, it surprised him when the woman returned with a brush and soap, and began bathing him. Rory called through the curtain, "El Paso is swankier, but the personal service is better here."

He heard E.B. chuckle and order, "Whiskey."

After his bath, Rory expected to find his friend waiting, but E.B. was nowhere about. "Where is my friend?" He asked the woman. She wrapped a towel around his waist and led him down the hall. She stopped at one of the rooms, and rapped lightly on an open door. Over her shoulder, Rory peeked inside the cramped room. On the single piece of furniture, a tiny bed, laid a brunette dressed only in a black transparent gown. The woman who bathed him now stood behind him and gently pushed him into the room ....

It was Rory's first time. Finished, he lie next to the woman and let his thoughts wander; they went to the conversations about life and women on the trail with Father Herberto.

****

It was early the next morning and Rory cooked breakfast. He waited for the coffee to brew before he woke the priest.

Herberto stirred, and his nostrils flared as he sniffed the beckoning aroma of the dark rich brew. "Ah," he said, and started to rise, but fell back with a moan. "I believe I'm crippled."

Rory laughed and moved to help the priest to rise. "You will be healed once you walk around and work out your stiffness. Today you will be too tired and sore to fight the rhythm of the horse's gait—it will be an easier day."

Herberto's expression conveyed his doubt as he stretched and then massaged his butt. "I shall walk awhile and give the horse a rest from yesterday's ordeal." They both laughed, but when they departed from their campsite, the priest walked and led his horse.

Over the days that followed, they settled into a routine. Herberto improved his horsemanship, and the mare mellowed in her attitude toward him. Rory loved the priest much the same way he did his uncle Bidzil. Their relationship, always one of mentor and protégé changed to friendship. At night, seated next to their campfire under the glimmering stars, Herberto told stories of his youth, and why he decided to become a priest.

"My parents died when I was young and left me an orphan. Wild and filled with anger, I terrorized the small village in Spain where I was born. The magistrate wanted me sent to prison, but Father Antonio, our local priest, rescued me and gave me a home. It was he who brought me to the church, and showed me the happiness that can be attained from doing God's work. Eventually, I joined the Franciscan order and never looked back."

Rory listened intently. He never considered or imagined this side of Father Herberto, and he asked many questions, "Have you been to Rome—did you meet the Pope—what's the Sistine chapel like?"

Herberto raised his hand to halt the barrage of questions. "We still have many days of travel. I will answer your questions, but one at a time. Now ask me one question only and we'll proceed from there."

The revelation that Herberto hadn't always been a priest sent Rory's mind reeling with questions. He settled on one. His face blushed when he asked, "What about women? I mean did you ever—don't you miss them?"

The priest chuckled. "Youth—it's not the first time I've been asked this question." Herberto stared off into the evening sky; his eyes welled with tears. "Yes, there was a girl. Her name was Anna Mari, and we were in love—very much in love. We secretly planned to marry, but her parents found out and sent her away to Madrid. By the time that I located her, and made my way there, she had died giving birth to our son. He died a short time later. Without Father Antonio to help me through the grief—I don't know the direction my life might have taken."

"I'm sorry, Padre. I didn't intent for you to return to a painful place."

The priest focused his watery blue eyes on Rory's worried face. Herberto's expression was peaceful, and he smiled. "To the contrary, My Son, my memories of her are pleasant—filled with love. Time has softened grief's pain, and I now choose to dwell only on our time together—the love we shared was wonderful. Truly, it was God's choice. I know that she and my son are in heaven, and I plan to be with them one day." The priest remained silent for a long while. At length, he said, "I'm tired now—goodnight, Rory."

Rory watched his friend and mentor settle down into his bedroll for sleep. Hopefully, Rory prayed, Herberto would visit his Anna Mari in his dreams.

The smell of wood burning and coffee brewing woke Rory from his sleep. Herberto was awake before him, which was rare. "Good morning, Padre—did you sleep well?"

"I slept very well, thank you. Now roll out of that bedroll you lazy oaf and help me with breakfast."

Pleased to find the priest in such high spirits, Rory smiled, *my prayer must have been answered.* Rory slipped on his moccasins and looked around for his sad excuse for a hat; worn beyond usefulness. Its crease around the crown was frayed, its ribbon hatband long gone, and its floppy brim hung as if wet.

****

Later, they went to the Mexican restaurant across the street from the Cactus Hotel. They sat at a rough-hewn table far removed from the elegance of the El Paso International Hotel, and they talked quietly. E.B. smiled, leered with an impish glint, and asked, "How was your bath?"

Rory's face colored. "It was an experience."

"An experience—that's all you have to say?"

"Yes." Rory would say no more on the subject.

E.B. shrugged, but his smile remained. They order their meals and while they waited, the bounty hunter shared what he had learned from the prostitutes. "It seems that Flynt got the fort's payroll—nearly $20,000. Wells Fargo is hoppin' mad and wants this fella in the worse way."

"Is he from around here?"

"I don't think so," said E.B. "It seems he drifted into town and hung around for a few of weeks to learn the fort's routine. Later, he robbed the stage. The soldiers think he went north probably headed for the Indian Territory to hideout for a while and then east to Fort Smith. Hell, with that much money, there's no telling where he'll go."

"The robbery happened nearly three months ago. Do you think we can find him?"

"It's been my experience that when someone like Flynt hits it big, he runs only long enough to feel safe. He'll want to spend some of that money and there aren't that many places to have a good time between here and Fort Smith. Flynt probably did head north after he robbed the stage, but if he's a Texas boy, he'd turned east and south after he lost the posse chasin' him. He's headed for San Antonio or Austin."

"How do we know which?"

"We follow the money."

"I don't understand."

"How do you track an animal?"

Rory considered the question. "You go to where they habitat, scout their feeding areas and water holes until you find tracks."

"We'll head east for Austin. At every cantina along the way, we stop and look for Flynt's track."

"The money," said Rory. "He'll spend the money."

E.B. smiled and nodded. "Fresh minted gold coins stand out."

Chapter 6

Four days riding from San Angela put them on the east side of the Colorado River. "We'll follow the river road south to Austin," said E.B. He stood in his stirrups and rubbed the small of his back. "If he's not there we'll move on to San Antonio, but we'll rest a day or so first."

"What makes you so positive he's not in Fort Smith by now?"

"Texas—if he's indeed from Texas, he'll want to stay in Texas. If he was smart, he'd use the money to buy a small ranch somewhere and give up bein' an outlaw."

"But you don't think he's smart—right?" Rory asked.

E.B. nodded. "I think we'll find him livin' the grand life in Austin."

The next day, they halted at the road's junction. The road signs indicated one way led to Austin, and the other to Dallas, Fort Worth, and Houston; a small town of sorts had grown up there. E.B. assumed its general store catered to the needs of the local ranchers, and a saloon and two whorehouses attended to their wants. Principal among these businesses, according to the sign hung from the porch, was 'Lil's Entertainment for Men.' Evidently, with the essentials covered, no one saw a reason to expand the village. They stopped at the saloon first.

"Same as last time," said E.B. "I'll do the talkin'."

Rory nodded. They dismounted, casually tied their animals, and entered the saloon. It wasn't payday, so the saloon was empty except for the man behind the bar.

His manner was pleasant enough, but his gaunt features, long nose, and overbite made him appear rodent-like.
"Ah, gentlemen," he said as they entered. "Please come in
and make your selves comfortable. Would you like whiskey,
or maybe a beer?"

The bounty hunter took in the room with a single
glance and saw a man seated at a table in the far corner.
E.B. said, "Fresh coffee and food—if you have it."

"Of course, Gentlemen, are eggs, steak, and beans
okay?"

E.B. nodded and said, "Make those four eggs each."

With an eye on the man in the corner, E.B. selected a
table where they could watch the room and both entrances
to the saloon. As his habit prescribed, E.B. had already removed the keeper loop from his pistol's hammer when they
entered the town. As he sat, he checked to make sure the
revolver was loose in its holster. Rory did the same. E.B.
preached, "Once you're known, you have to presume that
someone's gunnin' for you and shoot first—be ready if want
to survive."

The saloonkeeper returned with a tray. On it were two
cups, a pot of coffee, and a jar of honey. "My wife is cookin'
the food. She'll bring it out shortly."

"Sit with us for coffee—we've been on the trail for several days," said E.B. to the saloonkeeper, but his true focus
was on the man seated in the corner on his left. "We'd welcome news and the conversation."

"If you like," said the man. He went back to the kitchen
and returned quickly with his own cup. He seated himself
and poured a cup of coffee. Adding honey, he stirred the
dark brew and asked, "Where're you headed?"

"Austin," said E.B. "We're lookin' to find work there."

Abruptly, the man seated in the corner erupted from
his chair, flipped his table, and drew his revolver. "You'll
never take me in, you Son-of-a-bitch."

The man fired without aim and his bullet thudded
harmlessly into the wall behind E.B.

Without forethought, Rory's practice with E.B. triggered, and he sprang backwards from the table, and caused his chair to skid across the floor. As he rose, he palmed his Colt, cocked the hammer, aimed, and fired. His bullet punched a neat hole in the man's forehead.

A split second sooner, E.B. drew his revolver, from a seated position, aimed, and punctured a hole in the man's vest.

The man plopped down in his chair. The weight of his revolver, still gripped in death, pulled him to the floor.

E.B. holstered his weapon. Rory's Apache enculturation took over. Though his heart pounded from the surge of adrenaline racing through his veins, and the understanding that he'd helped kill a man began to sink into his thoughts, he calmly holstered his Colt, righted his chair, and sat down—neither looked at the dead man on the floor.

The barkeeper sat motionless mid-stir of his coffee. E.B. said, "You were sayin'?"

To his credit, the saloon owner's hand didn't tremble as he resumed stirring the coffee, nor did his voice break when he spoke. "Ahem." After he cleared his throat, he said, "Were you after that jasper? I mean—he said something about you takin' him in—you lawmen?"

E.B. glanced at the dead man. "Never seen him before. If he's wanted, it can't be for much. Now, I was askin' about Austin."

"Ahem," said the saloonkeeper, and then he swallowed hard and returned his attention to E.B. "It's grown some since the war ended. If you're lookin' for honest work you should do alright."

"We're mostly law-bidin'—if you know what I mean." E.B. winked. The man nervously smiled back. Sure that he had the saloonkeeper's attention, he asked, "A friend of ours came through a while back. He said if we had money to burn, a fella could have a right good time here and not be bothered by overly law-bidin' people."

"Whiskey and food at my place—none better. You can have a good time at Lil's place and a room to boot—if you can afford it."

E.B. patted his jacket. "We can afford it all right."

A thin angry looking woman entered from the kitchen with their food; she paused to stare at the dead man on the floor. She nodded toward the body and asked her husband, "He paid up?"

The saloonkeeper twitched his nose while he considered. "His horse and saddle will more 'an cover his bill. Send in Jack from the stable, he can get the jasper planted."

She turned back towards the men, carried the two large plates of food, and placed them on the table. "Need anythin' else?"

Rory smiled. "Have you any milk?"

The angry expression on the woman's face softened and she chuckled. "Sorry, Son, this is cattle country right enough, but we ain't got no milkin' cows. I got herb tea or water."

"Water then," said Rory.

The saloonkeeper studied Rory.

"He's got a grouchy stomach," said E.B. "Milk settles it down before he eats."

"That's too bad, a young man like you with stomach troubles. Try chewin' mint. That's what I do when her cookin' gets a bit spicy—settles it right down, so I can sleep like a baby."

Sheepishly, Rory glanced at E.B. "Thanks, I'll try that," he said and tended to his plate. The conversation with the saloonkeeper was fruitless. He soon ran out of topics for conversation and left the table to help his stableman drag the dead man out of the saloon.

Outside, they stood by their animals, and E.B. began to laugh. "It ruins the image of us bein' bad men—you askin' for milk."

Rory grinned. "I'll keep that in mind," he said and then asked, "Now what?"

"Lil's," said E.B. with a thumb pointed over his shoulder at the two houses.

As they rode up to the Lil's, a hard-looking generous-sized woman, who'd painted on too many layers of makeup, stepped out onto the porch. To Rory's way of thinking, she wasn't fully dressed. She removed the cheroot that dangled from her mouth, and studied them closely. Finally, she forced a smile and asked, "What can I do for you gents?"

"I'm Parker and this is my associate Rory. Man at the saloon said we could get rooms and entertainment at your place—if you're Lil."

"You can and I am. Step down and come into my parlor, the boy will take care of your horses."

A Mexican boy maybe ten-years-old appeared. His intelligent dark eyes and winning smile offset his age. "I take care of your horses, Señor's—no problem."

E.B. tossed him two bits. "Make sure they're curried and fed—oats would be nice."

"Si, Señor." The boy led the animals around the side of the house.

Rory watched after them. Lil noticed and said, "There's a stable out back. The boy knows what he's doin'." She smiled and revealed her lip-rouge discolored teeth. "Now—come on inside."

The parlor was cool. Four scantily dressed women sat on a bench, their wares on display. "Five dollars a night for a room, when the cowhands aren't here, includes a woman of your choice. Whiskey and a bath are extra. You get your food at the saloon."

E.B. appraised the women. He nodded and said, "Sounds reasonable." He handed Lil a twenty-dollar gold coin; then he held out his hand to a redheaded gal and said, "My name is Parker—yours? She giggled, took his hand, and followed him upstairs.

Next to the kitchen doorway, Rory spotted a younger woman whose skin color was mahogany, and her eyes were as dark as her raven hair. Lil saw him stare. "That's Sally. She's Cherokee, least ways her mother was—not everybody is comfortable doin' it with an Indian gal."

The girl cast her eyes at the floor. Rory walked over to her and said, "I'd be pleased to have your company—if you're agreeable?"

Barely lifting her face, she smiled and said, "Yes."

She took his hand, and led him upstairs to her room. It was small ornately furnished, with bright purple and gold wallpaper. Rory had never before seen so much color in one room. Between the two windows overlooking the street sat a canopy bed on a red, black, and yellow rug three-foot larger than the bed on all sides. A wardrobe stood to the left of the room's entrance. A vanity piled with rouges, powders, and perfumes with strong floral scents, occupied the far corner and a washstand was next to the door. On small tables beside the bed were lamps covered with gold-colored silk shades that shimmered in the light.

She released his hand, went to stand by the bed, and began to disrobe. Rory sat beside her and put her hands in his. She turned to look at him, and he asked, "Could we talk first?"

She seemed confused. "Don't you want me?"

"Yes, but I'd like to talk first," he said. "Tell me about your tribe?"

She sat on a chair at her vanity and brushed her hair while she stared at him in the mirror. Rory could see that she was making up her mind about him. Finally, she said, "My mother was Cherokee. My father was a half-black runaway slave, who they lynched near the end of the war. We was stranded here, and when my mother died, Lil took me in."

"Did you mother's people give you a name?"

She studied him further. "Why do you ask?"

"I was raised by the Apache. My name is Kilchii. It means Red Boy." He lifted his brow and looked up indicating his bright-red hair. She laughed, and it sounded genuine and was infectious, so he laughed too.

Their laughter waned to smiles. "Mine is Salali, it means Little Squirrel."

Rory asked, "The whites changed it to Sally?"

She shrugged and looked away. "It is easier for them to say."

Compassion and desire to be with her filled his heart; his smile moved to his eyes, and he came to her and took her in his arms. After a few moments, he led her to the bed where she again started to undress. "Not yet," he said. "Let's just lay here and talk for a while."

The morning light beamed through the bedroom window on Sally and Rory. He awoke with her head laid against his chest—she slept still fully clothed. He smiled. He had been lonely, and it was a pleasant night of conversation as they relived their happy childhoods with their Indian families. His attempt to rise without waking her was unsuccessful. She startled when he moved and quickly sat up in the bed.

She looked down at her clothes, she asked, "We did nothing more than talk until I fell asleep?"

Rory ignored her question and asked one of his own, "What do you do during the day?"

"Why?"

"I hoped we might go for a ride. There's a glen near a stream northwest of here. My friend and I rode passed it yesterday—we could have a picnic."

"What is a picnic?"

Rory didn't laugh or even smile. He patiently explained, "We pack a basket with food and drink and go to a pleasant location and eat it there."

"What is the point?"

This time Rory smiled. "Well—" Blood rushed to his cheeks, and he paused. "If two people want to be alone to talk without interruption they can go on a picnic."

"We will not be interrupted in this room," she said.

He felt frustrated and a little angry. Dejected, he said, "It was just an idea. You don't have to if you don't want to."

She watched him intently for several seconds. "Do you mean like a courtship?"

Rory's face flushed even a deeper red with embarrass‧ment—he could feel his cheek's burning. He was sure that his face color now matched his hair. "Sort of like that—I guess—I just—well I—"

Salali reached out for his hand and moved closer to him. "I would like very much to go on a picnic with you. What time do we leave?"

Rory grinned and jumped up with excited. "I'll get the food and horses. Can you be ready by ten?"

Her excitement more composed, Salali rose from the bed and sashayed to the door. "Yes I can, Rory," she said, and left the room.

****

Salali lingered outside the room, as she thought about Kilchii. He may be a grown man, but he's still a young one, and naïve about many things. Their reminiscing about their similar childhoods made him homesick for his Indian family. When she thought about it, she decided that so was she.

Rory was sweet and she wanted to make him happy, so she went to the room she shared with another girl, who was still asleep. Quietly, she went to her bed, where she slept when not entertaining guests, and removed a rolled bundle from beneath it. Stealing away, Salali took her bundle and headed to the washroom. On the way, she stopped by Lil's room to see if the woman was awake—she was. Lightly, Sa‧lali rapped on her door and called, "Lil, can I talk to you?"

"Come in, Sally," said Lil.

She opened the door and entered. The older woman asked, "What is that you want so early in the morning?" Lil sat at her dressing table wearing the royal purple silk nightgown and robe that she specially ordered from New York. Her hair pulled back and tied in place with a matching ribbon, while she applied her make-up.

Salali didn't wear any, save the lip-rouge that Lil forced her to wear when the cowboys came to town on their paydays. She thought it was rude to conceal who you were with paint and powder.

"Well, child—what is it?"

"Rory has asked me to go on a picnic with him, and I wanted to make sure it was allowed."

Lil frowned. "He's payin' for your time. Whether it's here or on a picnic—it's all the same." The madam saw that her harsh tone and indifferent manner upset Salali, so in a softer voice, she said, "Tell the boy to hitch up my horse and buggy for you two, no extra charge."

"Thank you, Lil." Salali darted out of Lil's room to clean up and change for her picnic with Rory.

****

At the saloon, Rory hadn't found the rat-faced man very accommodating, but his wife thought his request quaint and agreed to prepare a picnic lunch for the couple. With his basket packed, he returned to Lil's to ready the animals and collect Salali. The Mexican boy stood by Lil's buggy. "The Señora says you can use the buggy."

Pleasantly surprised, Rory said, in Spanish, "Thank you, young Sir. And please thank the señora for me."

The boy nodded. Then he looked passed Rory his eyes grew large with awe and a toothy grin spread across his face. "The señorita, she is beautiful," he said in Spanish.

Rory turned. Salali stood on the porch; she wore her native Cherokee deerskin ceremonial dress decorated with
beads of many colors and carved bones. The women of her
tribe spent many hours to adorn the dress, which she only
worn for celebrations, or her marriage. Braided, her long
black hair rested on her shoulders. A hint of red rouge
tinged her lips.

When Salali smiled, Rory couldn't remember when he
had ever seen anything or anyone so beautiful. His presents
of mind returned, and he moved to the porch to escort her
to the buggy. Rory took her hand, and walked her to the
buggy and helped her up to the seat. He climbed in beside
her, took the reins from the boy, and slapped them across
the horse's rump, and they were off.

As the buggy bounced alone neither of them spoke.
Rory's fanciful idea of this morning, which had seemed so
clear at the time, was now confused. His only thought was
to reach the stream; beyond that, he had no idea of what he
should do or say. Salali broke the silence. "Do you like my
dress? I don't know why I've kept it—I never expected to
have a chance to wear it again."

"I think the dress is beautiful—I mean you are beautiful in that dress." He paused to clarify his thought. "What I
really mean is that the dress is lovely, and you are beautiful." Rory blushed, but he didn't stammer.

Salali slid her arm through Rory's and squeezed it.
"Thank you for saying that."

They reached the glen near the stream. Rory pulled the
buggy under the shade of several large oak trees that
formed an umbrella across a grassy place. "There," he said
and pointed to a spot near the water. "We'll have our picnic
there." He jumped from the buggy, lifted the hitching
weight from under the seat, and tied the horse. Then he
came around to help Salali step down. Arms filled with the
basket and blanket, he walked to the stream's bank, and
she followed.

They spread the blanket on the ground and anchored the corners with loose stones from the stream. Seated on the blanket, they inspected the basket to see what they were to have for their picnic meal. There were two bottles of sarsaparilla, which he put in the stream to cool. From the dinner served the night before the rat-faced man's wife gave them fried chicken, cold biscuits, sliced tomatoes, and apple pie for desert.

"This smells good," she said. "Eating outdoors always seems to make the food taste better—don't you think?"

"Do you want to eat now? I'll get the bottles from the stream, and—"

"I'd rather talk for a while," she said. "But—"

He stared into her dark almond-shaped eyes; they reminded him of a doe's eyes; so bright and alert. "No. I'm not hungry either," he said, then rolled onto his side and supported his head on his hand, and they talked. He felt comfortable with her, as if he had always known her, so he spoke freely of his past, and about why he was there.

"Flynt, the man you're searching for was here, but he left several weeks ago. He stayed a month or so. He spent money like it would never run out—he did it with all the girls." She blushed. "Except me and Lil—"

Rory sat up with excited interest. "Do you have any idea where he was headed?"

"No, but you could ask Lil. She might know."

He smiled at her. "I don't want Lil to know that we talked about this. Is that alright with you?"

Salali nodded and then leaned over and untied her moccasins. She tugged them off, stood, and said, "It's getting warm and this dress is hot." She pulled it over her head revealing her smooth mahogany skin. Rory stared and was at once aroused. "Let's see how cold the water is." And she ran to the stream and waded to the center where the water was deepest and splashed her breast making her nipples jut out like small thimbles.

Rory jumped to his feet and nearly tripped and fell as he skinned his clothes and ran for the stream. Diving into the cold water, his manhood shrank almost as fast as it erected. They laughed and play in the water awhile before they returned to the blanket and let the hot afternoon air dry them. After they made love several times, they sat naked on the blanket and ravenously consumed the food from the basket. They returned to the stream one last time to cool off before they dressed and drove back to Lil's place.

E.B. sat in a rocker on the front porch and waited for them. "It's about time you got back here. What have you two been doing that you couldn't do here?"

Rory's face flushed, he took umbrage with E.B. tone and questions. "We could talk without your interruptions."

E.B. smiled and rubbed the back of his neck. His tone was gentler, when he said, "I guess I forgot what it's like to be a young man. When you're free, Rory, maybe we could get a bite and talk business?"

"Sure. Give me a few minutes with Salali and I'll meet you at the saloon—okay?"

E.B. nodded pushed up out of the chair and walked off the porch towards the saloon. "Don't forget your Colt." There was criticism in his tone.

Rory looked down. He had bolted out of Lil's without it, and thinking only about the picnic hadn't realized that he wasn't wearing it. That was the kind of mistake that E.B. preached about not making. He was sure there would be more conversation on the subject later. In the meantime, he walked Salali to the house, kissed her, and then shot up the stairs to his room for the Colt.

His friend sat at a table in the rear of the saloon nursing a glass of beer. As Rory walked to the table, he noted E.B.'s obvious stare at his Colt and steeled himself for a lecture. E.B. said nothing about his mistake. Instead, he asked, "Did you two have a good time?"

"Yes. I've never had a more enjoyable and satisfying day. Salali is wonderful, beautiful, caring, and—"

Stop there," said E.B. "Women and this business don't mix—ever."

"But—"

"Ever, I said. You've got to get her out of your mind."

Rory clenched his jaw tight and waited for his rising anger to subside. "I didn't plan on a long courtship and marriage." He paused—surprised at the sarcasm in his voice. But I do like her—a lot." He knew he had broken his mentor's cardinal rule when he let his guard down and left without his Colt. In another time or place, it might have gotten him killed. He wished he could change the subject, and then he recalled what Salali said. Rory gave E.B. a halfhearted smile. "Salali told me that Flynt came through here a month or so back."

"So that's what Lil meant when she said, 'It's good to have a big spender in the house again.'" E.B. stared east. Nodding, he said, "His three month lead is now a month. If he turns out to be true to form, we'll find him in Austin."

"When are we leaving?" Rory's voice held no excite-ment.

E.B. smiled. "Morning is soon enough. Let's get packed."

****

Rory brooded over Salali for the first two days of their ride to Austin, so E.B. let him be. He suspected that living in a monastery didn't offer many opportunities for a young man to enrich his knowledge regarding the other sex. E.B. watched Rory as they rode, *he'll get over it in time.*

The third day, E.B. woke to the aroma of fresh brewed coffee, and the smell of a rabbit roasted over a wood fire. "Mornin', Rory, breakfast smells good."

"I snared a fat juicy rabbit early this morning. Now that you're finally awake, I'll warm the beans and make some biscuits."

E.B. saw that Rory was contrite over his behavior, but decided not to bring up the girl or say anything further. "What do you mean, 'finally awake'? You should be mindful of your elders, not to mention betters."

"Yes, Sir—I was raised to respect seniors, and I do humbly apologize, but I don't know about the, 'better part'."

"If I wasn't so old and tired, I'd come over there and demonstrate who the better man is." They both laughed. E.B. had missed Rory's good-natured company these last few days, but hadn't realized it, until now. Sometime over these past weeks, he had started to think of Rory more like a son than he did a friend and partner.

Rory poured a cup of coffee and brought it to him. "I'm sorry about being so moody for these last few days. It's just that I never—"

"Everybody's young once and we all make the same mistakes. The trick in this business isn't to let them get you killed."

"Understood," said Rory, and then grinned at his friend ending their tension.

Chapter 7

On the porch of the Waterloo [18]Hotel and Saloon, John Flynt enjoyed his cigar. Smoke curled out of his nostrils then he carefully sipped the last of his morning coffee; leaving the fines in the bottom of the cup. He looked northward on Congress Avenue at the state capital building. The huge stone structure was damned impressive. Austin had grown rapidly since the war ended, and he intended to become an important part of the community as a ranch owner. He still had most of the $20,000 from the payroll robbery and was through with pissing it away on whores and whiskey.

Flynt arrived in Austin, over a month ago. The town was larger—more metropolitan than he'd remembered. Though two and three-story limestone buildings replaced the old wood structures, Congress Avenue was still just a wide dirt road.

He'd checked into the Waterloo and deposited the holdup money in the City Bank of Austin. Since then, he'd dealt with Mr. Jackson, a local attorney, to find and purchase an existing ranch. He didn't know much about how ranches operated as a business, so he figured that the thing to do was buy a working one. That way, he could just start out being the boss and let his foreman handle the day-to-day details. How hard could it be?

---

[18] Named after the settlement's name that was later changed to Austin.

Ha, if only pa could see me now. His father was a sharecropper back in Mississippi just like his father before him. John left home to fight in the war and never returned. As far as they knew, he was probably dead.

The army showed him how easy it was to kill. Most of the other men squeezed their eyes closed when they fired their rifles not wanting to see if they actually took another man's life, but not him. He picked his targets and smiled as he watched the blue coats fall. He liked killing, especially from ambush, and became good at it. An evil generated within John Flynt, and he felt no desire to restrain it. When they fixed bayonets for the first time in battle, he was terrified. However, he proved to be skilled at that as well. His adversaries tended to hesitate; he didn't. He watched the fear well up in their eyes as realization came to them that they were dying from the thrust of his blade. It thrilled him to a near orgasmic point of pleasure.

When the war ended, he felt a sense of deep loss. His comrades assumed, like them, he was saddened because the South had lost the conflict, but he knew the truth. It was because he could no longer kill with impunity; to enjoy the thrill of watching men die as he willed.

John Flynt changed his name and went west to join the Union Army. He assumed killing Indians would be the same as whites and blacks. He never got to find out—there was too much army bullshit to suit him, so he deserted after a month. Later, broke and hungry, he encountered a couple on the trail. They were trying to catch up to a wagon train they speculated was two days ahead. He relished the memory of the woman's begging, "Please, Mister, don't hurt us." She screamed when he shot her husband. She jumped from the wagon and tried to escape, but he caught her easily enough.

She thought he wanted to rape her at first and implored him to be gentle; she would cooperate. When he pulled his knife and put it to her throat, she called out, "Dear, God, help me—" He slowly cut her throat. His loins stirred when her eyes grew wide with the understanding that she would die; his manhood roused now at the memory.

After he pulled the wagon off the trail and released the horses, he moved on. Over the next few years, he drifted from town to town where he would spend his loot on women and booze. When the money ran out, he hit the trail watching for opportunities, which always seemed to be available. He invariably made it a point to kill his victims; that way there were never any witnesses. It was bad luck that the stagecoach driver got away and even worse recognized him.

San Angela was two hundred miles away. And since it was the army's payroll, the locals there didn't care. He led the Army north for several days before he managed to lose them, then he made his way to Austin and changed his name to John Sanders from Mississippi. Wells Fargo made good the lost money, so in the end it was only Wells Fargo, who was after him.

He felt confident that starting a new life hidden in plain sight was his best bet. It had been over three months since the robbery and there wasn't even a hint that anyone, including the sheriff, suspected who he really was.

The cigar nearly done, its concentrations of nicotine left a bitter taste in his mouth. He removed it from between his teeth, and spat on the ground then expertly dropped the tobacco stub into the pool of spittle. When he glanced up, he noticed two men looked at him as they rode by. "Howdy," he said, then turned, and strolled into the hotel's lobby. The two men reined up ....

****

"We'll stay at the Waterloo," said E.B. "I know the owner, she's a friend."

Rory glanced at E.B. with just the inkling of a smile. "At how many hotels are you known?"

"A few, Rory—just a few— it's important in our business to have a few select acquaintances." A smile came to his face. "Her name is Sara Atkinson—you'll like her."

They dismounted, gather their gear, and stepped onto the boardwalk. In the lobby, they saw the man who greeted them when they arrived. He sat in a chair with a cup of coffee and read the local newspaper, but he stopped and watched them closely. The man stared at Rory's moccasins and when he looked up, Rory looked back.

"Sorry—didn't mean to stare," said the man, "it's not often that you see a white man wearin' moccasins."

Rory nodded, and said, "They're comfortable so I wear them on the trail—it's boots in town."

The man rose and approached them. Mimicking the speaking manner of the officers he served under during the war, he said, "My name is John Sanders. I'm staying here as well, and it would be my pleasure to buy you gentlemen a drink."

E.B. finished signing the register and turned to face the man. He paused to inspect the man head-to-foot. "Maybe later, Mr. Sanders."

John nodded and turned to walk into the saloon just as Sara Atkinson came through the passageway. When she saw E.B., she lit up like an excited child who had found a favorite toy. "Well as I live and breathe. E.B. Parker, how the hell are ya?"

E.B., occupied with Sara, didn't notice that at the mention of his name, the man hesitated before he entered the saloon, but Rory saw it. He made a mental note to say something to his partner.

Sara embraced E.B. and then leaned back to look at his face. "How long has it been?"

"A long while," he said. "Sara, I want you to meet my partner Rory McLeod."

"Partner—you with a partner," she said. "I never thought I'd see the day when you would have a partner." She released E.B. and turned to face Rory. Sticking out her hand, she said, "Welcome Rory McLeod. Any friend of E.B. Parker's has a room here." She turned back to E.B. "Will you eat with me later—both of you? It'll be a private lunch in my room."

"I was afraid you wouldn't ask," said E.B. "What time?"

"11:30 sharp." She smiled at E.B. "You remember where my room is—don't you?"

E.B. grinned, and his eyes twinkled. Rory watched their exchange, and despite his best efforts to the contrary, he blushed bright red. Sara was a voluptuous blonde who apparently said whatever came to her mind.

Rory's flushed face only seemed to egg her on. She smiled at him impishly, but her eyes were suggestive. "We're just talkin', honey," she said. "There's no need for ya to worry. Now later—that's another story."

Independent of his conscious intent, he felt his manhood stir, and his face burned a deeper red, and he looked away. "What's our room numbers? I'll take our things up and then tend to the animals."

Later, after they had taken much-needed baths and put on clean shirts, they had an early lunch with Sara. Her suite was equal in size to two hotel rooms plus the width of the hallway. Rory couldn't see into her bedroom, but he was surprised to see how tastefully decorated the living room was—not at all like Lil's rooms.

His thoughts drifted to Salali—her pleasing smile and her gentle touch. But, then he pushed them away and returned to what E.B. and Sara had to say.

E.B. and Sara brought each other up to date on their lives, which included Lucy Parker, his daughter. Sara asked, "How old is Lucy now?"

E.B. paused. "Nineteen."

"Is she still at the boarding school in Saint Louie?"

"Yes."

"When's the last time you were there to see her?"

Again, E.B. paused and then surprise shone on his face. "It's been over two years—but I write often."

"Is she seein' a man on a regular basis, or talked about marriage?"

Rory watched as E.B. stiffened in his chair and a shocked expression shone on his face. Disquieted by Sara's questions, he said, "Lucy is a good girl. Besides, they don't let men enter the school."

"E.B. Parker," said Sara, her tone stern. "Nineteen makes Lucy a young woman, and she has the same urges and thoughts as a man." She stared at him with her mouth set firm and waited for his response.

Rory watched their exchange. His friend's face reddened, and then his eyes widened realization shone through; Sara was right. Finally, he responded, "When I think of Lucy it's as my little-girl, not as a woman. I guess I need to get back there and have a talk with her about men and—"

Sara cut him off. "Livin' in a girl's school—I'm sure she understands everything she needs to know and how to use the knowledge."

"We have to finish this hunt, but then I'll head back to Saint Louis."

"Who are you lookin' for?"

"A man who goes by the name John Flynt," said E.B. "He's slight build with dark hair and around five-eight."

"What's he wanted for?"

"He robbed an Army payroll of $20,000," said Rory, joining the conversation for the first time. "And he killed the stage guard. The driver reported he would have shot him too, but he escaped while Flynt opened the strongbox. We've trailed him to Austin."

E.B. asked, "Been any big spenders in the last month or so?"

"Not that I've heard of," said Sara. "But a Mr. John Sanders, the gent you was talkin' to down stairs, deposited $18,000 in gold at the bank."

Rory asked, "How do you know that?"

Sara smiled at him. "Well, in the first place I own this hotel and word gets around when an important business man is in town. Secondly, I know the banker and Mr. Jackson the lawyer who works with Mr. Sanders—let's say they spend money here." She looked steadily into his eyes and caused him to blush once more.

Attentive and curious, Rory asked, "What does he need a lawyer for?"

"He wants to buy a ranch, but from what I hear, he's not havin' much luck. Since the war, people back east want beef, and we have plenty. The ranchers around here are finally makin' money and aren't too keen on sellin'; least ways for what he's offerin'."

Rory remembered the man's response when he overheard Sara's call to E.B. "I meant to tell you earlier, but when Sanders heard your name, he stopped cold for a full second."

"That's not so uncommon," said E.B. "I'm known in these parts."

Sara perked up. "Sanders told me he was from back east somewhere. How would he know your name—you're not that famous?"

"Valid point, Sara," said E.B. "We'll look into Mr. Sanders tomorrow." Turning to Rory, he winked. "Rory, why don't you go downstairs, and if he's there keep an eye on him."

Rory didn't catch on at first, but when he did, he stumbled all over himself graciously trying to leave the room. Sara watched him closely and began to giggle, which caused him once again to blush deeply. At the door, he managed to say without stammering, "I'll see you later, E.B."

"In the morning for breakfast downstairs," said E.B.

Rory ducked out through the doorway without further comment. He could hear their laughter beyond the door and smiled at his own buffoonish behavior.

Downstairs, he found a table in the rear of the saloon and ordered coffee. He wore his Colt, and as E.B. schooled, he'd already removed the hammer loop from his revolver. From his view, he watched the men inside the barroom not making eye contact with anyone. The bar's business was slow, which he assumed was because of the time of day.

The Waterloo was nicer than the Cactus Hotel, but not a grand as the El Paso International, but the patrons looked the same. Men sat at tables and talked while they smoked cigars and sipped whiskey or beer. One old timer, mindless of his actions, curled his moustache while he gambled at the poker table. Another ran his fingers through his long greasy hair as he watched roulette wheel spin. In the corner, a piano player dressed in a plaid suit pounded the keys, and the bar girls danced with cowboys.

On his third cup of coffee and bored, Rory glanced up just as Sanders entered into the saloon. He stood by the entrance and scanned the room. When his eyes landed on Rory, he nodded and approached the table. "It's Mr. McLeod isn't it?" he asked, "May I join you?"

Rory nodded. As Sanders sat down, Rory studied him closely on guard for weapons. There wasn't anything visible; however, there was a telltale bulge under the left side of his chest. *He has a hideout gun*, Rory thought.

"May I buy you that drink I promised?"

"Coffee is it for me. I have an early day tomorrow."

The bartender, having seen Sanders come in, now stood at the table with a bottle of expensive whiskey and two glasses. Sanders said, "Just one glass." Then with a patronizing tone added, "Mr. McLeod here doesn't drink."

Without conversation, the bartender, a tall lanky man, his neatly trimmed hair pasted to his skull with perfumed oil, sat the bottle and one glass on the table and departed. Sanders waited for the bartender to depart. "Where is your associate Mr. Parker?"

"He's upstairs—retired for the night," said Rory, he chuckled to himself at the joke. "It was a long ride and a man his age tires easily." *There is no sense letting Flynt think otherwise.*

"That's unfortunate," said Sanders. "I hoped to speak with Mr. Parker. He's quite infamous you know. I'm sure I would find it exciting to hear his stories about the men he's captured."

"He doesn't talk about his business endeavors."

"Oh—that's too bad. Well, we'll just have to talk about something else then." He paused. When Rory didn't respond, he continued. "I'm from Mississippi here to buy a ranch. What brings you to Austin?"

****

Sanders focused closely on Rory's eyes, he watched for any sign that the he lied.

"We're headed back to Saint Louis to visit Mr. Parker's daughter."

"I wouldn't think a man in Mr. Parker's profession would have a family."

Rory didn't respond, but sat relaxed and sipped his coffee.

"Who's next on his list of men to hunt for bounty?"

"He hasn't told me. As far as I know, he may not have anyone in mind. I suppose he'll select someone when we return."

Sanders become slightly irritated with Rory's lack of participation in the conversation. "Come now. He must have a list of possible candidates?"

"Well—we were entertaining a leader of a band of Comancheros, but then Wells Fargo's after a murdering holdup man. He was headed north the last we heard."

Sanders clinched his jaw tight and tried not to react to Rory's, 'Well Fargo,' comment. *They think I headed north, so I got away clean. But then, E.B. Parker is no fool and when he's after a man, it's just a matter of time ....* Again, he studied the young man. *He seemed harmless enough, but ....*

"It's been a pleasure, Mr. Sanders, but I'm afraid I must call it a day—it was a long day's ride for me too." Rory stood to leave.

"Maybe I'll see you two at breakfast," said Sanders.

"Anything is possible. Thanks again, Mr. Sanders. Good night."

****

Rory woke early. He listened for sounds of E.B. being awake in the adjoining room—it was silent. Light streamed through the hotel room's window, reflected off the wash-stand's small oval mirror, and brightened the space. He rolled out of the rope bed, despite the down-filled mattress the rope left visible marks on his back. Rory stretched and scratched his way to the washstand. *I'm not sure that sleeping on the ground isn't more comfortable,* he thought. Inspecting himself in the mirror, he decided that he needed a haircut. He would get one today.

There was a knock on the door followed by a familiar voice. "Rory, are you up?"

"Yeah—doors unlocked, E.B., come in."

E.B. stepped through the doorway, his shirt still unbuttoned; his holster slung from his shoulder, and his boot in his left hand. Besides appearing unkempt, he looked tired. Rory smiled at his friend and mentor. "I see you didn't get much sleep."

"It's been a long time since I've seen Sara," said E.B. followed by a chuckle. "I had forgotten how demanding she can be."

Rory looked away, but he didn't blush. He was still a little uncomfortable with the casual conversation about sex and changed the subject as he began to dress. "Sanders sat at my table last night. He was curious about your whereabouts and wanted to know who we're after."

"What did you tell him?"

"That you had gone to bed early, and that we were traveling back east to see your daughter."

"Did he believe you?"

"Not entirely, I think, but he didn't dismiss my comments either. I don't want to jump to conclusions, but—"

"But you will. You think Sanders is Flynt—right?"

"Yes, E.B., I do."

"Why?"

With his shirt not fully buttoned, Rory paused to consider. "There are several reasons." He held up his hand raising fingers as he spoke. "He resembles the description provided by the people of San Angela plus Lil and Salali. His arrival here coincides with when he left Lil's place. Then there is the $18,000 in the bank, and finally—I have a feeling about him. Being near him is like being near a rattle snake."

E.B. nodded his head as Rory spoke. When Rory concluded, he said, "Those are all well-thought-out reasons. The last one is the most important though—you need to learn to pay attention to your gut. Don't act solely on your gut, but listen when it tells you to be on guard. My gut has saved my arse more than once or twice."

Eagerness sounded in Rory's voice. "So you agree?"

"Not so fast. We'll spend a day or two to watch and learn, and then we'll decide. Meanwhile, let's go downstairs for breakfast and some much-needed coffee."

****

As they strolled through the doorway of the saloon, Sanders stood. He was at the table Rory had chosen the night before. The other tables were occupied by, hotel guests, and local businessmen eating their breakfast. Sanders waved for them to join him. "I do the talkin', Rory."

Rory didn't respond or react.

"Good morning, gentlemen," said Sander. "Please won't you join me for breakfast?"

Sanders already sat in the chair that faced the entrance and the people in the room. E.B. looked uncomfortable about the situation and surveyed the room for his second best option. "Please, Mr. Parker, take my chair," Sanders offered. "I understand a man in your profession has to be on guard at all times." He moved to the second best location, which left Rory's back to the door and men at the tables. However, he was confident that E.B. had his back covered. Rory smiled at E.B. when he saw his left thumb caress the hammer of his Colt to ensure it was free of the leather loop—he did the same.

With a glance at each man, Sanders grinned, as they performed their ritual. "Like I said, 'on guard all the time' Ay?"

E.B. met his gaze and smiled. The man's eyes were cold and unfeeling. He'd seen that look before on the battlefield; he understood what Rory meant about watching a snake. Further, he concluded that Rory was correct—this was Flynt. *So, what's his game?* He wondered. "Thank you for allowing us to sit at your table, Mr. Sanders," said E.B.

"Please. I would consider it an honor if you would ad-dress me as John."

"As you prefer—most folks call me Parker and this is Rory."

"Since I didn't get to buy you that drink I promised, let me buy you breakfast."

"It's not necessary, but as you wish," said E.B.

Sanders waved for the bartender. E.B. noted that the bartender had been watching since they sat down, and that he moved quickly when Sanders summoned him. "What'll be, Mr. Sanders?"

Sanders deferred to E.B. "Gentlemen?"

"Eggs, bacon, biscuits or cornbread, and black coffee—hot."

The bartender turned to Rory. "I'll have the same please—and some molasses and butter—if you have any."

"We do," said the bartender.

He looked at Sanders. "My usual."

"Right away, Sir," said the bartender, and he hurried away to the kitchen. He returned almost immediately with cups and a pot of hot coffee.

Sanders grabbed the pot and filled both their cups. "As I explained to Rory last night, this is quite the treat to meet you, Mr. Parker—I mean Parker. If you don't mind my saying it, you're infamous back east. I hoped to learn the details of some of your escapades."

"Is that so, why?" asked E.B. He gave Sanders a deadpan stare.

"Well—you're the first bounty hunter I've met. Frankly—there's been nothing of interest to write home about. Meeting you and retelling your adventures would really be something back in Mississippi—don't you see?"

E.B. studied the man. The hideout gun didn't go unnoticed. *Flynt is working awfully hard to convince us that he's truly is a dude from Mississippi—why? I'll play along—for now.* "There's not really that much to bounty huntin'. Most outlaws are stupid and make mistakes. We just wait til they do then we capture or kill them—depends on the circumstances."

Rory saw Sanders' eyes flash at the comment, but he recovered quickly. "Come-come, Parker," said Sanders. "You're just being overly modest. Is the person you're hunting now your typical—stupid outlaw?"

So that's it, E.B. thought. *He doesn't think we've recognized him and he's tryin' to find out who we're after.* "Presently, we're not hunting anyone," said E.B., and gave Sanders his most disarming smile. "We're headed back to Saint Louis to see my daughter. It's been a while."

Sanders' shoulders lowered ever so slightly, and he leaned back on his chair. E.B. noticed the slight change and continued. "When we return, if he isn't already been captured, we plan on going after a Comanchero name of Cain. He's been raiding in West Texas along the Texas-New Mexico border."

Sanders leaned forward onto the table and asked, "How do you propose to capture this Comanchero? Don't they travel in bands of several men?"

E.B. noted—*he seems genuinely interested.* "Sorry, John—that falls under the heading of professional secrets."

Chapter 8

Flynt watched them as they left the saloon. He wasn't completely satisfied with their story, or that he fooled them with his alias. They had just arrived in Austin, and except for Sara, they hadn't spoken to anyone else; that he knew of. He would have to be watchful.

He had a meeting scheduled with Jackson this morning to discuss the purchase of the Rocking-K ranch from Mrs. Kramer. She was a widow with two daughters, who wanted to go back east to find husbands. Jackson thought he could buy it for a good price; less than $8,000 was Flynt's budget.

Flynt glanced at his watch as he arrived at Jackson's office; 10:00 sharp. Inside, Jackson and a mature woman sat behind a table. Her iron-gray hair pulled back from her lined and tanned face confirmed she was a hands-on ranch owner. Jackson rose when Flynt entered the office. The lanky man moved to greet his client and enveloped Flynt's hand with his long bony fingers. "Right on time, Mr. Sanders," he said, "May I introduce you to Mrs. Kramer?"

Mrs. Kramer's clothes hung from her thin sinewy body, but surprisingly, her handshake was as firm as any Flynt had ever shaken. He paused as she scanned him with her steely light-blue eyes. Flynt asked, "How do you do, Mrs. Kramer?"

"I do fine, young man. Jackson here tells me, you're interested in buying my ranch. Is that so?"

"Well, Mrs. Kramer, it's true I'm looking to purchase a working ranch here in Austin. If the purchase price is within my budget, then your ranch is the one I'll likely select." Flynt smile patiently at the old woman. "Mr. Jackson and I rode out to your place last week and looked the ranch over and—"

"Yeah—my men told me you was there. They know Jackson, so they didn't bother to see why you was there— they know I want to sell the place."

Flynt nodded and smiled pleasantly.

With stern eyes fixed on his, she asked, "What do you plan to do with the hands I got workin' for me?"

"Keep them on the payroll, assuming your operation is profitable and they're capable."

"I brung my books. You and Jackson can go over them while I do some shoppin' at the feed store. When you are done—make me an offer."

She sprang up, caught both off men guard, and forced them to jump to their feet. "Never understood why men felt like they has to stand up just cause a woman does." She tromped out of the office shaking her head.

They watched her leave. Jackson turned to Flynt. "Pioneer stock and tough as nails; her grandmother settled here when Mexico owned Texas. She's not too happy about going back east, but her daughters insist."

"What's her place worth?"

"Hard to say positively, but the house and buildings are in good repair. A sure water supply—they've never lost livestock during dry times. Their foreman, assuming he stays, is a top hand. He's been there over ten years. According to her books, they got money and working capital in the bank. They should equal or beat last year's income when they sell their beef."

"Okay, but what's it worth—what do I have to pay to buy her out?"

Jackson scowled at Sanders putting on the spot. "I say $12,000 would be a fair price."

"She takes the money out of the bank?"

Confused, Jackson said, "Why of course. It belongs to her."

"So how much 'working capital' do I need to operate the ranch and continue to make money?"

Jackson pinched his brow. "She's kept $5,000 in the bank for the last ten years."

Flynt sat down and massaged his temples. "Okay—offer her $8,000."

"That's only seventy-five percent of the value."

"Yeah, but who around here is going to pay that? Besides, she getting pressured from her daughters to sell—make the offer."

Jackson shrugged. "As you wish—wait here." Jackson left to find Mrs. Kramer. Flynt relaxed into his chair, he felt well satisfied with himself. As he observed Jackson cross the street, he caught a glimpse E.B. Parker as he stepped back into the shadows of a building. *Why would he do that ... is he following me ... has he figured out I'm not Sanders?* He asked himself, and then remembered what Parker said, 'outlaws are stupid and they all make mistakes'. *Well I'll just have to be careful and not make a mistake.*

Flynt glanced out the window and saw Jackson's return. Only twenty-minutes had passed since he left, but his face bore a triumphant grin.

As he came through the doorway, he said, "Mr. Sanders, she's accepted your offer. We'll have to get the paper work ready today—"

"Hold off on that. I've got something else to take care of first."

Jackson stared at his client. His smile faded replaced by an expression of disbelief. "But I thought—"

"Never mind what you thought. Just do as I say."

"But Mrs. Kramer—"

"No one else is offering to buy her ranch. She'll accept the delay—she has no choice."

Crestfallen, Jackson left his office to find Mrs. Kramer. Flynt followed him out, but headed instead to the City Bank of Austin. As one of the bank's largest depositors, Flynt bypassed the tellers and went directly to the bank president's office.

Walter Peterson, a prosperous looking man, stood to greet him. "Mr. Sanders, to what do I owe the pleasure?"

"I'm closing my account. Have my gold ready by 1:00 today."

Peterson fell back into his chair and blustered, "Closing your account—gold? Mr. Sanders, I can assure you that a check drawn on this bank is good anywhere."

Flynt glared at the banker. "Peterson, I deposited gold and gold is what I mean to receive." Leaning over the now seated Peterson, Flynt asked, "Is there a problem?"

"No, no, not at all," said Peterson. "It's just highly unusual, that's all. Are you leaving town then?"

Flynt stopped before he answered. *Taking my gold out the bank will be all over town by noon.* He said, "No. I'm negotiating a deal to buy Mrs. Kramer's ranch and I want my gold to pay her off."

Peterson smiled. "That's not necessary, Mr. Sanders. Mrs. Kramer is a founding depositor with our bank. I'll just issue you a letter of credit and—"

"I want my gold by 1:00." Flynt noted the confused expression on Peterson's face, and added, "I drive a hard bargain and I've found that the sound of gold coins clinking provides more appeal than a piece of paper from a bank. Understand?"

The banker stood and grasped the lapels of his pinstriped jacket. His smiled returned and he nodded. "Precisely, Mr. Sanders, and your funds will be ready by 1:00."

Peterson escorted Flynt out of his office to the bank's entrance. Extending his hand, he said, "Until 1:00, Mr. Sanders."

Flynt stood outside the bank and looked around. Specifically, he was on the lookout for Parker or McLeod. Not seeing either of them, he casually strolled to the livery. There, he checked on his horse and made arrangements to have it saddled and waiting at 1:00. Then, he returned to his room at the Waterloo, changed clothes, and waited.

At 12:50, Flynt came down the stairs to the lobby. Dressed in trail clothes, his shirt opened at the collar with a bandanna tired round his neck and a fringed buckskin jacket. He carried his bedroll under one arm, and saddlebags slung over his shoulder. Flynt was armed—a Remington .44 nestled in its holster, and he carried a matching caliber Winchester carbine. Sara sat behind the desk. "I'll be out of town for a few days," he said. "Hold my room."

When Flynt entered the bank at 1:00, Peterson had the gold stacked on the desk in his office. "If you'll just step into my office there is some paperwork, and of course you need to count the money."

Flynt's gaze conveyed his meaning. "No need. If it's not all there I'll be back."

Peterson swallowed hard. "Please, Mr. Sanders. I really prefer that you count the funds to ensure there isn't a mistake."

Inside the banker's office, Flynt saw eighteen stacks of twenty dollar gold coins of equal heights—about six inches. "How much is each stack?"

"One thousand dollars," said Peterson.

"Okay, it looks right." He asked, "Where do I sign?" Flynt had a fleeting thought; *I should have brought my horse here and robbed the bank. If things don't work out, I may do just that.* He signed the papers and stack-by-stack shoved nine stacks into each side of his saddlebags. Hefting the load, he figured it weighted about sixty pounds. He'd forgotten how reassuring the weight felt.

By 1:30, he was mounted and riding south out of town.
****

Nestled in a grove of cottonwood trees, they sat their mounts and watched unseen from the road. Rory asked, "How'd you know he would head south?"

E.B. smiled. "If he suspects that we are onto him, then he'd head for Mexico. If he didn't think it, he might be going north on business, and we'd have no problem picking up his trail."

His tone rich with eagerness, Rory asked, "When do we take him?"

"We'll let him make camp for the night and when his guard is down—we'll take him then. He's been taking it easy for a month or so, so I'm betting he'll make camp early. There'll be plenty of time for us to scout him out."

Four hours later, they smelled smoke. E.B. checked his timepiece. "It has to be him—I'll stay here with the horses and you scout his camp."

Rory slid from his horse, and pulled his carbine from its scabbard; he gave a nod to E.B. and trotted off down the trail. A breeze blew from the southeast and carried smoke from Flynt's campfire. *That's a lot of smoke for a campfire. I would have thought he'd use drier wood.* Easing towards the camp, Rory spotted Flynt through the trees crouched by his fire brewing coffee—seemingly unaware that he was about to be captured.

E.B. gave a start when Rory stepped from the trees. "Damn it—that's a good way to get shot."

"I can't help it that you're getting old and your hearing gotten poorly." Rory laughed out loud—he couldn't help it. He had deliberately stolen his way behind E.B. intending to startle him—it was the kind of humor the Apache enjoyed.

E.B.'s response was a glare, he asked, "What did you find out?"

"It's just like you predicted. He's made camp for the day. It'll be several hours before dark. Let's move back up the trail, the winds blowing from the southeast, and make camp for coffee and grub. When we move, we'll leave the horses there—no sense in taking a chance of his horse getting wind of ours."

E.B. nodded. With their horses at an easy walk, they backtracked nearly a mile before they set up camp. Rory found plenty of dry material for a fire. Once again, he thought it strange that a man used to being on the run would use green wood in his campsite, but it passed as he focused with the tasks at hand. They made a small fire for coffee and chewed on jerky and hardtack.

Rory drew lines in the dirt to diagram Flynt's camp. E.B. studied the layout for several minutes. "Okay. Here's what we're goin' to do. We'll leave the animals here and go in on foot. At his camp, you work your way around to his horse and keep it calm. I'll ease into his camp and get the drop on him."

After dark, with only moonlight to see, they made their way to Flynt's camp. As agreed, Rory circled the camp to find the man's horse—but it wasn't there. Before he could make his way back to E.B., the bounty hunter entered the camp. Rory squinted to focus through the grey smoke. A fleeting thought crossed his mind, *How could Flynt sleep so sound with all this smoke?* E.B. stood over Flynt's bedroll, and nudged him with the toe of his boot and cocked his pistol.

A shot fired—Rory watched Parker's moonlit features. He read the momentary confusion on his mentor's face as E.B. glanced at his Colt—it hadn't fired. Abruptly, E.B. collapsed to the ground landing like a heavy sack of feed. Rory heard a commotion among the trees behind where E.B. fell, and he fired four shots blindly in that direction. Seconds later, he heard a horse gallop away north—back towards Austin.

****

Flynt knew they would follow him. That's what he intended. He wasn't going to be one of Parker's stupid outlaws, '—— who made mistakes, and got caught.' *I'll get
him first.* Several hours south of Austin, he began to watch
for a place to set his ambush. North of San Marcos he found
a thickly wooded place next to a creek—it was perfect.

A game trail led him through the trees from the road to
a shaded clearing near the water. An ash-filled ring of
stones indicated that he wasn't the first to select this location for a campsite. He saw to the needs of his horse and
then built a fire. To make sure they would have no trouble
finding him, he used damp wood to produce plenty of
smoke. With his scene ready, he lounged against a log sipping his coffee.

The sun began to slip below the treetops—it was time.
He added more damp sticks to the fire, which caused a
smoky haze, and then, using debris and his hat, he built a
form under his blanket. In the darkness with only the
smoky fire light to see by, it would fool Parker. He saddled
his horse and moved into the trees nearer the trail to wait.

Propped against a tree, Flynt's attention was drawn to
movement in his campsite. A large dark figure slowly circled the fire. *He moves quiet for such a big man.*

E.B. stopped short of Flynt's dummy bedroll. Flynt
raised his rifle and aimed at the center of the bounty hunter's back. He put tension on the trigger. It surprised him
slightly when the cartridge exploded, and the rifle bucked—
sending death down the barrel.

Flynt smiled. He enjoyed watching Parker drop to the
ground. Splayed across the dummy he had used to trick the
bounty hunter. *Did he remain alive long enough to realize
that it was he who made a stupid mistake?*

Bullets thudded into the surrounding trees. Momentarily, he forgot about the young man. *No matter—Parker is
dead, and the boy is no real match for me.* He swung up on
his horse and bolted to the trail, north back to Austin.

****

Rory rushed from the tree cover to his friend's body. He put his hand on the bounty hunter's back and felt it expand with breath. "E.B., can you hear me? How badly are you hurt?"

E.B. stirred. "I can't feel my legs."

In the poor light, Rory moved his hand down Parker's torso until he felt the sticky gel of fresh clotted blood. He put his finger into the bullet hole, fully expecting E.B. to cry out. E.B. made no sound or gave indication he felt Rory's probe. "I feel the slug. It's lodged in your spine."

"Can you get it out?" E.B. asked and then paused for a deep breath. Even in this faint light, Rory could make out the beads of sweat on his friend's face. E.B. continued. "The longer you wait—the swelling will make it more difficult."

"I can't see anything in this light—I don't see how—"

"You don't need light. Use your fingers and a knife—feel for the bullet. Get the kit from my horse. I'll talk you through it—if I can."

Rory returned with Parker's horse and rifled through his saddlebags until he found the kit. Loosening the tie that bound it, he unrolled the kit. "Tell me what you see."

He held the kit close to the light. "There are two thin bladed knifes, four hooked probes, long-nosed pliers, and an assortment of curved needles. There's some thread too."

"That's catgut for closing the wound," said E.B. "You said you could feel the bullet?"

"Yes."

"That's good. Take one of the hooked probes and see if you can dislodge the slug and fish it out of the wound."

"What about the pain? If you jerk—I'm sure to make it worse."

"I don't feel anything," said E.B. "I don't know if it's shock or worse, but the sooner you get that slug out the better. Now get to it."

With his knife, Rory split Parker's jacket and shirt and washed away the blood. He was surprised at how little bleeding there was. He eased his finger once again into the bullet hole until it touched the slug. Using his finger as a guide, he tracked the probe down alongside. He sensed more than felt the object. Gently, he hooked the curved point over the lead and pulled. "It won't budge."

"You'll have to use more force. It's lodged in there—just get it out."

Rory removed this finger and placed his hand on Parker's back. Pushing down with his left hand, he tugged on the probe with his right. It broke free and came out in one motion. The point of the hook was stuck in the deformed lead slug. "I got it."

Even though E.B. said he didn't feel any pain, his body none-the-less seemed to be shutting down. Soaked with sweat, Parker's skin tone had turned pallid—Rory was worried. He built up Flynt's fire and covered E.B. with all the bedding available to keep him warm.

From the medical knowledge taught him by his Apache mother, Rory set water to boil while he searched through the herbs he carried in his saddlebags. From the assorted small leather pouches, he selected one. He shook out a palm full of white willow bark chips and dumped it into the boiling water to brew a tea. E.B. slipped in and out of consciousness throughout the night. Rory sat by his side and periodically forced him to sip the herb tea.

****

Sunlight filtered through the trees and settled on the bounty hunter's face. He opened his eyes, looked around, and saw Rory slumped forward asleep holding a cup in his hands. The smell of burnt wood drew his attention. Turning his head, he saw the frosted embers that remained of the campfire.

E.B. started to rise, but his legs seemed restrained. *The covers,* he thought and struggled to throw them off his legs. He pulled his elbows in order to prop himself up, and he stared at his feet. They were there, but he had no sensation of control. It was as if legs and feet were asleep, asleep to his waist. He fell back onto his bedroll. "Damn that back-shootin' son-of-bitch!"

Rory's head jerked up and he looked to E.B. "What is it, E.B.? Are you in pain?"

"No. That's just it. I don't feel anything from my waist down—except I got to pee."

"At least you're alive. There were times last night—"

"You call this living? What am I suppose to do now?" E.B. pounded the ground with his fist. "You should have just let me die."

"Take it easy," said Rory. "You don't want to reopen your wound." Rory stood and walked to their horses and re-trieved one of their canteens. After he poured the last of the water into the coffee pot, he handed it to E.B. "Use this to pee and make sure you don't get them confused."

E.B. scowled. "I assume that was a joke, but I don't see the humor."

As Rory moved about the camp making breakfast and performing the numerous mundane activities that one takes for granted, E.B. grew resentful and angry. *Is this the way the rest of my life will be? Pissing in a jug and lay-ing about having others care for me. I'd be better off dead.*

Gently, Rory propped him up against a log, so E.B. could function and feed himself. Then he left camp, return-ing with two long saplings and several branches. E.B. watched him for a few minutes. Finally, he asked, "What's all that for?"

Chapter 9

Lamps flickered through the windows of houses and the few businesses that remained open after dark. Slowly, Rory rode into town. He led a horse with a body tied atop a travois pulled behind.

A few men outside the saloons watched as he passed. One called out, "Who is it?"

Rory didn't answer—he continued down the street headed for the doctor's office next to the general store.

Another of the men trotted alongside the travois until light beaming through saloon doors illuminated the bounty hunter's face. "It's E.B. Parker."

Someone from the crowd called, "Is he dead?"

"Looks like it—can't tell for sure." The man trotted ahead to Rory. "Say, Son, is your friend dead?"

Rory stared down at the man and loosed the leather loop keeping his Colt holstered. The snoop took the hint and dropped back, but he continued to follow—at a distance.

A hand carved wooden sign protruded from the column that supported the roof over the boardwalk. It showed an apothecary jar next to the name, Paul J. Benson, M.D.

Rory dismounted, tied the horses, and checked on E.B.; he shook him gently. "E.B., are you awake?"

"Are we there?"

"Yes. You lie still while I go inside to get the doctor." He patted his friend's shoulder before leaving him.

As he reached the door, the man from the saloon called to the crowd, "He ain't dead yet."

Rory whirled with his hand on his Colt. Even in the dim light, Rory saw the curious bastard's eyes grow large. He put his hands into the air and quickly backed away. Rory watched as he ran to the safety of his friends at the saloon.

Doc Benson appeared at the door. He combed his long boney fingers through his graying dark hair. "What's all the commotion about?"

Rory turned to the doctor. "It's my friend. He's been shot."

The doctor looked past Rory. He grabbed his stethoscope and came out into the street. Benson held Parker's wrist and then put the instrument to the bounty hunter's chest and listened. "His pulse is strong, and his heart sounds fine. Where is he wounded?"

"He's shot in the back, Doc. I got the slug out, but he can't feel his legs."

"I can't do anything out here. We need to get him inside."

With Benson outside, the inquisitive men from the saloon felt it safe to investigate. The doctor surveyed the crowd. "You two," he said. "Give us a hand to get this man into my office."

One of the men asked, "Why'd you pick us, Doc?" Benson didn't respond—he just stared. Sheepishly, the two men did as instructed.

Inside, on the treatment table, Benson examined the wound. "The stitches are crude, but otherwise I couldn't have done better."

Rory visibly relaxed. "What about his legs?"

"Nerve damage I expect. Spinal trauma is tricky. He may regain the use of his legs, or he may not. Bed rest and time will tell."

E.B. spoke to the doctor for the first time, he asked, "How long?"

Rory and Benson turned to look at E.B. "Hard to tell," said Benson. "We'll have you stay here for a few days, where I can look after you, and later we'll move you to the hotel."

E.B. raised his head and looked around the room. "Whose is the 'we'?"

Benson chuckled. "My wife Rebecca and I are the 'we'. She's also my nurse."

****

Flynt watched as Rory came out of the doctor's office and led the horses to the livery. *I should have doubled back and taken care of McLeod,* 'he thought. *If Parker pulls through, I'm finished here.'*

Flynt flipped his cheroot butt out onto the street and downed the last of his whiskey before stepping from the shadows and into the hotel Waterloo. Sara Atkinson was behind the counter checking ledgers. *She hasn't heard the news.* He said, "Pardon me, Sara, but young McLeod just rode in with your friend Parker and it seems that he's been injured."

Sara jumped to her feet. "Where is he?"

"McLeod took him to Doc Benson's office."

She rushed past him and out the door.

He chuckled. *That's it. Run over there and see how bad he's hurt and then come back here and tell me.*

"What's so funny, Flynt?" He hadn't heard Rory move in behind him.

Flynt raised his hands. "What now?"

Rory stuck the barrel of his gun hard into Flynt's back and then patted him down with his free hand. He pulled the shoulder-holstered pistol from beneath Flynt's jacket and stuffed it into his gun belt. "One at a time put your hands behind your back." Flynt did as instructed and Rory clicked the Tower[19] ratchet cuffs around his wrist. "I should shoot you in the back they same way you did E.B., but I'd rather see you hang for killing the stage guard. Now move."

"To where?"

"The sheriff's office."

Flynt still had one chance—if the deputy was on duty. As they approached the jail, Flynt strained to see through the window. He was in luck—Deputy Toll sat behind the desk.

Rory pushed Flynt through the door. "I have a prisoner for you to lockup, Sheriff."

Toll stared at Rory with his mouth agape. He blinked several times and then finally spoke, "I'm not the sheriff. He's at home in bed I imagine."

"You've got keys to the cell don't you?"

"Yes—"

"Then you'll do. Which cell do you want the prisoner in?"

Toll looked at Flynt, who was smiling. "Mister, that's Mr. Sanders. He ain't no prisoner."

"I tried to explain that he was making a mistake, Matthew," said Flynt. He knew Toll preened when addressed by his given name.

Toll looked back to Rory. "What's Mr. Sanders supposed to have done?"

"Robbed Wells Fargo of an Army payroll and killed the stage guard in cold blood."

---

[19] Tower Manufacturing was the leading US supplier of handcuffs until after WWII.

Flynt continued smiling and he shrugged as if to say this is all a mistake. "You know me, Matthew. Do you think I could rob a stagecoach and kill someone?"

"No, sir, I don't." Toll turned back to Rory. "Son, I'm afraid you've made a mistake. Now let Mr. Sanders go."

Rory reached for his inside pocket. "I've got the wanted poster on him—"

Toll was quick; he drew his revolver and held it on Rory. "I said to let Mr. Sanders go—now do as I say."

"Deputy—"

He cocked the pistol; Rory unlocked the cuffs.

Flynt unconsciously rubbed his wrist as he turned to Rory and smiled menacingly. To Toll, he said, "Thank you, Matthew. I don't hold any ill will towards this young man, but I wouldn't like to have any further trouble. Could you keep him in a cell for tonight, and we'll get all this settled tomorrow when the sheriff is available?"

"That seems reasonable." Toll pointed his pistol to a heavy wooden door. "It's empty back there—your choice. The first cell on your right has the most comfortable cot."

"Deputy, you're making a huge mistake," said Rory. "Put us both in cells for the night. When the sheriff comes in then we'll get this situation settled."

Toll considered this and looked back to Flynt.

Flynt smiled innocently. "Matthew, I don't want to cause you any concern. If you think I should spend the night here as well, then I will."

Flynt stood next to Toll's desk where the deputy laid his and Rory's side arms. He'd go for his gun if the deputy called his hand.

"Nah—it'll be alright. You just be here early, Mr. Sanders."

Flynt casually retrieved his pistol and holstered it. "Right after breakfast—that okay?"

"You bet, Mr. Sanders."

****

Back at the hotel, Flynt found Sara seated behind the reception desk. She was quietly staring off into the distance, lost in thought. "How is your friend, Sara?"

Sara jumped and turned to the sound of Flynt's voice. "Oh, Mr. Sanders, you startled me." She put her hand to her bosom to slow her racing heartbeat. "E.B. was shot in the back by someone they were trailing. He'll live, but the doctor doesn't think he'll ever walk again." Tears spilled over the lids of her eyes and she sobbed, "It's a mixed blessing I guess. He'll have to stop bounty hunting, which was sure to get him killed—but he can't walk."

Flynt smiled inwardly. It turned out to be better than he planned. Parker was out of commission and no longer a danger. The best part—Parker knew it was he, John Flynt, who took away the use of his legs.

Sara sniffled. "I'm sorry to hear about Mr. Parker," he said. "Though it was bound to happen sooner or later—he'd run into someone better than him. Did he say who he was after?"

"I didn't ask. The doctor has him drugged with laudanum, so he's not talking straight."

"What about his young associate?"

"Rory wasn't there. I don't know anything about what they were doing. They played their cards close to the vest."

Flynt nodded. He faked a show of sympathy for Sara and her misery. "I'll say goodnight then, if you'll excuse me."

Sara smiled at him. *Bravely,* he thought. Flynt left her and entered the saloon through the connecting door. When he was sure that she couldn't see him, he left through the street door and headed for the livery and his horse. He'd retrieve his gold and be long gone when the sheriff showed up. And since he only had Rory to worry about, he figured San Antonio was far enough for safety.

****

Sparely furnished, the jail cell had a bucket for hygiene and two lumber framed beds. The oak frames held wooden slats for support, which held straw-filled mattresses. Based on his itching, Rory had no doubt that the straw needed to be changed. A hot bath at the barbershop would be his first stop when he got out of the Travis County jail.

"Deputy," Rory called. "Deputy, you're making a huge mistake holding me here."

"There ain't no sense you talkin' to me. I ain't goin' to let you go until the sheriff says so—now hush and leave me be."

The office door swung open, and a big man filled the doorway. His shoulder length thick black hair hung uncombed, his handlebar moustache drooped, and he was unshaven. The man had stuffed his nightshirt into his trousers and one of his braces had fallen free. Without Toll jumping up and addressing the man, Rory wouldn't have known who he was.

"Sheriff," said Toll. "What are you doing here this time of night?"

Rory watched patiently as the sheriff surveyed the office. When his eyes stopped on Rory, he nodded to the sheriff. The sheriff kept his eyes on Rory. To Toll, he said, "The doc sent word that someone had been shot. Have you heard anything, Matt?"

"I don't know any more than you, sheriff."

"What's his story?" He nodded towards Rory.

"He's waitin' on you, sheriff."

The sheriff finally took his attention off of Rory. He asked the deputy, "Why is he waiting for me in a locked cell."

"Cause of Mr. Sanders."

Sadness fell across the sheriff's face followed by frustration.

Rory rose from his cot and stepped to the bars, and asked, "If I may, sheriff?" The sheriff turned back to Rory. "My partner, E.B. Parker, was shot yesterday by John Flynt who's wanted by Wells Fargo for robbery and murder. He's living here in Austin under the assumed name Sanders. When I brought him in under arrest, he talked his way out of it. At Sander's suggestion, Toll is holding me pending my explanation to you."

The sheriff looked back at Toll. "Is that right?"

Toll nodded vigorously. "That's what happened." The sheriff's expression hardened, and the deputy quickly added, "You don't believe what he says about Mr. Sanders do you?"

The sheriff exhaled deeply and rubbed his face with both hands. "Matt, did it occur to you that he could be correct?" He pointed at Rory. "—and that you should have held them both until I arrived?"

Rory butted in. "Flynt can be pretty persuasive, sheriff. I wouldn't be so hard on the deputy." Pulling out his watch, he checked the time. "I've only been in here an hour or so. Flynt could still be in town."

The big man stared at Rory for several seconds. Finally, he said, "I'm C. H. Page. Sheriff of Travis County and you are?"

"Rory McLeod."

"Mr. McLeod, you stay put while I check out your story."

The minutes ticked by slowly as Rory kept checking his watch. After half an hour, Page returned. "Okay, Matt. Let him out of the cell and return his weapons."

"But, sheriff—"

"Damn it, Matt, do as I say."

The deputy jumped to his feet and rushed to the cell, doubling back to get the key.

As Rory came out of the cell, Page stuck out his hand. "Sara vouched for you, quite highly I might add. Sanders—I mean Flynt isn't at the hotel, and when I checked the livery, his horse was gone. I don't think he's got more than an hour's lead."

Toll handed Rory his holster and Colt. He strapped it on and immediately checked the load—another of Parker's rules. *Never assume your weapon is loaded—check it.*

"Thanks for the information, Sheriff."

Page's brow pinched. "I'll get a posse together in the morning and we'll track him down."

"He'll be long gone by then, Sheriff." Rory looked around for his hat, which hung on a peg near the door.

"You can't track him in the dark," said the sheriff. "How do you expect to catch him?"

"I think I know where's he's going." Rory left the office and headed for the livery—the hot bath would have to wait.

Hours passed—the going was slow on the trail, and Rory still hadn't reached the place of the ambush. *The sun's coming up and if Flynt's already recovered the gold ....* As the air began to warm with the sun's rising, a breeze moved along the trial. *Smoke ... I've got him now.* Rory reined his horse and dismounted. He tied his animal to a tree, then shucked his carbine from its boot and headed on foot towards the smell of smoke. As he crept forward, he wished he had at least taken enough time before leaving Austin to get his moccasins from the hotel.

At the path to the campsite, Rory paused and listened. He discerned the crackling of burning wood. The other noises were the normal sounds of morning. His patience rewarded him. Someone stomped among the trees to the south of camp. *He's fetching his gold.*

Farther down the path, Rory halted just short of the clearing. Flynt's horse, unsaddled, hobbled, and quietly nibbled at the grass that grew along the stream. The aroma of coffee drifted to his nostrils, and he compulsively glanced to the fire. Nestled near the flames a pot of coffee brewed. *Flynt hasn't been here long.*

The stomping noises stopped—replaced by the sounds of digging. *He's found it.* Rory circled to the north where he could see the camp and watch Flynt's horse. Several mi-nutes passed—Rory fought the impulse to check his watch.

From between the trees, Flynt appeared. Slung over his shoulder were his saddlebags—still dirty from burial. Flynt dropped the gold to the ground next to his saddle and moved to the fire.

Rory raised his rifle and took aim. He pulled the ham-mer back, the click barely audible, but enough to cause Flynt to freeze for a spit second. It was all the time Rory needed, and he squeezed off a round. Flynt stumbled and fell.

He curled up in pain, and held his leg. "My knee," he screamed. "You, No-good-fucking-shit-bastard, you shot my knee."

"Let's see your gun, Flynt, or I'll shoot the other knee." Rory levered another round into the chamber.

"Don't shoot. Here's my gun."

Rory recognized it from the night before, so he started to lower his rifle when he heard E.B.'s voice. *Never assume your man is unarmed until you've checked.*

"Keep your hands where I can see them." Rory stepped out from behind the tree. Flynt squirmed on the ground moaning in agony. "Lie on your stomach and put your hands behind you." When he complied, Rory dropped his knee on Flynt's back and for the second time clicked the cuffs around Flynt's wrist.

He searched Flynt; he found a knife in his boot, and a Derringer concealed in the watch pocket of his trousers. Satisfied Flynt was completely subdued—Rory poured a cup of coffee and sat back on his haunches to enjoy the brew.

Flynt's eyes flashed with hatred. "What about me? What are you going to do about my knee?"

Flynt shrank back when Rory turned to face him. Rory's mind recalled his time with the Apache, and he remembered what they did to an enemy who had harmed a member of his tribe. He felt no sympathy for Flynt and fleetingly considered inflicting more pain on the man.

"Be quiet while I drink my coffee. I'll tend to you when I'm finished."

Tied across the saddle of his horse, Flynt said, "I can ride. Sit me in the saddle."

Rory didn't respond. He merely mounted and pointed his horse north toward Austin. Whenever Flynt began to speak, Rory brought their mounts to a trot, which knocked the wind out of his captive. Flynt was a slow learner. After several attempts, he understood that he was to remain silent; Rory smiled.

Hours later, Rory stopped in front of the Wells Fargo office. With Flynt's saddlebags draped over his left shoulder, he entered the office. The agent busy with paperwork looked up as the saddlebags thudded on his desk. The agent asked, "What's this?"

"That's what's left of the San Angela payroll robbery. I've got Flynt outside."

The agent opened a file drawer and rummaged through wanted posters until he found the one he wanted. "This isn't much of a picture. How do you know it's him?"

"There's your money and he confessed after bushwhacking my partner."

The agent rose and walked around Rory to go outside. A crowd had gathered around Flynt's unconscious body. "Is he dead

Rory stepped to a nearby horse trough and dipped his hat into the water. He lifted Flynt's head and let his face fall into the water. Flynt coughed and spewed as he regained consciousness. "No. He's still alive."

Flynt moaned, "My knee. He shot me in the knee. I need a doctor. Please, won't someone help me?"

Two men came forward with their arms extended obviously intent on getting Flynt off the saddle. Rory turned on them and freed the hammer loop on his holster. In unison, they stopped, lowered their arms, and stepped back.

Sheriff Page parted the crowd. "What's going on?"

The agent said, "This young man has captured John Flynt and returned Wells Fargo's money."

Page looked at Flynt's wounded leg and decided he wasn't that badly hurt. He pointed to one of the men and said, "Go tell doc that I got an injured man at the jail—there's no hurry."

Rory smiled at Page.

Page explained, "Never had much sympathy for back shooters." He began to lead the horse to his office, but stopped and looked back at Rory. "How much money did you recover?"

"Don't' know I didn't bother to count it."

The sheriff nodded. "You and the agent count it together and get a receipt. Wells Fargo gives rewards for recovered money."

"I was just about to explain that to the young man, Sheriff."

Page grinned at Rory and continued on to the jail.

Chapter 10

Propped up with pillows, E.B. smiled when Rory entered the room. The whitewashed room hadn't a window and aside from the single chair that Rory perched on, the only furnishings provided were his bed and a side table to hold an oil lamp. "The doc said he was goin' to let me return to the hotel tomorrow. My wound's healed and whether I walk or not—only time will tell."

"Don't talk like that, E.B. You just need rest and someone to take care of you—that's all."

"Yeah—well—"

"What about your daughter?" Have you written to let her know that you've been hurt?"

Parker's expression saddened and he looked away. "No," he said. His response was quick, and his tone was final.

Rory didn't understand his friend's reluctance to be with family, so he persisted. "Why? You've told me often how much your daughter means to you and that you are looking forward to seeing her. I don't understand."

E.B. looked at Rory; his eyes welled with tears. "That's just it." His voice broke with emotion. "She has her whole life ahead of her. It would be unfair of me to burden her life with takin' care of a cripple."

He's feeling sorry for himself and wants to give up. "It's only your legs that are hurt. The rest of your body is fine. You'll learn to get around. Doc ordered you a Bath[20] wheelchair from Saint Louis and it will be here any day now. You have accumulated a considerable sum of money, so that won't be a burden. Why, back in Saint Louis, I bet you'll find a nurse to take care of you and your daughter won't be bothered."

A weak smile was the best Rory could coax from E.B. "Maybe I just need to get out of bed for a while."

Rory stepped out of the room and returned with a wooden chair with arms, and sat it next to the bed. E.B. asked, "What are you doing?"

"You're going to sit out on the porch for a while. Now help me get you into this chair."

After several minutes of trial and error, they wrestled E.B. into the chair. With a blanket across his lap, E.B. sat erect in the chair looking at Rory. He asked, "Now what?"

Again, Rory left the room without a word, and he returned with two able-bodied men. They lifted the chair and carried E.B. out to the porch in front of the doctor's office. Rory offered them two bits each, but they declined saying, "Glad to help."

E.B. surveyed the town and people passing by. "Rory, I feel exposed sittin' here like this."

For the third time, Rory disappeared and returned. "Here," he said and handed E.B. his .45. "Stick it under your blanket."

Quick as a snake, E.B. reached out, and snatched the revolver and placed it on his lap under the cover on his legs. He smiled; Rory thought it was a contented one.

"You know, Rory. It's a little early, but a libation would seem to be in order. What'd you say?"

---

[20] In 1783, John Dawson of Bath, England, invented a wheelchair named after the town of Bath.

"I'll be back shortly."

****

Later in the afternoon, Sara came by for her daily visit with E.B. She found him seated on Doc Benson's porch sipping whiskey from a flask and smoking a cheroot. "It's nice to see you up and about," she said. "How'd you get out here?"

"It was Rory's doin'. I was feelin' low, so he dragged me out here for some fresh air and sunshine."

She asked, "And?"

E.B. chuckled. "I'll admit I feel better and my mood has improved."

Sara smiled and raised a brow. "When you get to the hotel tomorrow, I'll see what I can do to make you feel even better."

He returned her smile, and said, "As far as I can tell everything down there still works. We'll have to make some changes as to who's in charge."

"I'll figure somethin'," she said and they both laughed.

Rory came out of the doctor's office and asked, "What's so funny?"

E.B. and Sara made eye contact and burst into near hysterics. After a few moments, they gasped for breath and wiped tears from their cheeks, but when they saw the confused expression on Rory's face, they had another fit of laughter. This one didn't last as long and when it ended, E.B. sipped from his flask and passed it to Sara.

Rory waited patiently for his answer. Finally, E.B. said, "I made a joke about my situation, and it seemed very funny. I guess the truth is I really needed to laugh."

"See if you can find Doc Benson, Rory. I think I'm ready to move back to the hotel this afternoon." E.B. looked up at Sara and winked.

Safely settled into her bed, Sara left E.B. and Rory alone to talk. E.B. watched Rory stare out the window. He feared he'd become a burden to his young friend. "By the way—you did a good job bringing in Flynt."

123

"He bamboozled the deputy and nearly got away. If the sheriff hadn't shown up, he would have."

"Aw, but he didn't—that's the point I'm trying to make."

Rory reached into his pocket. He retrieved a leather pouch and tossed it to him. "The gold in his saddlebags counted out to $18,236. The finder's fee was ten percent. Your share with the reward money is $1,412."

E.B. hefted the bag and threw it back. "It's yours, Rory. You're the one who brought him in."

"You've been taking care of me and my expenses since you found me. By rights, the whole thing should be yours."

"I appreciate your sentiment. I tell you what we'll do. You take me back to Saint Louis and we'll call it even."

"I was going to do that anyway, so—"

"Then it's settled. No more discussion on the matter—except to say that you're going to need that stake if you plan to stay in the bounty business."

Sara entered the room with a tray of food. "Sorry," she said. "There is only enough for two and I'm not leaving."

E.B. looked at Rory and raised his brow. "Oh, I get it. I'll see you later, E.B."

"Make it morning, Rory," said E.B. to his partner as he left the room quietly shutting the door.

****

The Bath wheelchair arrived, and E.B. was once again mobile, albeit confined to the second floor of Sara's hotel. With the aid of a knotted rope attached to the ceiling near the bed, E.B. could get in and out of the chair without assistance. The chair's design of two huge rubber tires on either side with a smaller single pivoting wheel in the rear allowed him to whirl about as he pleased.

Given his confinement to the second floor, E.B. and Sara spent time together at odd hours of the day. So, Rory made sure to knock on the door of Sara's bedroom before entering. "Yes," E.B. called.

"E.B., It's me."

"Come on in, Rory. Sara is downstairs taking care of some business or another."

Rory stopped cold at the sight of E.B. fully dressed, his sidearm strapped on, and the hammer loop freed. "Were you expecting someone else?"

"Just because I'm stuck in this chair doesn't mean that there aren't people who would still like to see me dead. So, I've been practicing."

"How's it working out?"

E.B. bumped his elbow against the arm of the chair. "I want to get the blacksmith up here to modify this chair. These armrests hamper my access to the wheels too. I can reach them alright, but I can't get the leverage I need to roll myself easily."

"I'll see when he can make time to come up. I've found a buckboard carriage that has the springs between the axles and frame. If we removed the rear seat and figured a way to get your chair in and out, that's what we use to get you Saint Louis."

He cast his eye up to Rory. "I haven't fully decided to go to Saint Louis," said E.B.

"But Lucy wants you to come home. She said if you didn't agree she'd sell everything and come out to you."

E.B. narrowed his eyes and looked hard at Rory. "And how does she know anything about my situation?"

He couldn't help himself, Rory grinned. "I've been corresponding with her since you were shot."

"You've told Lucy I was shot? Who the hell do you think you are? It's not your place to tell her something like that, or anything else for that matter." E.B. continued to fume.

Rory stood patiently by and smiled.

His anger spent, E.B. shook his head, and said, "Nothing I can do now but go."

"What were you going to do, E.B.? Just show up unannounced and surprise her in person about the fact that you're in a wheelchair?"

"Somethin' like that. I wanted to gauge her reaction in person—I don't want her pity."

"You're an ass, E.B. Maybe you should read these," said Rory as he handed him a bundle of letters. "She's written at least three times a week since she found out that you were injured."

He stared at the bundle a long time before he reached out to accept them. Gently, he placed them in his lap and turned his chair to face the balcony. He rolled closer to the light, and opened the first letter. He didn't seem to hear or care when Rory left.

****

He recognized her delicate hand,

'Dear Mr. McLeod,

Father has spoken of you in his letters. His praise of you is most high indeed. So, it is with that familiarity, I feel my addressing you by your given name isn't inappropriate.

Rory, I wish to convey my sincerest gratitude to you for your correspondence. Obviously, my father, whom I love dearly, didn't intend to share his condition with me, his daughter, and as far as I know only living relative.

Father isn't the only one with secrets. He still believes that I continue to live at the school for young women, but I haven't for these past three years. The matrons at the school have become my friends and the money father sends every quarter, they forward to me. I have in turn invested the money into a general mercantile, which, if I say so myself, has become quite profitable.

I know he has funds put away for his retirement. Those assets coupled with my income as a shop owner will more than meet our requirements, including a future surgery if needed.

Please, Rory, keep me informed as to every detail of his condition, including when you think he shall be physically able to come home to me.

Your friend,
Lucy Parker'

E.B. clutched the letter, but he could no longer see it through his tears. A single tear spilled over and plopped on the page causing the ink to run. He jerked the letter from harm's way. Using his bandana, he dried his eyes. With controlled emotions, he opened the second letter and read,

'Dear Rory,
Of course, you may address me as Lucy.
Thank you for sharing the wonderful things my father has told you about me. His letters to me are usually a bit stiff. After mother died, he changed. Maybe it was the war, or both, but father isn't the man I remember before he left.

I don't think he really has any idea of what to do with a daughter. It is silly of me, but as a child, I used to think he stayed away because he wanted a son instead of a delightful little girl. Now that I'm grown, I understand it was the war and then the need to provide for me that kept him away.

Dear me, I don't mean to carry on so. It is just that you are the only person I know that knows my father and can possibly understand my feelings for and about him. I do so hope you understand.

Regarding the wheeled chair, I have ordered the latest model from Chicago and made arrangements to have it shipped directly to you in Austin. I agree. It is best if father thinks Doctor Benson procured it for him.

Sincerely,
Lucy'

He dabbed at his eyes, and looked down at the wheelchair and then he caressed it gently. His emotions continued to swell, but he still took note of the familiarity devel-
oping between Rory and his daughter. E.B. wasn't sure how
he felt about that. Opening the third letter,

'Dear Rory,
You haven't yet received my last letter, but I couldn't
wait. I think I should close the store and come there to be
with father. To continue with this charade and not tell him
that I know about his injury seems silly, if not cruel.
Let me know your thoughts, please.
Lucy'

Startled by the prospect that his daughter might be on
her way to Austin, he ripped open the fourth letter.

'Rory,
Of course, you are correct. To close the store and run off
to Texas for who knows how long isn't a display of good
business sense. However, I disagree about father. I think
once he got over the shock of my arrival that he would be
happy to see me. Whatever else I know about my father,
I'm certain that he loves me and wishes only the best for
me.
It is good to know that Doctor Benson believes father is
well enough to move to the hotel. How long will he require
convalescence? I do so wish to see him, and of course, I look
forward to meeting you in person.'

E.B. rolled onto the balcony to finish reading Lucy's letters. Engrossed in his thoughts, he didn't hear Rory come
out to stand behind him. "Well?" E.B. nearly leapt from his
wheelchair; had his legs worked.
"Damn. You, scare me half to death. You know better
than to sneak up on me like that. Why if my legs worked,
I'd—"

"If your legs worked we wouldn't be here. I spoke to the blacksmith and he'll come up later this afternoon. We figured out how to get you and that chair onto the buckboard and he thinks he can have it done by the end of the week. So, the question is, when do we leave for Saint Louis?"

"Make arrangements and we'll leave when everything is ready. The hard part will be telling Sara."

"Telling Sara what?" Sara asked as she walked out onto the balcony to join them. She stood with her arms crossed and she glared at E.B. Rory snuck away.

"Sara, darlin'—"

"Oh. This isn't goin' to be good news is it?"

"Sara, please. You mean the world to me, and without your help, I would have never fully recovered, but—"

"But you're leaving—aren't you," she said and then began to cry. Through her sobs, she asked, "Where are you goin'?"

"I'm going back to Saint Louis to live with my daughter."

"Oh," she said. "That's different. Can I come to visit you?"

E.B. chuckled. *Women—as long as I wasn't leaving her for another woman it's all right.* "Sara, you practically saved my life, and you know I care for you greatly. I hope you do come for a visit. My daughter and I would enjoy that immensely."

"Really?"

"Yes really. Just give us time to get settled."

Sara rolled him back into the bedroom and next to the bed and smiled ....

****

It was the strangest looking buckboard carriage anyone in Austin had ever seen; many passersby said so. There was a single seat just large enough for one. He'd removed the rear seat, and guide rails installed to the dashboard. Rory pushed the wheelchair slowly around the contraption giving E.B. ample time to inspect it. "You say I'll be able to drive it too?"

"Yes, sir," said the blacksmith. "Let me put you up there and I'll show you."

E.B. watched as the blacksmith moved to the rear of the wagon and slid down three boards to form a ramp. Hooks attached to the top ends of the boards caught onto a bar added for that purpose. Rory rolled E.B. to the edge of the ramp. It was steep, but Rory had no trouble pushing the chair up the ramp.

The metal angle iron rails guided the chair to the curved stops designed for the chair's wheels. Keyed chocks designed to fit snugly at the rear. A leather strap ran across his lap, which restrained him and the chair's possible movement. Strapped down provided him a fixed leverage point, so he could control the reins. The boards used for ramps fit between the wheels of his chair and held in place by the wagon's tailgate. Lastly, the remaining space behind the single seat held their supplies.

Rory climbed up beside his friend and handed him the reins. "Try it out."

Cautiously, he popped the reins on the hindquarters of the two matched blacks and the wagon jolted forward. E.B. flew back into his chair, but it held fast. He eased back on the leather straps and the pair slowed to a stop. He started them again and they drove out of town. At the first clear straight away, E.B. slapped the reins and the team increased to a fast trot. He gave them their head and leaned back to enjoy the exhilaration of the wind blowing on his face as they rode along. A tear streaked from the corner of his eye, he had feared this feeling was lost to him.

"I think we should get back to the hotel," said Rory. "We have a lot to get ready if we still plan to leave in the morning."

E.B. halted the team and turned them around back to Austin. "Rory, I don't quite know how to thank you for all that you've done for me. I—"

"It's I that should be thanking you, E.B. If it weren't for you, I'd be dead. Plus all that you've taught me—there's no way I could ever repay that debt."

With nothing more to say, they rode back to the hotel in silence.

The next morning with everything loaded and ready to leave, Sheriff Page stopped by to see them off. "I thought you would want to know," he said. "I received word that the Army hanged Flynt last week."

"Thank you, Sheriff," said Rory.

"No less than the son-of-a-bitch deserved," said E.B. and then slapped the reins onto the blacks' rumps—they drove north headed for Saint Louis.

Chapter 11

The streets were paved with red bricks, the many com-
mercial buildings were constructed of brick or massive granite stones, and away from the center of town were lumber-
built small businesses and home. Shiny black lacquered
carriages bustled about, and narrow railroad track ran the
length of the city to guide horse-drawn trolleys. Everywhere Rory looked, there were people. Droves of colorful
humanity dressed in fashions Rory had only seen in a mail-
order catalog.

He'd never imagined this many people together in a
single place. The noise and the immensity of it all assaulted
his senses. Literally, everywhere he looked there was motion and sounds. At length, he overcame his awe, and
asked, "How—" A man in the street yelled to a passerby
and disrupted his question. "How many people live in Saint
Louis?"

E.B. smiled; amusement twinkled in his eyes. The last I
heard, there are over 300,000 people living here."

The Apache had numbers in their language, and Rory
had learned to count. Brother Fidel and the other friars at
the mission taught him higher math and science, but still;
this many anything, much less people, was hard for Rory to
fathom. "How do they live together? I know the river is
nearby, and it is large, but the waste from this many people
for a day?"

"They've had setbacks," said E.B. "After the last cholera
outbreak, the city relocated the cemeteries and built under-
ground sewer systems to discharge the waste further down-
stream, but I wouldn't swim in the river if I was you."

"How do all these people co-exist?"

E.B. shook his head, and said, "I didn't realize I knew so much about this town. To answer your question—Saint Louis is known as the, 'Gateway City to the West'. You can find anything in this place. Apples to zinc, and if you can't, then someone else will know where to get it and have it shipped in."

Rory felt uneasy among so many people, and he said what came to mind, "Living here would take a lot of getting use to."

E.B. laughed. "Not as much as you might think. Once you get beyond the crowds—the conveniences draw you in. It's when you leave and go west again that it takes time to adjust."

Rory didn't respond. He didn't wish to dispute his friend. Born and raised in the wide-open spaces of the southwest, he knew that no amount of time spent in Saint Louis would accustom him to the crowds, cramped vistas, and smells of the city. He knew that one day soon, that he'd return home.

"Whoa," said E.B. as he pulled back on the reins. "Hop down and tie them off, Rory."

Lost in his daydreams of home, Rory said, "Huh?" He looked up at the building. Carved into the stone lintel perched above the doorway, in large block letters, it read, 'CHATHAM HALL,' below the name in smaller letters was, 'Honor and Trust.'

He jumped down and tied the lead to one of the rings anchored to the masonry gatepost. "Why have we stopped here?"

"I need to talk with the head matron about Lucy, get directions to her store."

"Oh. Well, I'll just set the ramps in place."

After Rory rolled E.B. down the ramp and pushed him through the gates, he noticed the six steps that led to the entrance. He paused and looked for other options.

"Push me around to the side." E.B. pointed to his left. "There is a small garden as I remember and a ground level set of doors."

As they entered the garden, a mature woman stepped from the observatory attached to the school. "May I help you gentlemen?"

"I wish to speak with the head matron, please," said E.B. "My daughter was a student here."

"I'm the matron," said the woman. How may I help you?"

Confused, E.B. examined the woman closely. "What happened to Mrs. Rand?"

"Mrs. Rand retired some years back. I'm Miss Crown and I'm the current head matron. Now, how may I help you?"

They moved further into the garden, Rory sat on a bench to enjoy the flowers and listened. *At this pace, I'll be here a while.*

"I've started badly," said E.B. "My daughter, Miss Lucy Parker, until two years ago was registered at this school.

"Lucy. Of course, I know her. We've become friends since she left. I offered her a position here, but she had other ideas. Mr. Parker, she has spoken of you often."

"Can you tell me where her business is located?"

"Certainly, it isn't far. Continue up the road for six more streets and turn right. Her store is located in the center of the block, on the right. You can't miss it," she said and then smiled. "The sign over the door says 'E B Parker's Emporium.'"

Rory returned and stood by the wheelchair. Miss. Crown seemed only then to notice. "I was so sorry to hear about your um—accident, Mr. Parker. Lucy was very upset when she received the news."

Rory could tell by the way E.B. stared at the woman that he wasn't pleased with her condescending attitude. "I wasn't very happy when I heard about it either," he said. "Rory, we should go."

Rory tipped his hat to the woman and rolled E.B. back to the wagon. "You were a little rough on her, E.B. She just didn't know what else to say."

"Then she shouldn't have said anything."

At the carriage, E.B. was still aggravated about Miss. Crown's comment. He vented his frustration at the wheels of his chair—Rory hardly exerted any effort to get him up the ramp. "Whoa," he said. "If you've got that much energy maybe you should wheel yourself to the store."

E.B. glared at his friend. "Her attitude is one of the things I'll have to get used to livin' in a big city like Saint Louis. Damned do-gooders."

"Okay—good to know. I'll shoot the next one we meet."

"Speaking of shooting," said E.B. "I don't expect that you've noticed, but people don't wear their side arms exposed. We'll have to carry ours in our belts under our jackets—least ways you will. I'll keep this shawl pulled up over mine."

Rory unbuckled his gun belt and removed his Colt from its holster. He nestled the rig among their gear and shoved the pistol under his trouser's belt at the small of his back. "This'll take some getting used to. It feels like it might fall out."

"Just don't suck your gut in when you meet a pretty girl and it'll stay put," said E.B. and then he chuckled.

He's forgotten about Miss. Crown, Rory thought.

They made the correct turn onto the side street. Rory drove slowly to give E.B. time to work up his courage.

"It's been almost five years since I last saw Lucy. She was fourteen—I think."

"I thought it was three years?" Rory corrected, but E.B. seemed not to hear, or chose not to answer.

"She has black hair," E.B. continued, "her mother's eyes and mouth. Her nose comes from my mother—I think. Least ways it's not like mine."

Rory glance at his friend. "That a blessing."

Feigning Insult, E.B. said, "I'll have you know that women love my nose. It's a predictor of things to come."

"Oh. How do they handle the disappointment?"

This time it was E.B. who was nettled. "Why you little—"

"Now, now, E.B., were there," said Rory, and he pointed to the attractive young woman who swept the sidewalk.

Rory stopped the wagon and watched his friend's face as he worked through his confusion. He had to reconcile the girl he remembered with the young lady he saw. Finally, it came to him—he smiled and asked, "Lucy?"

The young woman turned to the sound of his voice. Her recognition was immediate. "Father, you're here. I didn't expect you for two more days."

E.B. glanced to Rory, who said, "I added a few days to our arrival date. I didn't want her to worry if we were delayed."

Amused, Rory watched Lucy. Her hands went over her mouth as she inhaled; the excitement over her father's arrival seemed almost to overwhelm her. He was cocksure she had to stop herself from jumping into the wagon.

E.B. seemed just as elated, and said, "Rory, get me down from here."

He pulled on the wheels trying to break free of the chocks. "Hold on, E.B.," said Rory as he removed the restraints and lowered the boards. He had to rush up the ramp to prevent E.B. from attempting to come down on his own. At the bottom, Lucy waited impatiently. When the chair halted, she and her father embraced for several seconds.

"Ahem," uttered Rory.

Lucy stood up and looked at the young man. Her dark almond-shaped eyes spilled tears that Rory assumed were joyous. "Rory, at last—I'm so very pleased to meet you in person." She stepped passed her father, embraced Rory, and lightly kissed his cheek.

The commotion began to draw a crowd. "Come to the rear of the store. I've had a ramp built to the back door so Father can come and go as he pleases."

"Rory, I can manage," said E.B. "Why don't you tend to the animals?"

Lucy added, "There is a small shed and corral in the back, and access is from the alley. At the street's corner turn right—then right again—you'll see it."

Strangely, Rory felt disappointed Lucy sent him away, but someone had to do the chore. He watched Lucy help her father maneuver the wheelchair to the rear of the store. He untied the team and climbed up to the wagon's seat. A light slap with the reins started the horses forward. He followed Lucy's direction, and quickly located the shed. It, like the store, and attached living quarters, was white. Rory guessed they'd recently received new paint to celebrate the arrival of Lucy's father. He saw to the horses and placed the carriage in the shed.

Rory's knuckles rapped against the door. It opened immediately, and Rory saw Lucy's smiling face.

"Rory, you're family. Please don't feel like you have to knock—just come in and make yourself at home."

He found the warmth from the kitchen inviting. It was small, but neat and clean. Coffee brewed on the wood-burning stove, on the table three places were set; cold biscuits and ham slices filled a platter in the center.

E.B. rolled into the kitchen from what appeared to be a bedroom. Lucy had the doorway widened to accommodate his chair and Rory could make out a grab-bar over the bed.

****

"Rory, come see my room."

E.B. led the young man into his room, which was of generous size. His chair turned 360 degrees freely. Lucy had a furniture maker build a short wardrobe and chest that E.B. could easily access. On the far wall was a writing desk deep enough to allow his chair to roll under. Behind a screen was another grab-bar hung over a chair with a chamber pot beneath.

Rory seemed impressed. He peeked behind the screen, he said, "She seems to have thought of everything."

"Yep," said E.B. his face beamed with a parent's pride. "She talked to one of the local doctors who spent time with soldiers after the war. And the carpenter she hired appears to be a pretty crafty fella in his own right."

From the kitchen, Lucy called, "Father, Rory, the coffee is ready."

****

Rory rolled E.B. up to the table as Lucy poured the third cup. "There's butter and jam to go with the biscuits. Please, help yourselves."

Rory piled his plate with the flakey morsels and ate heartily. Our many days on the trail didn't offer much variety, certainly not butter, and jams. Sipping the coffee, he thought, *it could have stayed on the stove longer, but it's still good.*

Lucy watched them consume all that she had prepared. "I'm not used to feeding men; I'll have the cook increase our food supplies."

E.B. asked, "You have a cook?"

"Yes, Father, I do. She comes in everyday but Sunday, and cleans the living quarters and cooks my meals. She's a widow, and I think she's a bit younger than you are. I've asked her if she'll help me take care of you, and she's agreed. She'll be here first thing in the morning."

"Well— I don't know about that—I mean the added cost and inconvenience to you—"

"Nonsense, Father. She's alone and needs the work. Who do you expect to help you bathe and get dress?"

Rory smiled as he watched E.B. blush. "Well—she's a woman, a strange woman and—"

"Father, are you telling me that besides mother, no other woman, strange or not, has seen you without clothes?"

Rory snorted and spewed his coffee across the table as he burst into laughter.

Lucy arched an eyebrow. "I believe Mr. McLeod has made my point. We shall speak no more about it. Agreed?"

E.B. didn't argue. His shoulders slumped with resignation and he quietly drank his coffee. When he finished, he retired to his room. Rory was sure it was to pout.

Lucy poured Rory another cup of coffee. "Would you like more to eat?"

"No thank you, Lucy. I'll be good until dinner and I'll get something at the hotel."

"Oh," Lucy looked towards the parlor. "I assumed you would want to stay here with father and me. I brought a cot in from the store and—"

Rory didn't hesitate. "I would prefer that, indeed," he said and then smiled at her. He held her stare with his. "You didn't tell me in your letters what your father said about me."

She didn't blush as he continued to stare. "It's not so much what he said, but how he said it. I got the impression he thinks of you as the son he didn't have."

Rory turned his reddened face away from her. "I care a lot for him too. He saved my life and taught me his trade—there's no way to repay that."

"According to him, you've repaid him and more. You need not have a guilty conscience on that score." She paused to study him. "Are you bound and determined to be a man hunter—like him?" Her tone sounded confrontational. "You've seen where it's gotten him."

He frowned, and his voice grew curt. "Maybe I should stay at the hotel—less conflict there."

Lucy drew back, and she blinked away tears. "I apologize," she said. "I've gotten used to being the head of my house and then there's the business. I meant no offense, please stay." Her dark eyes were inviting, her voice soothing.

He nodded and then said, "If for no other reason than to witness E.B. and your cook's first meeting."

An impish smile curled the corners of her mouth. Her eyes twinkled, and She leaned across the table and whispered, "Me too." They both began to giggle like conspiratorial children.

****

Mrs. Cavanaugh arrived promptly at 6:00 and began her daily duties as cook and housekeeper. Except for his socks and boots, E.B. was already dressed. The door to his room was ajar, and he positioned himself where he could see the kitchen. He watched Mrs. Cavanaugh bustle about the kitchen as she prepared breakfast. Tightly braided, she wore her thick salt and pepper hair coiled on the top her of her head. Stout, but not fat, Mrs. Cavanaugh handled the hefty cast-iron skillet with ease. *Pioneer stock,* E.B. thought.

Rory came into the room. Saw the woman, and asked, "Mrs. Cavanaugh?"

"Aye, it's herself you're speakin' to."

Rory pinched his brow confused. He pointed to avoid further miscommunication. "You are Mrs. Cavanaugh? Miss Parker's cook and housekeeper—correct?"

"Aye, that's what I said."

"Oh. May I ask where you are from—originally?"

"Lad, have you never heard of Ireland?"

"Oh—I mean, yes I have. It's just that I've never met anyone from there. Pardon me for saying so, but your accent is so unusual."

"O is it now. I've come to understand your manner of speakin', so you'd best learn mine, if you plan to stay about."

"Yes, Ma-am."

"My given name is Kathleen. My late husband—God rest his soul," she said, crossing herself and then glanced upward. "He called me Kate—you may do the same."

"I'm sorry to hear about your loss. How long were you married?"

"We were married for more 'an twenty years before the Comanche killed him in fifty-eight."

"But—I thought—"

"O did you now. Well—it's a sweet sentiment you're of-ferin', but no need. He's been gone these last ten years, and I've moved on."

E.B. bit his tongue to keep from laughing as he listened to Rory's initial encounter with Mrs. Cavanaugh. He opened the door and rolled into the kitchen. "Good mornin', Rory," he said and then rolled to where Kate stood. He leaned forward and extended his hand. "And good mornin' to you, Mrs. Cavanaugh, I'm E.B. Parker—Lucy's father. Forgive me for not standin'."

She took his hand and shook it with a firm grip, and then she looked down at his legs. He saw no special interest or compassion in her face. In a no-nonsense tone, she said, "We'll need to get you a pair of house slippers—fur-lined would be best."

"I can help you with those," said Rory. "I'll talk to Lu-cy."

"Good morning everyone," Lucy said as she entered the room. "Talk to me about what?"

"Does the store have leather pelts—preferably rabbit?"

Lucy said, "Yes. A local boy traps rabbits. He sells the meat to a restaurant and trades the hides to me. Why?"

"Mrs. Cava—Kate thinks E.B. needs fur-lined slippers," said Rory. "You have the rabbit hides, so I can make them for him—that's all. It won't take me any time to do"

"Coffee's ready," said Kate. "Take your places at the ta-ble and I'll finish cookin' the breakfast."

E.B. rolled his chair under the table. He selected a spot away from Kate and the stove and conveniently near his bedroom door. He sipped his coffee and watched his family—at least that's how he was beginning to think of them. The confusion from everyone trying to talk at once, the aroma of baking biscuits, the crackle of ham frying mixed with the smell of soap and water from freshly washed faces—it comforted him. For a fleeting second, his mind took him to his childhood home where he felt secure and loved.

Lucy turned to ask her father how many eggs he wanted, but he didn't respond. She spoke louder. "Father—Father, are you all right?"

E.B. snapped back to the present. "Yes, Lucy, I'm fine. Just day dreaming is all."

Kate brought the food to the table and took a chair with her back to the stove. E.B. reached for a biscuit. "Are you not grateful for this food, Mr. Parker?" Kate asked as he arched her brow.

"Why yes I am. Very pleased," said E.B.

"So, why don't you say the grace—then we can eat." Kate and Lucy looked at him expectantly. Rory watched his eyes twinkled with laughter.

"As you wish, Kate," he said. E.B. closed his eyes and silently collected his thoughts. "Lord, thank you for returnin' me home to my family and for this wonderful meal we are about to eat. Amen."

When he opened his eyes, he saw that Lucy smiled at him. Moisture filmed her eyes, but there were no tears. She reached over and squeezed his hand. I'm thankful you're home too—I love you so."

E.B. cleared his throat and choked back the sudden emotions he felt. Gruffly, he said, "Can we eat now? I'm starved."

****

Lucy watched Rory as he gently placed her father's feet, one a time, on the rabbit hides and traced the outlines of his feet. "Since they're more about keeping your feet warm and protected, I'll make them a little large. They'll be easier for you to slip them on and the fur inside will last longer."

E.B. nodded. "How do I get them on? When I bend over, I can't lift my leg. When I can lift my leg, I can't bend over."

"I thought about that," said Rory. "Boot hooks, but longer—I'll put a loop on each side. Then all you have to do is lean over to get them started and then use the boot hooks to pull them on. I'll have the blacksmith make them."

Still nodding, E.B. said, "Sounds like it should work—we'll see."

Lucy asked, "Is this something you learned how to do as a child when you lived with the Apache?"

Rory looked at her and then to E.B. "Yes," she said. "He told me in his letters about you being found and raised by the Apache. I haven't repeated it to anyone."

His smile put her at ease. "I'm not ashamed of being raised by Indians—it's just that most people don't under·stand—especially in Texas where folks are still touchy about the Comanche. Not everyone understands there are differences."

Rory moved to the table where he cut the leather piec·es. He didn't have to make leather lace. Lucy also brought heavy cord and an upholstery needle from the store. Deftly, he punched a hole in the leather with a sharpened awl, pinched the seam together, and laced the cord. Lucy was amazed at how quickly Rory finished the moccasins.

He isn't only quite capable, but he's handsome too in that masculine sort of way, she thought.

She flushed when she realized where her thoughts led. Lucy rose abruptly and turned to leave. "I've got to get back to the store," she said. "You'll have to excuse me please."

****

They watched her go, Rory asked, "What was that all about?"

E.B. shrugged. "Women—just because she's my daughter it doesn't give me any special insight to what she's thinkin'."

Kate, who knew Lucy best, had watched her closely when Rory was about. There was attraction brewing between them—at least on Lucy's part. *Rory seemed to be like most men,* she thought, *they're barely smart enough to find their willies.* "Men," she said and went outside with scraps from breakfast destined for the waste bin.

As she left, she heard E.B. say, "I haven't the slightest idea of what just happened or why. Women get that way—you know their monthly."

E.B.'s comment as she left got her Irish was up, and she knew better than return to the kitchen, so she walked around the building and entered the store through its front door. It was empty, save she and Lucy. "You'll pardon my sayin' it, but himself and that young scamp are thick as stumps."

Lucy looked up as Kate entered. "What did they say to make you so angry?"

Kate smiled at Lucy conspiratorially. "It's not so much what they're sayin' as much as what they're not—especially the redheaded young gentleman."

In a loud whisper, Lucy said, "Kate, I have absolutely no interest in Rory McLeod. He's merely my father's friend, so get that thought out of your mind—right now."

"Lucy, you're a beautiful young woman with needs and urges. Your mind may not have an interest, but your body does. If I was you—I'd pay attention. He's just like all men—he doesn't know what he wants until a good woman tells him."

That made Lucy laugh, she asked, "Say I wanted to investigate my feelings—how should I proceed?"

Kate didn't pause. "You have to give him some encouragement. Show interest in him and the things he likes. If he wants to talk about horses or farmin', then you listen and ask questions now and again. A man's ego is like his stomach; the more you feed it the bigger it gets." They both burst into hysterical laughter. So much so, E.B. wheeled into the store to investigate. The concerned expression on his face caused their laughter to begin anew.

Chapter 12

Rory and E.B. halted the wagon in front of the store. "We should hang a sign on that thing," said Lucy. "It would be a good way to advertise the store."

E.B. glanced up at the store's signage. "Maybe we should, and we could offer a delivery service too. It's been near a month of scoutin' Saint Louis—why, me and Rory could find anyone's house or business."

"They'd have to be close by," Rory smiled and winked at Lucy. "We have to be back here in time for Kate's lunch and your nap."

"Aw," said E.B. and elbowed Rory's leg. "You don't know what you're talkin' about. My belly's full, so why not take a nap to let the food digest—it's healthy. Why, if I wanted, I could drive this wagon from daylight to dark and never close an eye."

"You can't do that, Father. You've become a celebrity. Thanks to that reporter, and his dime novels, people expect to see you here at the store."

"Most of the tales you told that reporter are outright lies." Rory joined in. "You should be ashamed of yourself. How do you manage to keep a straight face?"

"Practice," said E.B. and then he became serious. "It takes lots of practice. If you're going to be a man hunter, you need to learn how to tell a believable lie."

Rory saw Lucy's expression change. She didn't like it when they talked about the trade—as he called it. He smiled at her and said, "We'll be back in a few hours. Tell Kate to make a big lunch, I'm already hungry." He slapped the reins and the team started forward for their daily exploration of Saint Louis and all its wonders.

"Enough of the side streets," said E.B. "Today, let's see what lies at the center of town."

They drove up and down the north-south streets for nearly an hour. When they came to Seventh Street, E.B. pointed to the west. "That's Hop Town, before the war, there was only one Chinaman living there. I guess a few hundred came later—and then they brought wives, and now it's a whole community. We have a couple of China restaurants in town—maybe we'll go to one for lunch one of these days."

"I see black men here and there," said Rory. "Do they also live separately?"

"Well, if you're interested." E.B. paused to gather his thoughts. "There have been free black men livin' in Saint Louis goin' back to when the French settled the city. A few have become wealthy businessmen—most own businesses down by the river. Things got pretty touchy when the Supreme Court handed down the Dred Scott rulin'."

"I'm afraid my reading did not include much American history."

E.B. had the floor, so to speak, and he provided Rory with a condensed version of American History; from his viewpoint. "We'll get you down to the library where you can find plenty to read on the subject."

Further south on Broadway, just past Market, Rory saw the Olympic Theater, which appeared to be a newer building. He read the attraction advertisement, 'Romeo and Juliet'. "Would Lucy enjoy going to the theater?"

"That's a good question," said E.B. with just a hint of playful sarcasm to his voice. "Why don't you ask her and find out? Maybe she would also like to be taken to dinner?"

"I just meant—"

"I know what you meant—you should ask her out for this evening. I'm sure I can get Kate to stay late and take care of me."

Rory looked at his friend suspiciously. "You and Kate have become very good friends. Do your Saturday afternoon bathes have anything to do with it?"

"Ahem," E.B. cleared his throat. "We were talkin' about you and Lucy. Don't try to change the subject. Now, what are your intensions toward my daughter?"

"Well, my good man," said Rory before E.B. cut him off.

"Rory, I'm serious."

"E.B., I like Lucy. I like her a lot, but at this point that's all it is. I wouldn't hurt her, or you for anything in the world—you know that. I saw the theater and thought she might like to go. I mean—she's been wonderful to me, and I just wanted to repay her kindness in some small way."

"Haven't you been payin' attention? You may not be able to help but hurt her. Haven't you noticed how she watches you when you come into a room?"

"That's insane, E.B. When I look at her, she's always staring at something or someone else. Hell, I think she goes out of her way not to look at me."

E.B. chuckled. "That's just the point—she does. She doesn't want you to catch her lookin'."

This was all news to Rory. He actually began to think he had done something that displeased Lucy, and she was avoiding him. The possibility that it was just the opposite never entered his mind. He asked, "What do I do now?"

"What do you want to do?"

"I don't know. All I know for sure is that I don't want to hurt her. Maybe I should leave sooner than I planned?"

"Is there any chance that you two would be a match for each other?"

"Well sure there is—Lucy's pretty, and she's bright." Rory looked sideways at E.B. "And I don't think her father would be opposed to our marriage."

"True enough, Lad."

Rory paused and smiled at E.B. with a quizzical expression, "Lad? You're starting to sound like Kate."

"She does a good bit of talkin'—I'll give you that. Some of it's bound to catch hold." E.B. sighed. "Let's get along home and you ask Lucy to see the play. I think she'll go."

****

"Thank you, Mrs. Blake. Your order will be ready next Friday." Lucy watched as the rancher's wife left the store. The morning brought a flurry of customers, and they all seemed to want special-order items, which meant extra time spent with each of them. She was tired and looked forward to having lunch with Kate, her father and Rory too, if they returned in time.

She shut the door and hung her 'To Lunch Returning at 1:00' sign, which she'd neatly printed on a salvaged piece of white cardboard that had a green ribbon tied at two corners. The ribbon hung over a small nail above the glass portion of the door.

She felt exhausted. It was at times like this that she questioned her choice of starting this business. Most women her age were married and starting families—she wanted a family. Her thoughts drifted to Rory McLeod. "Mrs. Rory McLeod," she said softly then quickly looked around to make sure no one heard. Suddenly not so tired, Lucy made her way to the kitchen. To her delight, Rory and her father were home.

"Father, did you see anything interesting today?"

"Nothing much—we have to get the lad down to the library. His knowledge of American history is woefully lackin'. But, Rory saw something interestin'." He nudged Rory, and said, "Tell her about it."

He seemed confused for a moment, and then understood. "He's talking about the Olympic Playhouse. They're
performing Romeo and Juliet."

Anticipation began to well and she looked directly into
Rory's eyes. "We read his plays in school, but I've never
seen one acted on the stage."

Rory broke their eye contact and looked down. He said,
"I would be pleased if you accompanied me this evening to
see the play and have dinner afterwards."

She saw that he was blushing, and it made her smile.
"That would be thrilling. What time shall I be ready?"

"The playbill said the performance starts promptly at
7:00 PM," said Rory. He turned to her father and asked,
"Can we get a cab from here to the theater and back?"

Kate was the one to answer, "Yes. I'll go now and make
the arrangements. I'm not hungry—you lot seat yourselves
and eat while I'm gone. I'll be back in two shakes of a
lamp's tail." She bounded out the door with the front of her
skirt lifted out of the way of her long strides.

In her excitement, Lucy spoke aloud, "Let's see—I'll
wear my dark-blue dress with the ruffles. When Kate re-
turns, she'll help me with my hair and— Oh yes, I'll wear
mother's pearl necklace and earrings—they'll look lovely
with that dress." She bolted up from the table, and without
eating a bite, she rushed upstairs to her room.

****

"See, I told you she would want to go," said E.B. and
punched Rory on the shoulder.

Lucy's response surprised Rory. He assumed she would
accept his invitation, but her obvious excitement concerned
him. Kate's hurry to arrange for a carriage was now also
suspect. *Were they all conspiring to arrange our marriage?
Aw, that's ridiculous.* He rubbed the back of his neck. *But,
then again ...?*

"What have you to wear to the playhouse?"

Roy turned to E.B. "What? Oh clothes, you mean?" E.B. nodded. "I hadn't really thought about—I mean. What do you mean?"

"Ideally, you should wear a fancy suit, but I suppose a decent jacket, and dark trousers will do," said E.B. "Let's see what Lucy has in the store." He rolled his chair through the common passageway into the mercantile area. There were a few people standing at the door waiting for Lucy's return; he ignored their presence.

On the shelves at the back corner of the store, were stacks of pants, shirts, drawers, and other sundries for men. There was also a rack with readymade suits. E.B. perused them one by one. Rory's suspicions returned. Just how much of this situation is coincidence and how much is contrived? "What made you want to drive to the downtown section of town today?"

E.B. didn't stop looking at the suits, and replied absently, "Just wanted to see something new." Changing the subject, he said, "Ah, here's something. What do you think?"

Rory lifted the suit off the rack and held it at arm's length for inspection. It was a complete suit, with a vest. He lifted the right sleeve to look at the price tag neatly pinned to the cuff—$22.75. "Twenty-two dollars and seventy-five cents for a suit of clothes," he blurted out. "Where would I wear it?"

"A man needs a good suit of clothes," E.B. grinned, "for bankin', marryin', and buryin'."

Rory saw in his friends face that E.B. enjoyed himself immensely. "Have you and Kate set this whole thing up?"

"Why, Rory, I'm afraid I don't understand what you mean?"

"Oh come on, E.B. You wanted to go downtown today and Kate's rush to get a coach, and now this suit, which appears to be my size."

"Don't be silly, Lad."

"Is Lucy in on this?"

"Absolutely not—"

"Then, you did set this up," said Rory, irritation heavy in his voice. Manipulation by his friends made him angry.

"I told Kate that you would catch on, but she persisted," E.B. sighed. "Lucy doesn't know anything, so please don't ruin her evenin'."

"Why did you go to this much trouble? How'd you know I would be interested in the play?"

"Slow down. First is the why. Lucy's in love with you, or at least thinks she is. Every time you come into the room—she nearly swoons. You haven't made any overtures, but neither have you been out chasing women, so there must be a little interest on your part." E.B. paused to let that sink in. "Then there's the how. That was easy. If you hadn't noticed the playhouse, I was prepared to point it out, and if necessary, suggest you ask Lucy out to the play and dinner after."

"When did you order the suit?"

"I didn't. Lucy runs the store—it must be a coincidence."

Rory stared at his friend. He tried to judge if had received the complete truth from him. He decided that he had, and said, "All right, I'll go through with this, but from here forward, you and Mrs. Cavanaugh keep your noses out of Lucy's and my business."

From the passageway, Kate said, "It's only because we love the both of you that himself and me bothered." She paused shaking her head with dismay. "For an intelligent lad, you're as thick as a stump when it comes to understandin' a woman." Kate walked to the storefront door, and removed the sign and drew down the shade with 'CLOSED' print on the street side. "The coach will be here at 6:00. I'll be upstairs with Lucy."

Rory spent the remainder of the afternoon preparing for the evening, which included a trip to the barbershop and bathhouse. His new suit fit remarkably well—for mail order—and he was even able to find a pair of shoes in his size to wear with the suit.

When Lucy came down the stairs at 6:00 on the dot, Rory was transfixed. Her eyes gleamed, and her smile radiated warmth with appreciation of him. She wore her hair up held in place with hair combs inlaid with pearls that matched her necklace and earrings.

The tops of her shoulders were bare with just enough of her chest exposed to accentuate her necklace. The floor length dark-blue silk dress shimmered in the light. Its bodice flared from the waist, like a vase, and displayed the gown's silvery ruffles covering her breast.

As she turned to show off her attire, Rory saw that she wore a small bustle. He saw pictures, but never one in person. He decided that he liked how it accented her femininity—then he wondered how she would sit with it tied to her backside.

"Lucy, you look— You look stunningly— I never would have thought—I mean—you're so beautiful."

She smiled warmly. "Thank you. You don't look so bad yourself." She studied his appearance closely, and then blushed. "It was silly of me, but I bought that suit with you in mind—I'm glad you found it."

"How'd you know I would have an occasion to wear it?"

"I didn't. I've seen gentlemen in town who wore similar suits and thought you would look good in one, so I ordered it. I was right you know—you look very handsome."

"Shall we go?" He held out his arm and they left through the store's front door where the coach waited.

****

She lay in bed too embarrassed to leave her room. It must have been the champagne. She'd had two glasses before dinner, and it was late. She hadn't eaten all day, and it made her tipsy, otherwise, she wouldn't have told him how she felt. What was she to do now?

There was a knock on her door. Kate asked, "May, I come in?" She didn't wait for an answer; she opened the door, came in, and saw Lucy in bed with the covers pulled over her head. "It's late, and you're still in bed. Are you ill?"

From under the covers, Lucy said, "No, but I'm never coming downstairs."

Kate placed a tray on the table next to the bed sat on the side of the mattress. She tugged at the covers. "Come now—out with it. Tell me what's happened that's got you holed up here like a scared rabbit."

The smell of coffee brought her from beneath the covers. Kate had brought her coffee and warm buttered biscuits. As she sat up and arranged the covers, Kate poured her a cup and handed it to her with a napkin for her lap. "Um—those biscuit smell good too." Kate passed her the plate and she took one.

"Well, out with it. What's got you cowered under the covers like a child?"

"The play was wonderful. He took me to Delmonico's and I had two glasses of champagne and—"

Kate gasped, "On an empty stomach?"

"I've never tasted it before, and the bubbles tickled my nose—it seemed harmless enough. Anyway, before I knew what was happening, I was tipsy and told Rory that I loved him, and that he should propose to me."

"O my, I was afraid the cause of your distress might be somethin' along those lines. Rory was gone when I arrived. Your father said he'd gone ridin'."

"I'm so embarrassed. What am I going to do, Kate?"

"Embarrassment aside, do you still feel the same way?"

Lucy didn't pause to consider. "Yes, I'm in love with Rory, and I want him to marry me. Is that so bad?"

"No, child, of course not—that's how it works. The man chases the woman 'til she catches him. In some case, where the man is a bit thick between the ears, the woman has to do the chasin' as well. Rory seems to be thicker than most, that's all. I know his feelings for you run deeply. Why else would he be out ridin' to clear his head?

"Now come on—get out of bed, get yourself dressed and come downstairs. Your father and I want to hear the detail of the play and the evenin' in general."

Lucy joined Kate and her father at the table where they sipped their coffee, tea for Kate. Kate poured a fresh cup for her as she sat. "Tells us how it went," Said E.B. "Rory left this mornin' without a word except to say he'd be back later."

Lucy was relieved, even reassured to learn that he planned to return. She looked to Kate, who nodded for her to start. Over the next half-hour, she told them about the elegance of the theater and the grand dress of the people she saw at Delmonico's restaurant.

Then she heard the grandfather clock chime 9:00. "Oh my," she said. "The store is closed—I should have opened an hour ago." Lucy jumped up from her chair and rushed through the passageway to the store's front door.

****

He left without a bite of food. Noon approached, and he felt the sharp pangs of hunger. But, he hadn't yet made a decision, and he was reluctant to return to Lucy without having made one. He had made up his mind that he loved Lucy, but that was as far as he got.

When he thought of them together, his thoughts switched to his birth parents, then Mosi and Sani, his uncle Bidzil, and finally Father Herberto. Everyone in his life that he cared about was dead—except E.B., and he nearly died.

It wasn't rational he knew, but he couldn't shake the notion that harm might come to her if they married. Or something could happen to him, and she'd be left a widow. He'd promised Herberto's spirit that he would avenge his torture and death. He'd also pledged to recover the treasure and take it to Santa Fe—it wouldn't be fair to her if they married.

He reached a decision; he turned his horse, and headed back to Saint Louis and Lucy.

She'd closed the store, and waited in the kitchen; she stood with her hands behind her back. When he walked in, she asked, "Are you hungry?"

He smiled at her tenderly. "Yes, but first I need to—"

"You don't have to say anything. I'm so embarrassed about what I said last night. I didn't mean to say all that—I had no right, and—"

Rory held up both hands to stop her talking. "I've spent all day riding across the countryside making up my mind that I love you and want to get married someday. Are you telling me now that what you said last night wasn't true?"

Lucy's hands excitedly came together, and she began to wring them as tears started to flow. "Did you just ask me to marry you?"

He paused. "Yes, I suppose I did, but if what you said last night isn't true—"

Lucy leaped into his arms and kissed him. She leaned back in his embrace, and said, "Yes, what I said last night is true—I love you. Yes, I will marry you, just tell me when."

E.B. rolled out of his room with Kate behind. "What's all the commotion about?"

Rory released her and stepped back embarrassed.

"Rory's asked me to marry him," Lucy said and then whirled around nearly dancing enraptured with excitement and romance. "Isn't that wonderful?"

Kate rush to Lucy and hugged her. "We've so many things to get ready. There's the dress, the church and Pastor Griffin, the guests, the food, and where should we hold the reception, and—"

"Hold on, Lucy, we need to talk," said Rory. His voice was stern, which dampened their excited conversation.

Lucy quickly moved to Rory, put her arms around him, and leaned back to look into his eyes. "You're right dear. It's just that I'm excited. After all, a girl's wedding is a big event—something we all look forward to, and when our beau asks the question—"

"Can we go for a walk?"

"Of course," she said and took his arm; they left the house.

They walked for a long time without talking. Near a small park, he guided her to one of the benches where they could sit. He sat, and looked down at his feet; his hands held together fingers interlocked. He squeezed them until his knuckles turned white.

Lucy became anxious, her voice fraught with worry; she asked, "What is it, Rory?"

"Lucy, I do love you, and I want to marry you, but I have something to do before we can be together."

Her eyes welled; she didn't cry, but her voice broke as she spoke. "What is it that would prevent our getting married?"

"Your father told you how we met, but I don't think he told you about Father Herberto."

"Only that he found a dead priest with you."

"Father Herberto was a priest from San Xavier Mission, south of Tucson. When I left the Apache, Father Herberto took me in and treated me like a son. He and Brother Fidel educated me and if not for them—I would probably be dead. I traveled with him to Santa Fe. Along the way, a group of Comancheros attacked us. Your father was after their leader, a man named Cain."

"I remember that name from father's letters, there's a $5,000 reward posted for him."

Rory nodded. "Yes, he's the one who tortured—" He paused for several seconds. "He used hot coals, and tortured Father Herberto to death."

Tears freely streamed down Lucy's cheeks. "Why would someone do that to anyone, especially to a priest?"

He hesitated only for an instant. "We transported a treasure for the diocese in Santa Fe. It was hidden in the stream near our camp, and Herberto refused to tell them where."

She asked, "Rory, can't you recover the treasure and take it to Santa Fe? That should fulfill your obligation to the priest."

"No. You don't understand, Lucy. The murder of my white parents by Comancheros went unavenged, my Apache parents, Mosi and Sani, ambushed and needlessly killed by the Army, and then Herberto tortured to death by Cain. Of all those I've lost, I know who kill him, and I want revenge—I need it." His repressed anger reared. He stood and paced back and forth; his fury raged, and tears of frustration streamed down his cheeks.

At length, he calmed and wiped his tear-stained cheeks with his sleeve. Lucy sat before him; she silently stared at him; waiting for him to say something to her.

"I sorry, Lucy," he said, and returned to sit beside her. "My anger burns greater than I knew. Without revenge, I fear it will never be quenched."

She took his hand in hers and stroked it gently. "Have you spoken to father about this?"

"Yes, but not for a while, I suspect he hopes that my desire to find Cain has passed."

"Will you seek his counsel—do it for my shake?"

"Of course, if that pleases you, but know that talking to your father won't change my mind."

Chapter 13

As they toured through the city on their morning drive, E.B. tried to get Rory to listen to reason. "Rory, this is madness," said E.B. "He rides with twenty killers. You won't have a chance to get close to him. If you must kill the bastard, take my Sharps and do it from a distance."

"That isn't the Apache way. He must know who kills him and why."

E.B. had never missed the use of his legs more than this minute. He desperately wanted to grab hold of Rory and shake some sense into the young fool's head, if that was possible. E.B. halted the coach at a park under a co-lonnade of cottonwood trees. The shade and breeze were comfortable, and one could think without distraction. "Rory, you've become like a son to me, but what about Lucy?"

"She has agreed to wait two years—we'll marry when I return."

"If you return," E.B. sighed. His shoulders drooped with resignation. "I guess I was stupid to think you'd let Cain slip from your mind. You've not once said a word about him since we left the stream and your friend's grave."

"I told you—the Apache know how to use guile when needed."

"If you're to get close enough to Cain to kill him, you'll require guile and much more. How do you plan to find him?"

"He will find me," said Rory.

E.B. snorted. "And just how do you plan to make that happen?"

"I will join his Comancheros. After I discover who there with him, I'll kill them first."

"Them," said E.B. He searched Rory's green eyes and found no humor. "Listen to me. You cannot succeed—they will find you out and torture you to death just for their enjoyment."

"Then I will try to die bravely like an Apache."

It was clear to E.B. he couldn't sway Rory's decision. Until now, he'd failed to understand just how much Rory's early life with the Apache contributed so much to the man he'd become.

"If you're dead set on doing this, then let me help." E.B. raised his hands to prevent Rory's rebuttal. "Just hear me out. Let me help you develop your plans. I also have money; much more than you suspect.

I should have quit the bounty trade years ago, but it gets into your blood." He looked up at Rory. "That's something we haven't talked about, Son. You haven't killed anyone—" Rory started to speak, but E.B. cut him off. "I know. We shot that man at the saloon, but that was sudden and in self-defense. It's the hunting and killing—"

"Flynt—"

"Yes you wounded him, but that's not the same, and killing a doe close up with an arrow, or breaking the neck of a snared rabbit isn't either.

"To end the life of another human being in anger or fear is a different thing than huntin' him down and killin' him while he stares you in the eyes. Most men can't do it." He paused and his eyes shone with regret. "Like I said, it gets into your blood. You start to like it. I saw plenty of it durin' the war—bloodlust they called it. After a battle, some of the men, laughin' and cryin', tromped through the bodies and bayoneted the wounded. Eventually, an officer would stop them—if he could.

"It's the fear of certain death followed by the sheer joy of being alive—one extreme and then the other. There is no other feelin' like it—it's impossible to describe fully." E.B. paused again. He struggled for words. "The fear is—primal. Your gut cramps and you near shit yourself. Being alive after the fight is like winnin' the biggest jackpot you can imagine, but more—far more."

"If I set my mind to it, I'll get it accomplished."

Rory didn't look away, and E.B. saw cold steel in those eyes. "Maybe you will at that. If you want to survive don't hesitate to shoot, and if you can, draw first; but remember, don't be too quick to fire; you could miss. Concentrate on accuracy—speed will take care of itself. Now tell me your plans."

****

Rory considered his mentor's question. The fact was he hadn't really developed a firm plan, so he offered his general idea. "I'll use my Apache name and join Cain's band of Comancheros. When I discover who was with him when he murdered Herberto, I will kill them one by one—close or far, it doesn't matter." Rory's face clenched his green eyes flashed with an intense focus. "When only Cain is left, I will gut-shoot him and while he slowly dies, I'll tell him why." His voice was cold ... no sign of anger. His actions were without hesitation, as he took the reins from E.B. and gently slapped their rumps to start them moving.

"How will you get Cain to ask you to join?"

"I will hunt down wanted men and kill them to build my reputation. I plan to take credit for their crimes and boast about them—all the while I'll hunt for Cain and his men."

"When you've killed him, then what?"

"I'll finish what Father Herberto and I started." His expression calmed and a light shone once more in his eyes. He grinned sheepishly, and added, "Then come back here and wed Lucy."

"Speaking of which, we'd better get back to the house. I bet they wonder where we've gotten off to."

It was 12:04 when they came into the kitchen. Kate was at the stove stirring a pot, and Lucy sat plates on the table. Rory watched as she looked to her father who slightly shook his head. Her face fell. She turned to Rory and asked, "When do you plan to leave?"

Kate kept her attention on the stove. She lifted a stove-top lid to check the fire, and E.B. rolled his chair over and pretended to help; the silence was awkward. Rory's heart ached as he stared at her saddened face. If she cried, so would he. "I thought Friday would be good."

Lucy sucked in a huge breath and exhaled slowly. "Would Monday hamper your plans?"

"No. If it will make you happier, I'll wait until Monday."

Her eyes began to well. "It would make me happier if you didn't leave, but what does that matter." Lucy turned, ran up the stairs to her room, and slammed the door.

Rory wasn't sure what he should do.

Kate said, "I'll go to her. You two fools stay here."

E.B. rolled his chair over to where Rory stood and squeezed his arm. "With women it seems worse than it is. She'll be all right and downstairs shortly—you just wait and see."

****

Kate opened the door to Lucy's room, and with purpose stepped in. "Lucy, me darlin', you shouldn't be wastin' your time up here bawlin' when your young man is set to be leavin' soon. Now dry your eyes and come back downstairs. There'll be plenty of days for weepin' after he's gone."

Lucy's sobs subsided. She sat up and looked at her face in the mirror above her dressing table. "Oh, my face is streaked and my eyes are swollen and red."

"You just stay put, me darlin' and I'll be back in two shakes." Kate gathered the folds of her dress and rushed downstairs. Rory still stood where he had been when she left and E.B. was pulled up to the table sipping coffee; or maybe something stronger. "Make yourself useful, Lad, and work the pump for me. I want the water near cool as the mornin' breeze."

Absently, he operated the pump's handle as Kate held her wrist under the stream to check its temperature. When she was satisfied, she filled a pitcher and hurried back up the stairs. Lucy remained at her mirror. "Lie back down on the bed me darlin'. We'll soon have those red puffy eyes clear as the mornin' sky." Lucy did as she was bid, and Kate applied a cool damp compress to her eyes.

"Mmm— Thank you."

"Think nothin' of it, darlin'. I shed many a tear over my man when we were courtin'." Kate patted Lucy's arm reassuringly. When you're ready, come down and we'll start all over again—and don't apologize. We don't want them to think there is anythin' amiss about a woman sheddin' a tear now and again."

Downstairs, Kate found Rory and E.B. as she left them. "Kate will be down in a minute," she said and leaned towards them menacingly as she wagged her finger. "There'll be no mention of her tears, is that understood?"

****

Lucy halted on the landing and surveyed the room. She tried to detect how they'd receive her after her earlier childish performance. Her father glanced nonchalantly. Kate smiled and nodded encouragement, and Rory beamed. She smiled back and came into the kitchen. She stopped at the hutch belonging to her mother and collected fresh linen napkins. Pressed to her breast like a shield, she stepped to the table where Rory waited. She rose on the tips of her toes, leaned in, and brushed her lips gently across his cheek, and despite Kate's admonition, she whispered, "I'm sorry."

Her show of physical affection in front of Kate and E.B. caused Rory to blush. "Well get on with it, Lad," Kate said. "You're among family and friends. Squeeze her and give her a kiss, so we can eat dinner before it's burned to a crisp."

Still blushing, he took her into his arms, hugged, and kissed her passionately. When they parted, his face burned red with embarrassment.

****

After their meal, E.B. and Kate remained at the kitchen table talking. Kate sipped a hot cup of tea, and E.B. imbibed a shot of aged Kentucky Bourbon. Lucy and Rory retreated outside to the porch-swing. His arm over her shoulder, they swung gently. Lucy broke the silence. "I really am sorry about my earlier outburst," she said, and then paused.

Not at all the fool Kate thought him to be; Rory understood the reason for her pause. "Lucy, I'm the one who should apologize. From your point of view, I'm certain it must seem that I'm mad, but it's who I am—how I was raised. I think about Herberto and the man who killed him every day. A part of me is stuck, and I can't move forward with my life until I've done this thing. Does it make any sense to you at all?"

The swing halted, and she sat up and turned to face him. "I understand you want justice for your friend's murder, but why does it have to be you to secure it? Surely there are lawmen or the Army that could track this criminal down?"

"Herberto was more than my friend." His voice was firm, but with feeling, he reached for her hand and squeezed it as he continued. "He treated me like his son, and I came to love him like a father." He remained quiet for a minute. It was important to him that she understood what the priest had meant to him.

"I'm sorry. I just knew that you cared for him. Until now, I didn't realize how much, I don't want you to go. You might not come back. Isn't there anyone else?

"There is no law outside the towns and cities through-out the southwest. If you want justice, you must seek it for yourself."

"Would Father Herberto want you to do this?"

That question derailed his argument. He leaned back onto the swing and started to-and-fro while he considered her question. At length, he stopped and turned to her, she waited in silence. "No. I don't think he would want me to seek revenge. If I could capture Cain and turn him over to the law, Herberto would agree to that."

"Is that what you plan to do?"

The Apache way now controlled his thinking. "No. Let's talk about something else. Where shall we go on our ho-neymoon?"

They spent the remaining days planning their future life together. There was any number of vocational choices for Rory, but he concluded his talents and interest would be in law. When he returned, he would study law and become a lawyer.

At daybreak Monday, Rory saddled the silvery grey-speckled roan. He had also purchased a mule to pack his gear. E.B. rolled his chair across the yard with the aid of Kate. Lucy followed, but stayed back while her father said his good-bye. "Son, I want you to take my Sharps and carry the Lang across the saddle." E.B. looked at Rory. "Don't forget what I taught ya—ya hear."

Kate stepped around the chair, hugged him, and then kissed his cheek. She held his face in her hands, and said, "You take care of yourself. Don't worry about himself or Lu-cy. I'll take good care of them." She leaned in closer. "By the time you return, I expect to be your future mother-in-law." Back to behind E.B.'s wheelchair, she winked.

Rory stifled his urge to laugh, but he couldn't stop himself from grinning at her. Lucy moved in close to him, and he put his arm over her shoulder and hugged her to him. He led his animals, and they walked down the alleyway to the street. Lucy asked, "What did Kate say that was so funny?"

"She expects to be your mother soon."

"Oh that—everyone knows but father—she'll tell him soon enough."

At the end of the alley, Lucy pulled back. "I don't want you to go, Rory."

Rory took her into his arms and kissed her passionately—crushing his lips to hers. "I love you, Lucy. I'll write often as I can—please wait for me." He swung into the saddle and urged the roan to move. Seconds later, he halted and looked back. Lucy wiped away her tears and waved.

Chapter 14

For the next several weeks, Kilchii meandered through Missouri and crossed the Arkansas border. He headed for Little Rock, which was still a tough rowdy town that carried only a semblance of civilization. From there, he planned to enter the Territories[21].

Along his route, he selectively compiled wanted posters and information on men allegedly hidden in the Territories. He returned to his buckskin shirt, trousers and well-worn calf-length moccasins. His shaggy copper colored-hair grew long, and his beard thick. Kilchii appeared well suited to his Apache name red boy. The transformation back to Kilchii was complete. The young man appeared as fierce as the reputation he planned to build.

Kilchii held the roan to a walk as he entered the town. Eyes straight forward, yet he still detected the town's people as their gaits hesitated to steal quick glances of the redheaded stranger. As he neared the older part of town and the White Elephant Saloon[22], the stares became bolder. The Lang rested across his saddle and dissuaded anything further.

---

[21] Oklahoma Indian Territories.

[22] An oft-used name for drinking emporiums.

After he stabled his horse and mule, Kilchii took his gear and walked to the Jefferson Hotel for a room. The accommodations were passable; he recalled the comment from E.B., 'The return to living rough was hard to get used to.' From the hotel, he went to the White Elephant Saloon. E.B. told him to begin there, he said, 'Be patient, and they'll come to you.'

The paneled walls and bar front were dark, almost an ebony. Oil filled lamps hung from the tin ceiling above by heavy cords tied high at the walls. Glass shelves in front of mirrors covered the wall behind the long bar manned by three bartenders.

In addition to small tables for patrons, there were two faro[23] tables near the rear exit. At the rear of the saloon, away from the entrance, he sat where he could monitor the establishment's patrons' comings and goings.

As he loosed the leather loop on the hammer of his Colt, one of the bartenders appeared. "What'll ya have?"

"Beer and something to eat."

The man's indifferent demeanor confirmed to Rory that he blended.

The bartender asked, "Stew?"

Kilchii nodded, and the bartender left and returned with a beer and a tin bowl of stew. "Before you ask—it's meat in the stew, but I don't know what type." He sat the glass and bowl down on the table. "That'll be two-bits."

Kilchii gave him a silver dollar, and said, "On account."

The men who frequented the White Elephant tended to mind their own business, so Kilchii ate his meal in peace. While he sipped his beer, he watched men, careful not to stare, as they walked into the saloon. He mentally compared their faces to the wanted posters he'd memorized.

---

[23] A popular card game of the era.

Throughout the day, he sat in the White Elephant and sipped beer. At night, after an evening meal in the hotel's restaurant, he sat inside his room and reviewed wanted posters; that became his routine.

E.B. proved to be right. Late afternoon of his eighth day, a trail weary rider stood at the entrance and assessed the patrons. Kilchii recognized him as Tom Dozier, road agent and horse thief. The reward offered $1,500, dead or alive. Dozier walked to the bar and ordered a shot of rye, which he tossed down. When his eyes returned to the mirror, Kilchii stared back.

The outlaw didn't react, but his left hand eased below the surface of the bar. The movement registered; Kilchii knew from the poster that Dozier was left handed. "Tom Dozier, there's a wanted poster on you—dead or alive."

Men on either side moved away from him. The bartenders ducked down behind the thick wooden bar. The faro dealer paused, and his patrons turned to watch the showdown. Dozier poured another drink using his right hand.

Dozier asked, "You aim to collect it?"

"I do. Put your hands behind your head or I'll kill you where you stand."

The outlaw smiled and lifted his glass. In the mirror's reflection, he gave a salute. He tossed it back and slammed the glass down hard, but Kilchii was ready. Dozier turned, his pistol drawn. Kilchii shucked his Colt and fired as Dozier turned. A neat black hole appeared above his center shirt button.

Dozier's pistol slipped from his hand, and confusion clouded his eyes. He slumped to the saloon floor seemingly unaware he was about to breathe his last. The bullet severed an artery and blood drained from his wound absorbed into the sawdust covered floor.

Two deputies responded to the shots fired. Kilchii waited with raised hands. They entered with their revolvers drawn. The older of the two, asked, "What's happened here?"

Kilchii pointed to the body, and said, "That's Tom Dozier. He's wanted dead or alive—look at your wanted posters."

"Fair enough, but in the meantime you come along with us to the jail." The younger office stepped around and retrieved Kilchii's Colt. "Now come along," said the older man.

At the sheriff's office, Kilchii explained the details of the shooting to the sheriff. "There is a wanted poster for a Tom Dozier dead or alive," said the sheriff. "The reward's $1,500 offered by Wells Fargo. Assuming you've gotten the right man, you'll have to collect the money from them."

The younger deputy said, "Sheriff, we questioned the witnesses and they all agreed that Dozier admitted who he was and that it was a fair fight." He pointed to Kilchii, and added, "The witnesses said Dozier drew first, but he was twice as fast."

The sheriff stared hard at Kilchii. "Alright, you can go, but don't give us any more trouble or we'll haul your ass in front of a judge. Do you get my meaning?"

Kilchii nodded. "Yes, Sheriff, I believe I do." They returned his Colt and the knife he carried in his boot. "One last thing, Sheriff—I need written confirmation from your office that I killed Tom Dozier and that I'm entitled to the reward."

"Come back tomorrow," said the sheriff.

"I'll have it now if you please. If it's the required language delaying you, I can write it out for your signature and a witness. I just need official stationery."

The sheriff glowered up from his desk. He pointed to the badge in his shirt. "I know how to write an affidavit, but the judge has to sign it, so come back tomorrow."

Reluctantly, Kilchii turned to leave. The sheriff stopped him. "What's your name—for the affidavit?"

"Kilchii, K-i-l-c-h-i-i."

The sheriff scowled. "What kind of name is that?"

"Apache."

"Well I'll need more than that for the affidavit."

"Mr. Kilchii," he said and walked out of the sheriff's office.

By noon the next day, Kilchii heard his name whispered as he walked by, he smiled.

Later at the Wells Fargo office, he presented the affidavit to the clerk behind the caged counter. The clerk studied the document several seconds before looking at Kilchii. "I've been expecting you," said the clerk. "Payment is a bank draft. What name shall I use?"

"Bearer."

"That's—that's highly unusual and I must tell you not very safe. Should you lose the draft anyone who finds it could redeem it for gold."

Kilchii stared hard at the clerk. "Please don't make me ask you a second time—bearer."

The clerk swallowed hard, grabbed his pen, and rapidly dabbed it in the ink well. "Yes, Sir. I, I mean no, Sir. I'll make the draft out to bearer. There's no problem, Sir."

From the Wells Fargo office, he went to the First Bank of Arkansas and asked to speak to the bank's president. There was a delay until he presented the draft. Soon after, Mr. Johnson, the bank president, appeared holding the draft. "What may I do for you, Sir?"

Kilchii asked, "May we speak in private?"

Johnson hesitated, and then glanced at the draft once more. "Certainly, we can talk in my office. This way please." He led the way.

Seated in a wood paneled office in front of a hand-carved walnut banker's desk, Kilchii noted that Johnson hadn't relinquished the draft. "Now how may the First Bank be of service?" Johnson asked.

Kilchii reached into the saddlebag he carried over his shoulder and retrieved a document. "I must know I can rely on the bank's confidentiality."

"Sir, we never disclose information about our depositors." He glanced at the draft. "May we open an account for you?"

Kilchii passed the additional document to Johnson. "Yes you may, and add this to it."

Johnson opened the document. It was a draft on Saint Louis Citizens Bank to the amount of $10,000 to Mr. Rory McLeod. Johnson looked back to Kilchii, and asked, "Mr. McLeod?"

"Yes. That name, my name shall be held in the strictest confidence. You shall address me as Kilchii or Mr. Kilchii if you like, but no one else is to know that I'm Rory McLeod." He paused, to make sure the banker looked at him. "Will that be a problem?"

Johnson glanced at the drafts, and back to Kilchii. "Not at all—Mr. Kilchii."

"I require $1,000 in gold coins now and will, from time to time deposit or withdraw funds as circumstance dictates. And I will only deal with you. Can that be arranged?"

The banker nodded. "Certainly, if that's your wish, Mr. Kilchii, we aim to satisfy our customers."

Kilchii stood and leaned across Johnson's desk. "You're aware how I earned that money?" Johnson nodded. "Then don't fail me—do you understand?"

Eyes wide and pale, he nodded, and finally stammered, "Ye—yes, Sir, Mr. Kilchii."

Kilchii turned to leave Johnson's office. At the door, he paused and said, "Thank you, Mr. Johnson. It's been a pleasure doing business with your bank."

Tomorrow, he would leave for the Territories. For rest of today, he would enjoy what Little Rock had to offer. He entered the White Elephant. Paused at the door, and looked to his usual table; the two men seated there immediately vacated the table. As was habit, he steadied his holstered Colt as he sat and checked to make sure the hammer loop was free. The bartender brought him a beer and asked, "Do you want something to eat, Mr. Kilchii?"

So they now know my name—good. He smiled at the bartender. "What's on the menu?"

To his left, standing at the end of the bar, he saw two men take notice when the bartender spoke his name. Before the bartender could answer, Kilchii said, "Never mind—the beer is fine for now." He sipped his beer and watched the two men, who were now deep in hushed conversation. They finished their drinks walked passed Kilchii's table as if to leave. One lagged the other and when they were abreast of his table, they turned and went for their guns.

Kilchii, who had already palmed his Colt, jumped up and to his left, he fired two shots, left to right. The man on his right got off a round, but it missed him, and it lodged in the wall behind where he sat. The total exchange happened in less than a second, giving no one a chance to duck. Consequently, several beers were spilled and glasses broken.

Smoke drifted from his gun barrel and the acrid smell of cordite lingered. Kilchii asked, "Who were they?"

The bartender who served them said, "They were askin' about Dozier—they said they was friends of his." The bartender's eye grew large and he held up his hands. "I didn't point you out Mr. Kilchii. Please, I have a wife and children."

And they're also afraid of me—even better. He holstered his Colt and looked at the other bartender. "Bring me a fresh beer and some stew."

"Right away, Mr. Kilchii."

The same two deputies from the day before rushed through the saloon doors, revolvers drawn. They stared at the two men on the floor and then at Kilchii. The older one asked, "What happened?"

Kilchii smiled. "Would you believe that they killed each other?"

The policemen looked down at the bodies. "But they were facing you, Mr. Kilchii."

Even the deputies now call me Mister. "I didn't think you would believe me, but it was worth a try. It seems that they were Tom Dozier's friends and they decided to ambush me while I sat here sipping a beer." The policemen glanced around the room and virtually all the patrons nodded.

Kilchii's bartender said, "Damnedest thing I ever saw. Those two acted like they was leavin' and quick as snakes pulled on Mr. Kilchii, but he killed 'em both. That one," he said and pointed toward the body nearest the door. "He got off a shot, but it plum missed."

"Sorry, Mr. Kilchii, but you got to come with us to the jail."

Kilchii shrugged and stood. "Am I under arrest?"

"No, sir," said the older deputy. "It's just a formality and some paperwork."

At the jail, the sheriff glanced up as they entered. "You, again. What is it this time?"

The older deputy provided the details to the sheriff, adding that the two men were most likely outlaws and there could be reward money involved. The sheriff set his jaw firm and stared hard at Kilchii. Finally, his face softened and he leaned back in his chair. "I tell you what, Mr. Kilchii. If you agree to leave our peaceful town—say tomorrow. I'll speak to the prosecutor so you won't have to bother with an inquiry. What do you say to that?"

"As you wish, Sheriff, I'll leave in the morning."

Chapter 15

Five-days southwest of Little Rock near the Ouachita foothills, Kilchii came upon a small farm-ranch. Its pasturage sparse and cattle few, their bones bulged against their hides with the threat of piercing through. At the weather-worn and unmaintained main house, he encountered a woman; he assumed the owner's wife. She stood within the shadows of the doorway aiming a rifle; two young tousle-haired boys stared out from behind her skirt tails.

Sun and wind made her appear older than her time; beaten down by her way of life, but he noted her voice retained spirit. "What do you want?" she asked.

Aware that his appearance didn't encourage trust, Kilchii smiled to try and relieve her suspicions. "I'd hoped to discuss a business matter with your husband, Ma'am. Is he home?"

The woman slowly cocked the rifle's hammer. "I'm askin' again." Her jaw flexed with determination, but her voice sounded calm and business like. "What do you want?"

He continued to smile, and put his hands out to his side. "I'd hoped to purchase a few head of your cattle. They're underfed, but I'll still give you a good price."

After she studied Kilchii for several seconds, she lowered the rifle and eased the hammer down on the pin. "My name's Betty Henighan." Once she began to talk, it didn't seem like she could restrain herself. She dragged the boys out from behind her and said, "These are my boys Joe, Jr. and Robert. Things around here were tough with all the men gone off to war. Then my husband, Joe, he up and died three years ago, and the farm has gone to seed since. I'd sell and move back east if I had a buyer."

"I'm pleased to meet you, Mrs. Henighan—you too, boys."

"Step down and come in for coffee," she said, and stepped back from the door.

Inside, the house was clean and bright. The coffee smelled good. Mrs. Henighan gingerly took a blue and white cup and saucer from her china cabinet. Kilchii recognized the pattern; it was the same as Lucy's dishes. "Ridgeway china—how lovely—you shouldn't go to that much trouble."

Mrs. Henighan smiled warmly, which softened her face. "If you know what they are, then it's no trouble—they belonged to my mother. How did you come to know china patterns?"

He chuckled. "I don't really, but a friend in Saint Louis has the same pattern, and she only uses them on special occasions."

"Mister, you're a contradiction. You dress like a half-breed, and your red hair and beard make you look like a wild man—you should shave if you're goin' to be around women. Instead of stealin' my cows like everyone else has— you offer to buy them—why?"

"It's a very long story, Mrs. Henighan. Suffice it to say I do try to be an honest man."

"Well, I've got plenty of time. She paused, settled back in her chair to examine him, and then asked, "What's your name?"

"Kilchii."

"Sounds Indian."

"Apache."

"You don't say. They're out west. Do you speak their language?"

"I was raised by the Apache after Comancheros murdered my parents."

Mrs. Henighan scooted to the edge of seat, leaned forward, and waited for him to continue. He said nothing more. Finally, after waited several seconds, she asked, "You don't talk much, do you?"

"No," he said and grinned. "There's not really much to tell. May we get back to the subject of the cattle?"

Obviously disappointed, Mrs. Henighan sighed, "If you must. How many head do you want and how much will you offer?"

"Twenty-head and I'll pay $25 a head."

She shook her head. "You don't know much about cattle, do you? For the shape they're in, that price is four times what they're worth."

"They're worth that price to me. I'll pick the healthiest of the bunch and change their brand before I leave, if it's okay to camp here a few days?"

"You're more 'an welcome. The bunkhouse is habitable. You can stay there, and I'll feed you here at the main house."

"Deal," he said and offered his hand.

"Deal," she replied and they shook hands.

Kilchii led his animals to the sagging structure she claimed was a barn. She called, "There's grain in the barn, help yourself."

He waved without looking back.

★★★★

Betty watched the redheaded young man walk toward the barn. His lean muscular body and the way he moved reminded her of a cat—a powerful dangerous cat. Absently, she touched her hair. *I must look a fright.*

Moments later, her son Joe ran out of the house with a bucket, intent on pumping water from the well. When he returned with it, she heated the water and took it to her bedroom to wash.

Toiletry complete, she looked at herself in the small mirror hung over her vanity. As she smoothed the front of her dress, she thought, *At least I still have my figure.* When she entered the main room of the house, her boys looked at her with curious expressions. "What are you two staring at?"

"You look nice, Ma," said her youngest son Robert.

Joe scowled his eye full of suspicion. "Why you dressin' up, Ma?"

"Now, Joe, you know why. Mr. Kilchii is joining us for supper, and we want to appear at our best when we have company." She inspected their appearance. "It wouldn't hurt a thing if you two washed behind your ears as well. Supper will be soon, so hop to it."

The boys grumbled on their way to the well with soap and towels. Kilchii came from the barn and joined them. Betty saw him through the window. She tried, but couldn't look away as she watched him strip down to the waist. He poured a bucket of water over his head; wet his hair's redness intensified. When he stood and shook his head to sling the water from his mane, his neck muscles rippled, and she once again thought him cat like.

Mesmerized, she stared as his taunt torso as it glistened in the glow from the afternoon sun. Not fully conscious of her action, she cupped her breast and with her thumb and index finger pulled at her nipple until it strained against her bodice. Her boys bounded through the door—it broke her trance. She turned away and faced the pot hung over the fire.

Minutes later, Kilchii followed the boys. He stood at the door and waited for permission to enter. After a deep inhale, he said, "That smells delicious."

Unable to face him after seeing him half-naked, she said over her shoulder, "It's just beans with a bit of pork for flavor. The bread was fresh baked today, and the vegetables come from our garden." Finally, she turned to face Kilchii. "Please come in and take a seat, supper's nearly ready."

"Is there anything I can do to help?"

"No. You're our guest. Please sit down."

Joe and Robert stared at him suspiciously, as he approached the table. He selected the chair furthest from the fire to be out of Betty's way.

"That's pa's chair," Joe said with Robert nodding his agreement.

"Boy's, mind your manners. Where else should Mr. Kilchii sit?"

Joe frowned, then shrugged his shoulders and looked away as Kilchii took a place at the table. Kilchii glanced around the house's interior. Its floor plan was simple, one portion dedicated for living and the other part for sleep. There was a fireplace located at each end for warmth from the cold.

Betty placed a large bowl of beans on the small table and sat down. She served food onto Robert's plate and then Joe's. Kilchii waited his turn. "If you'll pass your plate Mr. Kilchii, I'll serve you too."

Finally, she served herself and took the first bite. "Ma, ain't we going to say grace?"

Betty blushed. "We have a guess, Robert. I doubt if Mr. Kilchii wants—"

"May I, Mrs. Henighan?" Kilchii asked and laced his fingers together.

"Yes please, Mr. Kilchii."

"Bless us, O Lord, and these Thy gifts, which we're about to receive from Thy bounty, through Christ our Lord—Amen."

"I must apologize, Mr. Kilchii. Since you told me you were raised by Indians, I just assumed that you weren't religious."

"I left the Apache when I was sixteen, Mrs. Henighan. I went to live with a priest and the friars of San Xavier Mission south of Tucson where I went to school."

Joe and Robert perked up. Joe asked, "What was it like living with Indians?"

"Joe, I never—"

"It's fine Mrs. Henighan

"Please call me Betty."

"If you'll drop the mister in front of Kilchii," he said and then grinned. His strong white teeth looked like pearls in the nest of his fiery beard. She returned the smile and nodded.

"Joe," Kilchii said. "Living with the Apache is the best childhood I could ever imagine for a boy."

The boys flung questions at him faster than he could answer. Betty said, "Boy's, that's enough for now. Let Kilchii eat."

He gave her a grateful look. "After supper, if your mother says it's allowed, I'll tell you some stories then."

Their heads snapped to look at their mother, their expressions begging permission. "Alright—on one condition; mind your manners."

Joe and Robert raced to see who would finish first—Joe won. They rushed to the sideboard with their dirty plates and practically ran back to the table. Betty raised her hand. "Boys, no running in the house."

After Kilchii cleaned his plate and turned down an offer for seconds, she said, "Well then—what would you say to peach cobbler and coffee."

"I would say please."

Betty served the dessert and then tended to the supper dishes while Kilchii thrilled her sons with stories of life among the Apache. When she finished, she sat by the fire sipped her coffee, and watched Kilchii. *It's been a hard three years without a man to take care of the place and ... me.* She turned away. *Where are these thoughts coming from? He certainly doesn't resemble Joe, nor act like him. Why am I having these thoughts about a man I don't even know?* "It's time for bed, Boys."

"Aw, Ma," they begged. "One more story—please."

"I'll be here for a couple of days. If you boys are good and mind your mother, I promise to tell you more stories." They jumped down from their chairs and raced to their bedroom.

"Boys, no—," she called, but they slammed their door before she finished.

She switched her gazed to the fire where errant smoke stung her eyes. Hankie in hand she wiped away her tears. She couldn't find the words for a conversation, so she sat in silence.

"They seem like good boys, Betty."

"They are—it's been tough raising them alone. They're at the age where they need a man's influence though. If I could sell this place I'd move back to Ohio where my family lives."

They sat without talking for several minutes. Kilchii broke silence. "I guess I should turn-in. It's going to be a long day tomorrow."

As he rose to leave, she said, "Wait—I have extra bedding."

"Thanks, but it's not necessary."

"Please, Kilchii, it is no trouble. If I don't use them once in a while the moths will just eat them." She went to her room and returned with sheets and blankets. He accepted them with a grateful nod.

From the doorway, she watched him make his way to the bunkhouse; lantern in one hand and bedding in the other. Fixed on its warm glow, she watched the bunkhouse window until Kilchii blew out the light. As she leaned against the closed door, she shamelessly wondered what the rest of his body looked like. Distress seized her, and she shook her head violently to rid her mind of such immoral thoughts. Her mind quieted; she went to her room and got ready for bed.

Two hours later, she remained awake. Her mind recalled memories of love and lust that aroused her. Every time she started to drift off to sleep, Kilchii's strong arms embraced her, jolting her awake, hungry for a man's touch. She rose from bed and made her way quietly outside, and stared at the bunkhouse just yards away. The windows were dark; it was silent with only the sound of crickets beguiling potential mates with their songs. Was he awake as well? Her desires conquered, and she went to the bunkhouse.

At his door, she tapped lightly. "Kilchii, are you awake."

"Yes, I'm a light sleeper."

"May I come in?"

"Let me dress and get the light."

She opened the door, stepped through, and shut it behind her. "Please—no light," she said as she carefully made her way to the sound of his voice.

"Betty, I—"

"Please, Kilchii. Don't make me beg. I've been alone for three years and there's—"

Kilchii reached up and pulled her into his bed. "I'm lonely too."

****

The next two days ... and nights followed a similar routine. During the day, Kilchii gathered cattle and used a 'D-ring' to modify their existing brand. It was easy enough. The original brand was a lowercase 'h' over a rocker. He traced over the 'h' and rocker changing it to a circle. Then he added a line at an angle changing the 'h' to a 'k'. The only way to know for sure that he'd altered the brand was to butcher the animal and check the hide from the skinned-side.

At night, Betty came to the bunkhouse, her eyes aglow with passion. At dawn, she scurried back into the house and began making breakfast before her boys stirred.

After breakfast on the third day, Kilchii finished his coffee and watched Betty flit from one task to another. She no longer seemed like the old woman whom he'd met when he arrived. This woman was happy and looked forward to the days ahead. It pleased Kilchii that he brought so much happiness into Betty's life. The remorse he felt about Lucy was slight. He and Lucy were not yet wed, and his Apache upbringing understood and tolerated things like this.

"Betty, in addition to the $500 for the cattle, would you consider selling me the farm for $1,000? That would get you home to your family and help you start a new life."

She saddened. "Boys, forget your chores for now, and go outside and play. Mr. Kilchii and I have business to discuss." The boys bolted out the door. She sat down and leaned on the table. "There's another way you could get this land," she said as she smiled and arched an eyebrow.

Kilchii unprepared for her comment blushed. "That's not—"

"I know I'm older than you, but I still have my figure and the boys like you. The four of us could get this farm up and running again in a year, or two."

"Betty, I'm sorry, but—I have no long-term interest in this place. I have something I must do and this farm could help me achieve my goal—that's all the property means to me. If you don't want to be rid of it, then I'm prepared to lease it."

She sat upright in her chair, not happy but not sad either. "I didn't think you'd stay, but it was worth a try—you might have said yes."

"Will you sell?"

She hesitated only briefly before she extended her hand. "Yes."

"The cattle are ready. I'm leaving in the morning."

"That's what I thought."

Kilchii moved from the table to a small writing desk placed against the wall in the living area. Taking paper from a drawer, he began to write. "I'm giving you a letter of credit for $1,400. Here is $100 in gold." Five coins clinked as he dropped them on the desktop. "Also, there are instructions to the banker to draft a bill of sale for your signature. Finally, I've asked him to see to the boys and your comfort until arrangements are made for your travel back to Ohio." When he finished, he handed her the documents.

"Thank you," she said, as she turned and fled into her bedroom closing the door behind her.

That night, after the boys had gone to sleep, Kilchii heard the now familiar tapping on the bunkhouse door. She came to him, and they made love—never speaking. When they finished, she didn't stay but returned to the house.

Before dawn's rays began to warm the day, Kilchii rose from bed, dressed, and made his way to the barn where he readied his gear and animals. With his mule packed and his horse saddled, he went to the house to say his goodbyes. A huge spread of food lay on the table. Betty and the boys wore their Sunday best. Kilchii was confused. "I don't under—"

"You've done so much for us," she said, "that we wanted to show you how special we think you are."

Robert's cherub round face turned up to him, he said, "It's like a birthday—just no cake."

"Aw but there's pie," said Betty. "Please sit down."

After a huge breakfast, they stood on the porch. Kilchii asked, "How soon before you and the boys leave."

She paused, and then began to speak; thinking out loud. "Well—we have to pack, but there are just a few personal things. The only livestock that needs tending are the horses—"

"Sell them and the wagon in town—I won't need them."

"Well then, I think we should be away from here in three days—why the rush?"

"There could be some tough men passing through here, and I don't want you around. It would be too dangerous for you and the boys to remain."

"Oh," she said confusion in her eyes.

Kilchii smiled at her. "That's all I can tell you. Please—for your safety, Betty—you should leave as quickly as possible."

Betty reached up, grabbed his beard in both hands, and pulled his face down to hers and kissed him wetly on the lips. "You're such a dear," she said and rushed inside and into her bedroom.

The boys stood eyes wide and mouths open. Joe said, "Golly—did ya see that, Robert? Ma kissed him on the lips." Robert nodded.

Kilchii mussed their hair and stepped down from the porch. Mounted, he turned in the saddle. "Boys, you take special care of your mother. She's a good woman and needs your help."

After they acknowledged him, he reined his horse west; he didn't look back.

Down the trail, his herd milled about; they grazed in a grassy meadow. Driving them in the direction he wanted to go while leading a mule was going to be difficult, he hoped the men at Robbers' Roost would appreciate his efforts. After a while, he noticed that one of the cows led the others and that all he had to do was keep track of her. *Boss heifer,'* he thought.

Chapter 16

Before Rory left, he took stationery and envelopes from Betty's desk. Now, he sat cross-legged near his campfire trying to find the words to say to Lucy. He missed her awfully, but even more since being with Betty. He decided, he thought wisely, not to tell Lucy about Betty; she wouldn't understand. There had been no lust on his part; he only wished to comfort a lonely widow. Smiling, he thought, *they would probably like each other; if they ever met.*

'My Dearest Lucy,
I have missed you terribly these many weeks on the trail. If only my quest was done, and I could come home to you, Darling.' His mind went blank; he could think of nothing more to say that was romantic. Then it occurred to him that he should tell her about the things he recalled when he dreamed. 'Lucy, I remember how you smell of scented soap in the morning and exotic spices in the evening when you finished work at the store. I smile when I recall the crinkles at the corners of your eyes when you are angry and scold me—your finger wagging.
My heart aches when I think of the expression on your face the day I left. Darling, I long to be with you, and I think of you always.

Your loving fiancé,

Rory'

It was short, but he thought he had done rather well for his first love letter. His next would be better he was sure. He took out another sheet of paper.

'E.B.,

We now own a small ranch in eastern Oklahoma. You should receive the deed and other necessary documents in a few weeks. I bought the place for its cattle, part of my plan to enhance my reputation as a bad man. With twenty-head of cattle, I'm moving west toward Robbers' Roost. From there I plan to go south into Texas to start my search for Cain. My plan is to join his outfit and take him when the time is right. I know you disagree, and that I should take him with the Sharps, but I want him to know who is taking his life and why. I don't know when I will get another chance to write.

I pass by Fort Gibson tomorrow and will mail these letters. I don't think I will be near another Post Office for some time to come. Please explain to Lucy how difficult it is to communicate under the circumstances.

Your friend and soon-to-be son-in-law,

Rory'

He chuckled at the closing. E.B. would laugh as well—he was sure of it.

Chapter 17

Four men rode up; two of them slowly moved to his flanks. "Gentlemen," said Kilchii. "What may I do for you?"

The oldest of the bunch scratched his beard as he studied Kilchii. "State your business," he said and laid a rifle across his saddle, relaxed, but obviously pointed at Kilchii.

Reins held with both hands out and away from his Colt, he said. "I'm looking for a place to hole up, and I hear Robbers' Roost is as good a place as any."

"You don't say," said the older man. "What makes you think they'd let you enter their canyon?"

"Fresh beef," said Kilchii. "I figured you men would want whiskey or beef. I couldn't find enough whiskey, but I did find cattle."

"Hey Coe, these brands look fresh to me," said one of the men flanking Kilchii, "and no two look the same; they weren't done using a smith-made brandin' iron."

The man addressed as Coe smiled. "So you rustled 'em?"

Still smiling, Kilchii said, "Let's say I acquired them and that's my brand."

Coe looked to the man who examined the herd. "What's the brand?"

"Circle 'K'," came the reply.

Looking back at Kilchii, he asked, "What's the 'K' stand for?"

"Kilchii"

The man beside Coe, a half-breed Comanche Kilchii guessed, smirked. "It fits right enough."

"What do you mean, Crow?"

"Kilchii is Apache for 'Red Boy'," he said and nodded at Kilchii's head, "His hair color."

Crow spoke in Apache, and asked, "How long did you live with them?"

Kilchii replied in the same tongue, "I was raised by Mescalero Apache."

The other man who flanked him, moved so he could see Kilchii's face. "There was a man by that name who kilt Tom Dozier a while back in Little Rock—that you?"

"Depends—"

Coe leveled his rifle at Kilchii's mid-section, and asked, "On what?"

He was in a dicey situation—the shotgun lay hammers down across his legs and the leather loop held his Colt tightly in its holster. "Was Dozier a friend? I had to deal with two of them the next day—never got their names."

The man said, "That's right—I heard that too."

Coe's smile was more of a grimace. "I knew him. He's been through here a few times, but I can't say we was friends."

Unaware at first that he'd been holding his breath, Kilchii exhaled, his shoulders lowered, and he shifted to a more relaxed posture. To change the topic, he asked, "What about the cows?"

Coe scratched his beard again, and asked, "What's your price?"

"My price is room and board until things cool off."

Coe asked, "You wanted for shootin' Dozier?"

"No—that was self defense. There were problems when I acquired the cattle. I want to lay low until I know for certain that I got away clean."

Coe smirked, "You hope the owners won't report the theft—that it?"

Kilchii smiled, but his eyes were cold. "They're no longer there to report the theft. I just need time to see if they're missed."

Heedful, Coe asked, "How many?"

"A widow and her two sons."

Coe nodded. "Alright, you've got a deal. But, we're a little short handed, so you'll have to take your turn standin' guard and doin' other chores—you got a problem with that?"

Kilchii shook his head.

"Good. This is Crow," he said and pointed to the Indian next to him. In turn, he indicated the others. "The young fellow is Reb Hollister, and that hombre yonder is Logan. I'm Coe."

Kilchii nodded to each as he wondered; *what have I gotten into?*

"Kilchii, you ride with me and the rest of the boys will follow behind the cattle to make sure we don't lose any."

They rode for several hours, through one canyon to another along the mountain range, until they came out onto a high grassy meadow about 1,000 feet below the summit. It was a hidden valley. There was a small natural lake fed by a stream from higher up. On the mountain's slope sat a prominent stone fortress with a modest corral behind. Kilchii twisted in his saddle and examined the meadow and the building above; a rectangular structure with buttressed walls constructed of fieldstone, and a heavy timber-framed roof covered with tin sheeting. "You built that?"

Coe nodded. "Me and about forty men built it over a four-year period. The building is impenetrable. There's a corral behind and a trail leads over the ridge to the back way out of here." Coe pointed to the ridge behind and a rock formation over the entrance they passed through. Kilchii watched and men at both locations stood and waved. "They're guarded around the clock, rain or shine."

"Impressive—has the law ever tried to get in here?"

Coe conveyed a bit of pride in his voice. "A few, but they got turned back at the canyon, or killed outright."

"Crow said, "The passage down the backside isn't easy." Sarcasm came into his voice. "If you have to take it, you might want to ride the mule—if its saddle broke." The others laughed.

"Come on," said Coe. "Meet the rest of the crew." He led off up a series of switchbacks that took nearly twenty-minutes to ascent. The last leg of the trail opened onto a plateau. Behind the fortress were a corral and a lean-to shelter for the riders tack.

Kilchii looked about. "What about feed for the horses?"

Coe said, "Don't worry there's grain up here, but mostly somebody takes them down in the morning, and brings them back in the evening. That's why we've got a gate at the entrance." Coe looked at Kilchii. "I know it's a lot of work, but you can sleep easy here—besides when we have twenty or more men here the workload is light."

"What about food?"

"You've sure got a lot of questions," said Coe, "but then it pays to play it safe. Most of the men who come bring dry goods to share. Crow, and a few others that are good at it, hunt for game—deer or elk, mostly."

"Is that the same for ammo?"

Coe laughed. "Yes. We've even got some dynamite. They're for protection should the law ever make it this far, or it's for sale if you need some for a job."

Dismounted, Kilchii massaged the small of his back before he tended to his animals. "You've got a pretty good set up here. What's the monthly rate?"

Coe gave him a toothy grin. "Half of whatever you've got. If you don't have anything then you don't stay—there's no backin' out once you're here."

"Sounds a bit steep—I mean if you've made a good haul—"

"It's up to you. This is your first time here, so I'll make an exception. If you want to gather your cattle and go, you're free to leave."

"No, no," said Kilchii. "I'm fine with the arrangement."

"Most are," said Coe. "When you're unsaddled and done out here, come in and I'll introduce you to the others.

****

Inside, Coe motioned for Crow. "What do you need?" asked Crow.

"I need for you to keep your voice down," he said. "Now sit down." Crow did as directed and leaned in towards Coe. "Crow, I'm going to have the new man to work with you. If he's lived with the Apache, you'll know soon enough. I want you to keep an eye on him and see what he's up to."

"You don't trust him?"

"I don't know him or anything about him, so no—I don't trust him."

"We've got all those cattle he brung. We don't need to go huntin'."

"Then take him out to scout the area. We're gettin' too sloppy around here." Coe scratched his beard. "Now that I think about it, he could be a spy. You just keep an eye on him and let me know if he does or says anythin' suspicious—understand?"

Crow shrugged. "If that's what you want."

****

Saddlebags slung over his left shoulder, rifle in his left hand; Kilchii used the Lang's barrels to push the fortress door open. Without thought, he stepped out of the light that silhouetted his body, but didn't immediately shut the door. It was cool; the two-foot thick fieldstone walls at this higher elevation made it comfortable inside. It probably worked the reverse during the winter. He counted four fireplaces plus a small one with a Dutch oven over a modest fire and utensils hung from cut nails. The timber-built roof appeared sturdy and would easily carry a winter's snow-load, and the tin would resist most fires.

When his eyes adjusted, he scanned the room. Single bunks lined the far wall; several tables occupied the center, and a single corner dedicated for storage and cooking. He counted fourteen men. With the other two on guard-duty, it made a total of sixteen men staying at the fortress.

Coe waved. "Over here Kilchii," he said and pointed to an empty bunk, "Use that one."

Kilchii laid his long guns across the bunk and un-slung his saddlebags. Coe stood and began walking around the room. As he went, he stopped at each man and made the introduction.

"Crow, Hollister, and Logan, you already know." He pointed to a hulking man who sat with his back to them and played cards. "That big horse over there is Big Jake Louis. He's not the smartest in the room, but none better in a fight." The next man was normal size. "That's Big Jake, so this is Little Jake McNally." Little Jake nodded.

Kilchii asked, "Why not call them by their last names?"

Coe stared at him for a moment and then shrugged. "That's the way it is— Next is Swede." Coe leaned in close and whispered, "He's a little touchy, so watch yourself around him." Kilchii nodded.

Coe placed his hand on a man's shoulder. "This is Henry Starr—at the other table is Joker Malone, Dix Jackson, Carlos, and Juan Garcia; brothers. Black Joe is here full-time and mostly handles the livestock and cookin'. Last, we come to the 'Dandy', Mr. John R. Matthews." Coe scanned the room. "Big Nose Mike and Curly Bill are on guard. You'll meet them later. Meantime you'll be workin' with Crow until you've learned the ropes—that suit you?"

"Sounds fine to me," said Kilchii. He smiled at Crow. "Just let me know what needs to be done." Crow nodded and then followed Coe back outside.

Kilchii returned to his bunk, and stored his personables under the bed. His long guns, he hung across pegs set in the wall above. As he stretched out on the blanket to rest, he reviewed the names of the men he met—all were wanted. With the exception of Swede, he didn't think he had anyone to worry about so long as he stayed here. He would bide his time and get to know the men, and which if any knew of the Comancheros.

Chapter 18

Early the next morning, Crow rousted him out of his bunk. "We're goin' to scout the area outside the Roost."

Black Joe was also up. He had poured coffee and set out cold biscuits and bacon. Surprised by his appetite, Kilchii ate five biscuits and drank three cups of coffee. Joe watched him eat. Smiling, he said, "I can sees that with y'all here, I has to cooks extra. May bees y'all gots some more growin' to do?"

Kilchii popped the last bit of his biscuit and bacon into his mouth, and good-naturedly grinned back at the cook. "May be," he said.

Crow stood. "Let's go. I want to be outside the canyons at sunup. Just in case there's somebody breakin' camp, I want to know about it."

Outside, Kilchii found his horse saddled, he looked at Joe and nodded thanks. Mounted, he followed Crow's lead, and took a lighted torch from Joe. "These should bees good 'til suns up," Joe said as he handed the torch to Kilchii. "Good lucks to y'all."

Carefully, their horses picked their way down the switchbacks. They rode in silence, their torches held high above their heads to provide the most light. After a few minutes on the trail, Crow said, "Seems like Black Joe has decided to adopt you. He's not normally that friendly with strangers."

"Is it best to mind my own business and not ask questions?"

Crow smirked. "Generally, I would say that's best, but it really depends on who you're talkin' to. Swede—I'd advise you to stay clear of him. The Garcia brothers are friendly enough, so are the others, for the most part. Dandy likes to talk about his women friends, but not about how he's killed them for their money." Crow paused and looked at Kilchii, and asked, "What about you—hard-case or friendly?"

Here was what Kilchii waited for—innocent conversation. The advice from E.B. flashed in his mind, 'When you tell a lie make sure it's partly true. It'll be easier to remember and seems more believable.' "I'm friendly enough—there's just not much to tell."

"How long did you live with the Apache?"

"Most of my life—Sani sent me away when the band went to fight with Cochise against the Army."

"What did you do then?"

"Drifted around—ended up in Texas."

"What got you started on the outlaw trail?"

He paused to consider Crow's question. "This is starting to sound like an interrogation."

Crow ignored his objection. "That's another thing—the way you talk. You don't sound like you lived with the Apache."

"I went to a Christian school for a few years—learned to read and write."

"You didn't say anything about that earlier—why?"

"I didn't think it was any of your business—still don't. Where did you learn to speak English?"

"I learned at a missionary school on a reservation. They beat us when we didn't do as they said. When I was sixteen, I killed them and ran off and joined a band of Comancheros."

They were down the switchbacks. They rode across the meadow in silence. Kilchii spoke first. "It was different for me. I kept what I learned from the Apache, but added what the whites had to offer. I can walk in both worlds."

"So what put you on the trail?" Crow was persistent.

"I shot the man who ambushed a friend. They wanted to put me in jail, so I left town. I didn't have any money so I borrowed and sold things."

"Like cattle?"

"And horses—" added Kilchii.

"Are there any posters out on you?"

"Not that I know of—you?"

"No, I've always rode with Comancheros. I didn't see a need to stand out from the others."

Kilchii was mildly surprised at how quickly they had arrived at the subject he most wanted to discuss. He asked, "Do the Comancheros come here to hideout?"

"No—it's too far north."

'Careful, Kilchii, you don't want to spook him. He waited, but Crow didn't continue, so Kilchii asked, "How'd you end up here?"

"We came across the Rio Grande to raid a little town south of Val Verde; Langtry. It was a trap. Texas Rangers was waitin'. They shot us up pretty good. You can say a lot of things about them, but you can't claim they're bad shots—especially with repeatin' rifles," Crow said and shook his head. "Nope, you can't claim that at all. The Garcia brothers and me rode north and ended up here. I saw Cain and four or five more headed south, back to the Rio Grande."

It required every ounce of self-control to keep from attacking Crow. Crow had to be one of the two Comanches he saw the night before they killed Father Herberto. His mind jumped back to his trip with the priest.

****

As Rory and Herberto sat eating their breakfast, a lone dark figure, outlined by the sun, approached their camp from the East. He wore no hat, neither were there stirrups for his dangling legs, and he carried a lance and shield. "Apache," said Rory. "This is Cochise's land."

"Is there danger?"

"Not from a single brave riding so slowly."

The weary looking rider entered their camp. Rory rose and signaled welcome. In Apache, he said, "Would you share our food and coffee?"

At the mention of coffee, the brave smiled and slid off his pony and moved to the fire. Herberto passed a cup of hot coffee to their visitor. In Spanish, he said, "Good day, my friend."

The Apache nodded and replied, "Good day, Padre."

After they shared their food and poured two more cups of coffee for the brave, Rory asked, "How is the trail behind you?"

"It is filled with danger."

"Cochise?" Rory asked.

"No. Cochise has moved high into the mountains and bluecoats chase him. They will not catch him, but they pursue him just the same—they are stupid."

"Rory asked, "Then what is the danger?"

"Comancheros—with the bluecoats hunting Cochise, there is no one to stop them."

Quietly, the priest sat by the fire and watched their conversation. He understood only a word here and there. In Spanish, he asked, "Where do you go?"

The Apache didn't answer at first—he seemed sad. It was as if he didn't understand the question. "I do not know where the end of my trail lies. Cochise's war has no chance of victory. I no longer have a family, and to live on the reservation is not a choice." He stood and walked to his pony and swung onto its back. He gave the sign for peace, and rode out of their camp. The brave didn't look back.

Herberto watched him leave. "He sounds like a man who no longer has a reason to live."

"He searches for a good place to die." Rory explained.

"But he doesn't look ill. He—"

Knowing that the priest wouldn't understand or accept the warrior's intent, he changed the subject. "Padre, the Comancheros shouldn't be taken lightly. Do you wish to return to the mission?"

"God will protect us, Rory. We'll be watchful, but we need to complete this trip to Santa Fe."

When everything was packed, the priest waited while Rory obliterated the evidence that they had camped there. His efforts wouldn't pass close inspection, but someone casually riding by wouldn't pick out their campsite. He returned to the trail where Herberto waited. As he swept the ground with a brushy branch behind him, he erased the faint prints made by his moccasins.

Mounted, they looked back on the camp. "If I didn't know better, I would swear no one had ever camped on that patch of ground."

Rory held up his foot. "Still think I should own a pair of boots?" They both chuckled and proceeded on the trail eastward for Santa Fe.

"Your point is taken. I will not raise the subject again."

By the day's end, they were above 4,800-feet. The temperature and humidity were lower. The pine trees grew tall, and formed a forest broken only by sporadic granite outcroppings that punched up from the earth like the fist of some ancient pagan god. Still, even there, patches of bent and twisted scrub trees grew; they clawed the rock with their roots holding on against the winds that blew through the pass year round.

Rory raised his nose to the wind that blew from the east. "I smell smoke, Padre."

"I don't see any smoke, My Son. Are you positive?"

"It is from campfires, Padre. Close your eyes and focus on the aroma. What do you smell?"

The priest did as instructed. His eyes opened wide with surprise. "I smell bread baking and meat roasting over a fire. How far away are they?"

Rory shrugged and slid off his pony, and handed the reins to the priest. "Wait here and I will scout ahead."

"Be careful, My Son."

Nearly thirty-minutes of slow deliberate movement through the trees brought Rory to the edge of their camp-site. He counted sixteen men. Four stood guard while the rest lounged around the fires eating and drinking. The leader was a big white man who looked to be in his late forties or early fifties. Two were Comanche, and the remainder was Mexican vaqueros[24] turned bandits.

Herberto paced near where he'd tied their animals. Rory stepped out from behind a tree, and the priest startled, grabbed his robe, and jumped back.

"Where've you been all this time? I was worried that they had captured you."

"There are two Comanches with them, and they drink the white man's whisky—there was no need to worry. We'll wait here until dark and slip past their camp. I checked their back trail, and they're heading west. Once we're passed their camp, we should be safe."

They waited until long after the Comanchero camp bedded down for the night, but early enough that there were still night noises to mask the sounds of their passing. Under the light from a crescent moon, they led their horses down the trail.

As they neared the camp, their horses started to fidget when they smelled the Comanchero's animals. Rory moved calmly from horse to horse, stroked their necks, and whispered Apache words to each in a soothing tone. They steadied at the sound of his voice, and followed in single file while the priest brought up the rear.

An hour later, beyond the Comanchero's camp, they mounted and rode in silence; they followed the trail to a lower elevation.

---

[24] Mexican cowboys or wranglers.

Miles away by dawn, Rory reined in his pony. He pointed, and said, "There's a good place by the stream for us to stop and rest. It should be safe to have a small fire."

Nearly asleep in his saddle, the priest said, "I think we should stay here for the day and give the animals a rest."

Crinkles formed at the corners of Rory's eyes, and the slight upturn of his mouth indicated his playful attitude. "You're right," said Rory. "The horses are tired, and they could use a hot meal and a long nap in the shade." He raised a brow and smiled at Herberto, who finally caught on and scowled at the sarcasm.

Dismounted, the priest walked toward the stream and sat on its bank. "These boots are made for riding. I need my sandals for walking." He pulled off his boots, and eased his feet into the cold water. "Ah—surely this is one of God's delights." He leaned back on his elbows and then finally onto his back.

"Padre, don't fall asleep. The water is cold and your feet will go numb."

Herberto sighed and returned to a seated position, removed his feet from the stream, and dried each with the tail of his robe. Rory had a fire going and prepared to make coffee, he said, "I know you're a holy man, Padre, but I'll get the water upstream of your feet washing." The priest laughed and rose to help with the camp chores.

Hot coffee and food in their stomachs, the priest seemed rejuvenated. He looked about their campsite. "I'm concerned about the treasure. Let's find a place to conceal it." They found a spot where the rocks jutted out into the stream. "We can stay in the water and leave no trace that we were there."

"You would make a good Apache, Padre."

With the treasure safely hidden and the animals hobbled, they laid in the shade of a scrub oak to rest. Worn out, the priest began to snore. Rory hadn't the heart to disturb him, so he moved to the rocks near the stream.

****

He heard his mentor's voice in his mind, 'Take it easy, Kilchii. Do as the Apache have taught you—show no emotions. Just be patient'.

Kilchii turned to Crow and asked, "Cain?"

"Yeah—he was our leader. He's one cold bastard, too."

Kilchii feigned disbelieve and asked, "Yeah, what's he done that's so cold?"

"I doubt that you could think of something he hasn't done," said Crow. "Murdered his brother, he's raped and killed women and children—why he even tortured a holy man to death once just because he thought he carried gold."

"Did he? I mean did the priest have gold?"

Crow looked up quickly. Suspicion shone on his face. "Why did you say priest? I never said it was a priest."

Careful. Don't give yourself away. Kilchii returned Crow's gaze and kept his expression innocent. "I just assumed it was a Catholic Priest. Who else would be traveling with gold?"

Crow nodded and seemed to be satisfied with the answer. Kilchii showed that he was still interested, Crow continued with the details. "Hell, he killed one of our men when he tried to stop him." He paused stared off into the distance. "That priest had sand—I'll give him that. Cain stripped him, and staked him out on the ground. He started with his feet. Cain placed hot coals around his feet one at a time until they were burnt black and cracked open. Then he did the same thing to his hands—you could see the bones of his fingers." Crow shook his head and grimaced. "When he set a fire at his manhood, some of the vaqueros turned away.

"The Priest was long passed feeling pain, but Cain continued. He set a fire on the priest's stomach and laughed when it flared up burning the belly fat. He's one bad hombre. If there is a white man's hell—he's sure to go there when he dies."

Kilchii's face paled; all emotions left him except the cold desire for revenge. Evidently, Crow mistook his pallor and expression for shock on hearing the gory details of the priest's death, and asked, "You alright?"

He couldn't speak. If he tried, his anger would take control and Crow would know it was more than the sickening details of Father Herberto's death, but he would learn soon enough. *You will be the first,* he thought. He said, "No," and then rode ahead.

They neared the last section of ravines ahead of the flatlands. Crow called, "Kilchii, wait there. We need to put out our torches."

Crow dismounted and stepped past the rock face that concealed the ravine's entrance. The trial sloped down to the flatland. It traversed through boulders, and sprawled across an outcrop of granite. A good tracker who carefully looked for signs could find the place, but a passer-by would never see it.

When they reached the trail, he turned in his saddle. He knew the entrance was there, but he couldn't see it. Yesterday, when Kilchii arrived, with Coe and the cattle, he hadn't noticed the ravine's entrance couldn't be seen from below. He saw laughter in Crow's eyes. "Coe claims he was hunting a deer when he saw it disappear behind that rock wall—is that what you were going to ask?"

Kilchii nodded and then asked, "Now what?"

"We want to make sure that we don't have company in the general area, and if we do, we find out why." They sat their mounts and scanned the predawn-horizon. They searched for the glow of a campfire. As the sun crested, they rode south beginning a loop that would circle them back late in the day.

By habit, if for no other reason, Kilchii constantly examined the trail as they rode. Occasionally, he commented on the details the sign conveyed. But, in the back of his mind, he planned revenge, and it would begin with Crow.

For the next three-days, it was the same routine. Their only variation was to change direction when they started their circuit of the flatland. As with the first day, there were no signs of anyone's recent passage. On the morning of the fifth day, Kilchii awoke just after sunup with the other inhabitants of the fortress. Joe poured coffee for each man as he came to the table for breakfast. And when Kilchii took a seat at the table, Joe asked, "Sleep well?"

"I did, Joe—umm that coffee smells wonderful."

Joe grinned. "I bets you is hungry too—ain't that right?"

"There's no denying I could eat a bite or two," said Kilchii, also grinning. "What's on the menu?"

"Corncakes—bacon—and red-beans." Joe leaned in closer and said, "I gots honey if y'all want. Just don't let on that I gives it to y'all."

"Thank you, Joe, but I don't want trouble with the others, so give me the same thing they have."

"All rights then, but its powerful good honey," said Joe, and he went back to the cooking fire to plate Kilchii's food.

Crow sat down beside him. "No scouting today."

"I noticed. What do we do today?"

"Nothing today—Coe's decided that you're legit, so you'll stand guard in rotation with the others. You've got the main entrance 4:00 to 8:00 in the morning, so I'd turn in early if I was you."

"The new man gets the worse shift—that it?"

"Oh—I don't know," said Crow. "For me those are the best hours of the day. It's peaceful and you get to see the sunrise."

"I'll let you know."

Kilchii spent the day exploring the solidly built stone fortress and its grounds. Constructed from split timbers the corral was sturdy, but they could use a way to bring water up for the horses and the fortress. While he let the problem mull around in his brain, he strolled to the rear exit from the fortress.

He looked down the gorge and then the ledge that led to a slopping rock face, both appeared treacherous. *So that's what was so funny. The situation would have to be desperate, before I tried this way out—and not with a mule,* he thought. Then it occurred to him—he had the only mule at the fortress. If there were trouble, he'd have to keep an eye on him.

He studied the trail, but couldn't determine where it came out on the flatlands below; he needed to know.

Joe woke him just after 3:00 in the morning. "When do you sleep, Joe?"

"I gets my sleep durin' the day. Y'all don't needs to worry none about old Joe. I knows how to takes care of me."

Kilchii rose and went to the table for coffee. Joe had warmed the corncakes and set out the honey. "That's to hold y'all over til breakfast. Y'all eats that while I gets your horse saddled."

The moon was full, so Kilchii didn't need a torch to ride down the trail. He tied his horse to the scrub tree at the base of the climb to the guard's station. He replaced Swede. Kilchii asked, "Anything to report, Swede?"

Swede shook his head, stood and walked off without saying a word. Shrugging his shoulders, Kilchii positioned himself to wait for the sunrise and his replacement. From his viewpoint, he could see the flatlands beyond the outcropping and down into the ravine itself. Noises in the ravine amplified and echoed both ways; not even a whisper would go unheard. There was little to no chance of anyone using this way to sneak into or out of the meadow without detection. The hazy-gray stria that hangs over the horizon just before dawn reminded Kilchii of the last hunting trip with his uncle.

****

Rory helped his uncle carry firewood to the mission's kitchen. The silver in Bidzil's hair seemed to come over night as now it was hard to find any black, and his posture stooped beyond that caused by the armload of firewood. As they neared the woodpile, Rory said, "Uncle," He used the Apache word. "I think we should go on a hunt. The friars could use something new to eat. Maybe we could kill a deer or even an elk."

Bidzil didn't respond at first. With the aid of his hands placed at his lower back, the aging warrior stood erect and puffed out his chest. The lost look in his dark eyes faded, and he turned to his nephew. "Yes, I would hunt again. We shall go tomorrow." His uncle walked away taller and displayed the pride he once carried.

Before dawn, the door to Rory's sleep chamber slowly opened and dim light from the hall shone through the doorway, and silhouetted a figure. "Nephew, it is time to go. Are you ready?"

Rory rolled over and sat up. Activities began early at the mission, but not before dawn. "Give me a few minutes, Uncle. I will meet you at the stables."

"There is no need. The ponies are outside the gate, and everything is ready. I will wait there."

He struck a wooden match, and lit the candle that sat on his small stand next to his bed. At his writing desk, he penned a quick note to Herberto to explain that he and Bidzil had gone hunting, and would return in a few days. Then, he dressed, propped the note against the inkwell and left to meet his uncle. At the gate, his uncle was already mounted and seemed eager to get started. They rode without talk eastward under the light of a full moon.

Miles from the mission, they stopped and built a small fire to make coffee. They ate bread taken from the friar's kitchen. "I miss having agave cakes," said Bidzil, "They would be good with this hot coffee."

Rory saw the serene expression on his uncle's face. "It is good to get away from the mission."

"All they do there is women's work," said Bidzil puffing out his chest. "I'm a warrior and shall do it no more."

Rory, who, after so many years, was now accustomed to the friar's ways, was sad for his uncle. As gently as he could, he said, "Uncle, they live a life without the need for warriors. All who live in their community have to work. No one is kept except for the sick, and you are not ill."

"Then I shall return to the Apache."

"Where will you go? Sadly, Cochise wants only young warriors."

Bidzil turned to look at Rory. There was no reproach in his eyes. "I have cousins with the clans that now live on the reservation, and I shall go to live with them."

"As you wish, Uncle, I shall miss having you near."

The old warrior's eyes sparkled in the firelight, and his grin was big and sincere. "As I will you, Nephew. It isn't so far that you couldn't come to visit."

"That is true, Uncle. I shall come, and come often. That is a promise."

The sun peeked over the horizon and the surreal vista of the desert and its wildlife halted their talk. After several minutes, Bidzil stood. "It is time."

Their ponies already hobbled, they extinguished the campfire and moved out into the desert scrub to search for tracks. It wasn't long before they came across deer tracks. The cactus berries[25] were in bloom, and the deer's trail led from one plant to the next. The deer's lips and digestive tract were tough enough to handle the hair-like thorns that protected the sweet-tart pulp in the center of the fruit. The Apache, who also enjoyed the berries, had to be vigilant if they wanted to harvest them before the deer had their fill.

---

[25] The red/purple fruit of the Prickly Pear cactus.

When they saw the doe, she was selectively eating only the ripe berries; she left the unripe ones for a later time. From his kneeling position, Bidzil notched an arrow and pulled back the string made of sinew, his thumb touching his cheek as he sighted down the shaft.

The doe jumped as the arrow sunk deep into her chest. Rory rose intending to shoot his arrow, but she had begun to run. His uncle's arrow was a killing shot; they only needed to track her for a short distance. Bidzil sprang through the air and howled, and then he set off running after the doe. Rory smiled. It pleased him to see his uncle so happy; it had been too long.

Rory returned to their campsite for their ponies. He knew his uncle would have started butchering the deer. The deer's and his uncle's tracks was easy to follow in the sparse scrub. Rory found his uncle knelt at the deer's body, but he hadn't begun the work. *Fair enough*, he thought. *Uncle killed the deer—he would do the work.*

At his uncle's side, Rory knelt. "It was a good kill—I will prepare the animal." His uncle was silent and stayed very still. Rory leaned forward to see his face better. "Uncle." There was no reply, so louder, he said, "Uncle." But still no response, then he grabbed his uncle's shoulder, and shook him hard. When Rory released him, his uncle fell to the side. Bidzil, 'He is Strong', was dead.

Rory placed his ear to his uncle's chest and listened. His heart no longer beat. *It must have been too much strain running after the wounded doe.*

Rory laid his uncle on a blanket; Kilchii chanted a warrior's prayer to Ussen for his uncle.

Later, that day, Rory rode into the mission leading his uncle's pony with the deer tied over its back. Herberto came out to meet him. "Where is your uncle?"

"He is buried according to Nde custom; in a hidden grave so no one may find it."

Stunned by the gravity of the news, the priest said, "Here—let me take your horses." Rory slid off his pony's back and landed softly on the ground. Herberto signaled to a passing friar to come, handed him the reins, and gave him instructions. Rory stood silently and waited. The priest took Rory's arm, and escorted him to the covered veranda where he sat him in a chair. He felt that it was childish to notice, but Rory saw that the chair was the one he used on his first visit to the mission.

The priest left Rory for a few minutes and returned with a tray. On it were a bottle of brandy and a small ornate glass. Herberto poured the glass three-quarters full and gave it to Rory. "Here—drink this it will help you."

Rory knew what alcohol was and that the friars drank wine with their meals, but he didn't like the taste, so he drank water, or more often, goat's milk. This alcohol tasted different; it was sweeter and burned his throat as he swallowed. Within a few minutes, he felt its effects. His face flushed, and his brain seemed to slow down—he could sleep. "Can you tell me what happened?"

The young man turned to his friend and mentor, seemingly to notice him for the first time. "He shot a deer. It was a well-placed arrow, but even though mortally wounded it ran, and he pursued. It wasn't far, but the exertion was too much for his heart. When I arrived with the ponies, a few minutes later, I found uncle kneeling by the fallen deer, and they were both dead."

"Rory, words can't convey the sorrow I feel for your loss. I don't know why God chose to let you suffer yet another blow."

Rory looked at his friend. "I don't think God had anything to do with their deaths. My birth parents chose to
come to this land, and I must believe that they knew of the
danger. Sani and Mosi chose to join with Cochise, and I
know for certain that they were aware of the likely outcome. Bidzil knew his health was fragile, but still, he chose
to chase after the deer. They made choices on how they
wanted to live, and those choices led to their deaths."

****

He heard the sound of leather scraped against rock—
the sun was full, and someone climbed to his station. His
thoughts returned to the present. If he were to successfully
leave and return, without discovery, it would have to be
through the escape route. Today after guard duty, he would
come up with a pretext to climb down the escape route to
see if it had possibilities.

Chapter 19

Big Nose Mike peeked over the rocks. "I'm here to re-lieve ya, kid. Black Joe's got your breakfast waitin'."

Stiff from setting so long on the cold rocks, Kilchii pushed himself up and stretched causing a cramp in one of his legs. He hobbled aside to let Mike pass. "I don't feel like a kid this morning."

Mike smirked. "Talk to me in twenty-years."

"Is everyone here as grumpy as you and Swede?"

"Compared to Swede, I'm happy as a young colt kickin' his heels up in a pasture."

Kilchii smiled at the comment and turned to leave. Mike said, "Speakin' of Swede, you'd better keep your dis-tance. I don't think he likes you."

"How can you tell?"

Mike laughed. "Good one, Kid, but watch yourself."

"Thanks, I will."

A half-hour later, Kilchii sat down at the table, and Joe put a plate of food and a steaming hot cup of coffee in front of him. He held the cup in his palms to warm his hands, and sniffed the brew. "Mmm—Joe, you make the best damn coffee I've ever had."

"Y'all is just cold and hungry—that's all. Go on now, eats your breakfast."

Kilchii looked at his plate. "Eggs, bacon, beans, and bis-cuits," said Kilchii with more than a little surprise. "Where did you get the eggs?"

"We gots chickens, but they don't give many eggs. Mr. Coe and them usually eats the few we gets, but I saved y'all two."

"Thank you, Joe. I owe you a big favor for taking such good care of me."

Joe sat down and leaned in close and whispered, "Y'all wants to do Joe a favor—leave this place and don't y'all ever come back. Mr. Kilchii, y'all is a good boy—Joe cans tell. Leaves here afore it's too late."

"I'm afraid I can't do that, Joe, but I do appreciate your concern."

"Listens to me, Mr. Kilchii. Mr. Coe has business planned and he's goin' to takes you with him—don't y'all go. Y'all ain't wanted yet—go to California and starts new."

"I truly can't do that, Joe, but I will be on guard."

"Y'all watch Swede the most—he be the one to kill y'all if Mr. Coe says."

Kilchii nodded and turned back to his meal. After his third cup of Joe's coffee, he wanted to stretch his legs. Outside, he saw Coe. "Coe, I wanted to talk to you."

"What about?"

"The escape route; is there any rule against my climbing down to see where it comes out?"

"No, but why?"

"I took my first turn on guard this morning. True no one can get in, but no one can get out either. If the law finds this place, all they have to do is set out there and wait. Eventually, we'll run out of food."

"Thanks to you, that'll be a long wait. But, if it will make you feel any better, be my guest and have a look." He smirked. "I don't advise taking your horse though."

"I wasn't planning on it, but now that you bring it up that's one of my concerns. Escaping on foot down there isn't much of an escape option."

"I've thought about that myself. Let me know if you come up with a solution."

Kilchii nodded and headed passed the corral for the rear escape trail. At the trail's head, he looked up to see Juan Garcia on guard duty. He waved and climbed up to the guard station. Juan said, "If you're relieving me, you're three-hours too soon."

"Not me—I was curious about this way out of here and wanted a bird's eye view." Kilchii inched to the edge of the cliff where he could see the entire trail unobstructed. Mumbling under his breath, he said, "Whew—that looks scary."

Juan overheard, and said, "Sooner stay and fight than make that climb down."

"Not on a horse anyway," said Kilchii, "that's for sure."

****

Crow sat at the table with a cup of coffee when Coe entered the fortress. "Crow," said Coe, "Kilchii is goin' down the back trail. Go with him and make sure he's not up to somethin'."

"Aw he's alright, Coe, besides that way's dangerous."

"Crow, you've been up and down it before. Now go on, do as I say."

Crow stood, gulped the last of his coffee, and then went to the storeroom to collect gear to aid the descent.

****

"What's the rope for?" asked Kilchii.

"The ledge is narrow and I want to make sure we can make it back up here." Crow played out the rope and tied one end to a huge boulder. "I've been up and down. Coe says I should go with you and make sure you don't break your neck."

"Appreciate the company. Has Coe or any of the others been up or down?"

"Only me—far as I know, why?"

"What's the sense of having an escape route if you don't know that it works and what about horses? I don't think even a mule deer much less my mule could make this climb."

Kilchii held the rope with one hand, and moved onto the narrow ledge that skirted a crevasse, which went straight down; he estimated at least 1,000-feet. He stopped and ran his hand across the wall. "We could get Joe to modify a few horse shoes and wedge them into these cracks and lace a rope through them for something to hold onto." Crow nodded.

Once they passed the gorge, the rope ran out. Now they had to make their way down the sloping face to the flatlands below. The slope was so steep in places that they couldn't stand and had to use the rocky terrain for handholds. They paused several times to examine their path. "We could improve passage at these steep places with fixed ropes. What do you think?"

Crow looked back up the way they had come. "I wouldn't want to make it easier for someone to sneak up on us from this direction."

"You'd be a setting duck if you tried to come up this way," Kilchii said and jerked his thumb up toward the top. "A single man could hold off an army from up there."

"Where are you headed with all this?"

"Hear me out, Crow. That's a box canyon down there where this ends—how far to the flatlands?"

"Quarter-mile maybe, why?"

"We have extra horses—right?"

Crow's brow pinched. "I still don't follow, what are you saying?"

"We build a corral down there to hold horses."

"You're crazy," Crow said. "What about feed and water?"

"We could haul in feed and how do you know there isn't water down here—have you looked?"

Kilchii continued the descent to the canyon floor. At the bottom, he shaded his eyes with his hand and looked back up the rock's face. To a flatlander, he was sure it appeared daunting, but to someone reared in the mountains of Arizona it was but a mere scramble.

Crow stood beside him and asked, "So?"

"Let's scout the canyon and see what there is to find." Kilchii took off at a trot down the canyon. Soon, he found what he hoped would be there—vegetation. The earth was soft. Behind the plants, a steady trickle of water streamed from a crack in the canyon wall. He dropped to his knees and began to scoop the sandy loam back, and soon he had a small pool. When the silt settled, he tasted it. "It's good water. We can dig this out and line it with rocks—there'll be plenty of water."

"You found water, but you still got to get the feed down here and someone has to tend to the horses?"

Kilchii didn't have an answer. "Let's see what's ahead." They followed the sandy canyon floor past a bend, and out onto the high desert plain. They saw only the occasional bush destined to become tumbleweed. A quarter mile further, they turned back to face the mountain wall. From a distance, the canyon's entrance appeared as just another indentation.

Back in the canyon at the base of the climb, they examined the sloping rock face that from their position appeared to end at a sheer rock wall. The path across the ledge was hidden from the ground. "If nothing is done down here, and someone stumbles onto this entrance—chances are good that they'll think it's a box canyon, but, if the fortress came under attacked and taken. Eventually the rear escape would be found and those on foot easily hunted down."

"The fortress has been here a long time," said Crow, "and it's never been found much less attacked."

"That's my point." Somebody is sure to talk to the wrong person about how to find this place. Time is against the fortress. I for one don't want to be trapped like a rat when a posse shows up unexpectedly."

"What's your remedy?"

"Corral horses down here and make it appear as if a mustanger—"

"You mean horse thief don't you?"

Kilchii stared patiently at Crow, and then shrugged and continued. "Make it appear as if a horse thief has temporarily hidden them here."

"You still haven't explained how to feed them?"

"We'll bring some feed down here and once a week, or so, we change out the herd."

Crow looked doubtful. "Who's going to do all this?"

"I'll need some help with the fence, but I'll do the daily chores."

An hour later, they were back inside the fortress to confer with Coe. "What do you think, Crow?" Coe asked.

"I think he's right about the odds," Crow said. "The law may not be able to get in here, but what good does that do us it we can't get out? It's the same as jail."

Kilchii watched Coe's face as he look from one to the other trying to decide. *He still doesn't trust me.* "I'll start with my animals first," Kilchii suggested. "The others can make up their own minds what they want to do."

"Alright, we have extra mounts. You can put a half-dozen down there and let's see how it goes from there. Take Joe and the Garcia brothers to help with the work, but go in and out through the ravine. I don't need anyone gettin' killed."

Over the next few days, Kilchii and Joe gathered the materials needed to modify the canyon. They wanted to make the corral large as possible, but still unseen from the flatland. A narrowing after a bend in the canyon fulfilled the need. There, they built a split-rail fence with a gate only large enough to pass one horse at a time. They expanded and deepened the water source was easy digging. Next, they lined the small pool, but to get it to retain its shape proved to be the most work. After a week of hard work, the corral and water were ready. In a cave, really just a depression in the wall, they closed off the opening with a door to store grain and Kilchii's tack.

Kilchii brought his animals plus six of the spare horses to the new enclosure. Joe drove the wagon filled with feed and other necessities. Kilchii planned to start the next day; he would come down here twice a day and care for the horses. Once a week, he would change them out for another six. That was to be the routine, but Kilchii had other plans ....

So did Coe; it seemed. Kilchii asked, "You wanted to see me, Coe?" He nodded to other the men setting at the table.

"Sit," said Coe and then waved at Joe, who brought him a cup of coffee.

"Here y'all is, Mr. Kilchii. Now y'all remembers what Joe tells ya—it's hot and will burns y'all if y'all ain't careful."

Kilchii remembered Joe's words of warning; *this must be the job.* "I recall every word you've told me, Joe. There's no need for your worry, I'm grown, and will decide for myself what's too hot and what's not."

Coe listened and watched the exchange with a curious expression, and then said to Joe, "Get back to work before I decide to send you back for hangin'."

Joe shrank away, back to the cook's fire. Coe's words make Kilchii angry, but he controlled his temper ... for now.

"Were all here, so let's get started," said Coe, as he looked at each man in turn who confirmed he had their attention with a nod.

Crow sat to his right, then the Garcia brothers, himself, Dix and Joker—seven in total. "We need supplies and a little extra cash wouldn't hurt us any. Dix's has a job scouted near Van Horn. It's northwest of here forty-miles."

"What's the job?" Joker asked.

Coe turned to Dix. "It's your job," he said and waved his hand for Dix to begin.

Dix hunched forward elbows on the table, and then quickly looked around to make sure no one else was close. *He's paranoid even here,* Kilchii thought.

"The El Paso and San Antonio stage stops at Van Horn for food and horses," said Dix. "And once a month, the day varies, but they carry the payroll for the soldiers at Fort Bliss."

John Flynt's image immediately sprang into Kilchii's mind. "I'm not sure I want to be in on this one, Coe," said Kilchii. "The Army's not very forgiving when their payrolls go missing. Besides, how do we know his information is correct?"

Dix reared back from the table. "You, callin' me a liar, Kid?"

"No. Just asking a question, but I'm also saying that the Army will hunt us down. If they track us back here— think about it, if anyone has what it takes to wait us out it's the United States Army."

"That's just it," said Dix. "There ain't been no soldiers stationed at Van Horn since the war. And Fort Bliss is busy dealin' with the Comancheros. We don't have to worry about the Rangers either. They're on the border fightin' the Comanches and Mexicans; this should be easy."

"Alright," said Kilchii, "assuming all that is true, you still haven't told us how you know about the payroll date."

"I've got a friend who works for the stage line," said Dix; his expression showed he was pleased with himself. "He gets an equal share," he finished.

Kilchii asked, "How much is the payroll?"

Dix grinned. "It's more than payroll. There's procurement money too—should be close to $100,000."

"The first $20,000 goes to the Roost," said Coe, "and the remainder is split eight ways. That's $10,000 each. For a stage job, that's a really good haul."

He could see the greed light up in their eyes. Kilchii said, "Alright, I'm in—what's the plan and when do we leave?"

Dix hunched forward again and used a handful of small stones to show the town's layout, which was really nothing more than a stage stop. "We meet my friend here," Dix pointed at a place on the table, "he'll confirm everything's ready. We'll take the stage the next day late mornin' some-time. I figured you and Crow would scout their route and pick a good place for the ambush."

Crow glanced at Kilchii. Kilchii smiled and nodded. Coe looked around, and then said, "That's it then. We leave in the mornin' at first light. Three-days from then, we'll all be $10,000 richer—questions?"

"Do we come back here?" asked Kilchii.

"That's right—you don't know how it works. After we divvy up the loot, we head our separate ways for a week or ten days. Only after you're absolutely sure that the law's not on your tail can you return," said Coe, and then he leaned with a menacing glare. "Anyone brings the law back here he is killed on the spot. No exception—is that clear?"

Kilchii didn't flinch, he said, "Sounds fair."

Coe rose from the table. "Alright, be ready at first light. Kilchii, bring your animals up here for the night. We'll all leave from here."

Kilchii nodded and walked toward the rear door and out to the escape route to flatlands. Joe stood waiting at the trailhead. Mr. Kilchii, don't y'all go through with this. Joe's got a terrible feelin' that somethin' bad is goin' to happen—y'all listenin' to me?"

Smiling at his friend, he put his hand on the old man's shoulder and squeezed it gently. "Joe, you've been a good friend to me while I've been here. You needn't worry about me—after we're gone, you need to leave the Roost and nev-er come back. There are six good horses, feed, tack, and food in the canyon corral. Act like you're going down there to take care of the livestock, then just leave."

Joe's eyes widened. "I gots no place to go. They wants to hang Joe."

"What did you do, Joe, that's so bad?"

"Afore the war, I runaway. When I run, I done took the master's horses. More so he can't chase me than anythin' else. But, they hangs horse thieves."

"How'd you end up here?"

"I was lost and Mr. Coe founds me. At first, I thoughts he was goin' to hangs me, cause of the horses, but then he brung me here. He saved my life."

"Listen to me carefully, Joe. That was a long time ago. The war's over and slavery has ended—"

"I knows that, Mr. Kilchii."

"Listen—no one is looking for you now. Coe has just been telling you that to keep you here to do his cooking and other chores."

"That for true, Mr. Kilchii?"

"Yes, Joe, it's true. With your skill with animals and cooking, you can find an honest job at any ranch you choose. Just tell them to let you cook the meals for a day. If they like it, you stay—if they don't you'll move on. I guar-antee they'll ask you to stay."

"Y'all thinks so, Mr. Kilchii?"

"I do. When you leave here head southwest toward El Paso, you'll do fine, Joe." Kilchii left Joe lost in thought and made his way down to the canyon below.

****

Two days later, they waited at the agreed rendezvous for Dix's inside man. Joker, on guard, called out, "There's someone comin' in."

Dix stood and walked down the trail to where Joker waited. He shaded his eyes, and squinted to focus on the rider's image. "Looks like him. He'll be close enough in a few minutes to tell for sure." Gradually, the rider grew larger, and finally, Dix waved. "Hey, Buck, we was about to give you up—expected you this morning."

"Yeah—had a late night and wasn't my spry young self this mornin'."

Dix asked anxiously, "Everything still a go?"

Buck looked at him. "Sure, why wouldn't it be?"

"Well you bein' so late in all, I just—"

"Quit bein' an old woman; things are just as we planned. The stage will be through here tomorrow. Have you got the ambush spot located?"

"Two men are out scoutin' now."

Coe walked up. "Trouble?"

"Nah," said Dix, "He just got a late start."

****

Crow and Kilchii stood on a bluff overlooking the trail below. Crow said, "This looks like a good place, there's enough grade to slow the horses. You up here with that Sharps and the rest of us down there," he pointed to the far side of the road, "we'll have 'em in a crossfire. They won't have a chance." Crow glanced at Kilchii for confirmation. Kilchii stared at him and his expression unnerved Crow for some reason. "What?" He asked.

"You like it when they don't have a chance don't you?"

"I would be stupid if I did. What's wrong with you?"

Kilchii didn't respond. He walked back to his horse and mounted, and without further conversation returned to their camp where the others waited. Crow followed, but he didn't ride too close.

****

Back at camp, Crow reported on the location they selected. Kilchii didn't add to the report. As the details for the next day fell into place, Coe asked, "What do you plan to do with the mule?"

"I'll take him up to the bluff with me and hobble it and my horse in the nearby trees."

"Don't knows that I would go that far, Kilchii," Joker said. "You never know what's going to happen. I'd keep them handy, were I you."

"Thanks for the advice. I'll keep it in mind."

"One more time," said Coe, "let's go over the plan. Kilchii is on the bluff with his Sharps, and he kills the lead horse, just as they reach the top of the grade. Joker, you, and Dix kill the driver. Garcia brothers, you kill the guard. Buck, you steady the team while Crow and I take care of any passengers. The party starts when Kilchii kills the lead horse; any questions?" No one spoke. "Good. Let's get some sleep—big day tomorrow."

Everyone went to his bedrolls to sleep—except Dix, who stood the first two-hour guard shift. Kilchii didn't sleep. He spent the night working out the details of his plan for revenge on Herberto's killers.

At the bluff's edge, Kilchii lay on his stomach and looked down on the men below. They were concealed from view to the road, but not to him. The rocky grade behind them left them no place to maneuver, and if they came out on the road, they would be easy targets for the stage guard. He smiled; he couldn't have devised a better plan than the one Crow set into motion. The only thing is that Crow had no knowledge of Kilchii's goal.

He heard the clink of harness chains before he saw the team. Kilchii swung the Sharps .50 towards the sound and waited. The lead horse, struggled against its harness as it rounded the bend. When the coach came into view, the lead horse collapsed and then the thunder of the Sharps echoed down the hillside. For a long second, no one moved or said a word. At length, the guard yelled, "It's a holdup," and he leapt from the coach. A split second later so did the driver.

Coe cussed, "Damn it; what's wrong with him? The bastard shot the horse too soon." He scrambled to find a shooting position. Already tightly packed together in the gully, they had no space to maneuver. "Spread out you, sons-a-bitches. Some of you get across the road damn it."

Joker, Buck and Dix scrambled from cover to make their way to a better position. Men with rifles erupted from the coach and laid down rapid fire. Exposed, Coe's men dropped. Before he fell, Dix yelled, "Where the hell—"

Coe and Crow fired at the guards, while the Garcia brothers hunched low behind them. Kilchii watched the commotion and waited. When Coe and Crow fired, so did he, but at different targets. In quick succession, Kilchii killed Carlos Garcia and then Juan Garcia. It was only when Juan fell into him that Coe seem to realize they'd been killed.

Coe was in his sights. A split second before he squeezed the trigger; shots from the stage guards kicked up stone chips near his face caused him to flinch. Coe looked up just as Kilchii fired.

Startled when Coe fell into him, Crow glanced about, and he saw that only he lived. On the bluff above, Kilchii watched him. Then shots from the coach zinged by Crow's head, and he ducked for cover.

The big Sharps thundered in rapid succession as Kilchii fired at the coach; Crow was his kill. Splitters flew, and the guards sought cover. Crow saw his opportunity, and he bolted from the gully and down the trail to where they'd hidden the horses. Crow reached his mount, slung himself into the saddle, and raced away as fast as the horse would carry him.

Away from the bluff's edge, Kilchii now sat his horse and watched Crow through binoculars to determine his direction of travel. It was southwest, not back to the fortress.

Kilchii could tell that Crow worked hard to conceal his trail, but not so skillfully, that someone who knew what to look for wouldn't find it. Patiently, Kilchii followed. He knew that time was on his side. And he knew also, that after a while, Crow would lower his guard—begin to believe that he lost his pursuer.

From the hiding place in the tree above his camp, Kilchii dozed. Ten days he tracked, and ten nights he guarded against an ambush, or the possibility that Crow might double back; exhaustion began to take its toll.

He was tired and grew weak with hunger. Kilchii would have to catch Crow soon, or give up. The night sounds stopped, and then complete silence brought an eerie ringing to his ears. Like the sound, or lack of sound, you hear when you plug your ears. Then he heard, or maybe felt, movement below, and he strained to see in the darkness.

It wasn't that he saw something, but more like images were momentarily void of their reflections. It was Crow—it had to be. He drew his knife from its sheath and posed to pounce. Crow stood above the bedding that Kilchii so carefully made to appear as if it were he asleep bundled in a blanket without a fire for warmth.

Crow must have sensed that something wasn't right. The moment Kilchii dropped from the tree Crow glanced up, but too late. Kilchii knocked him to the ground. Astride Crow, Kilchii pinned his arms down with his knees, and held the point of his knife to Crow's neck beneath his chin.

Crow's involuntary swallow caused the knife's point to penetrate his skin, he asked, "Why?"

"Remember telling me about Cain's torture of a priest? His name was Father Herberto."

Crow didn't answer, but Kilchii knew that he did.

"Remember the redheaded man dressed like an Apache—the one Cain shot?"

This time Crow reacted. His eyes widened with recognition. "That was you?"

Kilchii responded with a swift plunge of his knife up to its hilt into Crow's brain. His last thought was of Kilchii and the murder of Father Herberto; that was Apache justice.

Suddenly, consumed by exhaustion, he pulled the blankets to him, covered his shoulders and lay back to sleep. When at last he awoke, it was late morning and his animals, hobbled, wanted his attention. He stood and stepped over Crow's body to his horse and mule.

He built a fire, the first in many days and brewed coffee, and began to prepare food. Crow's body remained where he died his eyes and mouth opened showing surprise. Kilchii waited for the satisfaction he expected to feel from the death of Crow, but it didn't come. Maybe, when he killed Cain ... maybe it would come ....

Chapter 20

The death of Crow and the others didn't provide him with the peace he had anticipated. Cain, when he killed him, it would avenge Father Herberto and put the priest's soul at rest, but would also ease the rage and sense of helplessness he felt? In the meantime, he needed supplies and rest, so he swung westward toward San Angela, Texas.

'My Dearest Darling,

My scheme to deal with the outlaws is going well. I visited the infamous Robbers' Roost, and I stayed there a while. I'm pleased to report that things didn't go well for them, and that I'm no longer welcome there. However, I did make one friend, and his name is Joe. He's an elderly black gentleman, who took me under his wing, and made sure that I ate properly, and that I got plenty of rest. We didn't get to say a proper good-bye, but maybe we'll meet again under better circumstances.

Tomorrow, I go south to Mexico where I expect to find Cain. I have learned that Texas Rangers killed many of the men I seek. The rangers are a tough lot. They were formed to fight the Comanche Indians and the Comancheros. Their reputation is legendary, at least in Texas.

I miss you so, my dearest Lucy. If only you could respond to my correspondence then I would have something tangible to touch until I can hold you.

Your loving fiancé,

Rory'

He addressed the envelope and put it aside. On a clean sheet of paper, he wrote,

'E.B.:

Robbers' Roost is done for. Coe, the leader, is dead. He died during an attempt to steal an Army payroll. Their ambush didn't go as planned. There are still several outlaws at the roost. Use the enclosed map and information as you see fit to root out the place. My suggestion would be to get the Army involved.

Regarding Cain, three of his men were holed up at the roost. All three are dead, but before they died, I found out that only a few of the men who killed Father Herberto still live. The Texas Rangers and attrition appear to be my allies. The Texas Ranger's ambushed the Comancheros near Langtry, Texas.

I detoured through San Angela for rest and supplies. Your friends send their regards. Tomorrow I head south in pursuit of Cain. If all goes well, I may be able to start back to Saint Louis within the next six months.

Please, only share with Lucy the generalities of this letter.

Your friend,

Rory'

Sipping the whiskey, he reread his letter. Satisfied, he shoved it into an envelope along with the location map and notes he made. *I hope Joe understood what I tried to tell him and got out of there.* He topped off his glass. *When did I start to like the taste of whiskey?*

Chapter 21

After he left San Angela, Kilchii went south then drifted southeast along the Rio Grande. He headed for the old mission town of Presidio, Texas, a border town north of Ojinaga, Chihuahua, Mexico. Rumor has it that Cain operates on both sides of the border near there. He stole cattle from Mexico and raided white settlers in the United States. Men who want to join the Comancheros gathered at Fort Leaton's trading post; Kilchii planned to join them there.

He held to the wilderness; Kilchii sought the healing attributes of its solitude. A conflict warred within him. The ways of the Apache and the Whites fought against Father Herberto's beliefs. Apache ways and the Whites' laws were not so different, at least in results. His execution of the Garcia brothers and Crow was just. His heart told him that Father Herberto wouldn't wish for him to seek vengeance. It also told him that until he found justice for his friend, the ache in his heart would never stop.

At the outskirts of Presidio, dust covered and weary, Kilchii halted and scanned the town—such as it was. The central whitewashed adobe structure appeared to be more a house than a fort. He'd heard that it was the largest still occupied adobe building in Texas. It was now home and headquarters for the Leaton family ranch and trading post. There were other buildings of more recent vintage, but none as impressive as the trading post.

As he rode into town, he drew the attention of the few men who conducted business at the buildings outside the fort. They appeared only mildly curious. *They think I'm just another gun for the Comancheros.*

As he rode toward the gate to the courtyard abutting the adobe trading post; an image from his youth flashed across his mind of Father Herberto, who stood at a similar gate, and waved; his face held a warm familiar smile. And he waited to greet him. A pang of longing to see his old friend struck him, and reinforced his resolve to avenge his death.

It was early afternoon, siesta time, and many lazed about out of the sun. Dismounted, he cradled the Lang in the crook of his left arm and entered the trading post. Once inside he stepped out of the doorway and waited for his eyes to adjust to the dim. In the far corner of the post's can-tina area, he found a table. With the Lang propped against the nearby wall, he positioned his Colt with his left hand and thumbed off the hammer's loop as he sat.

The bartender, a Mexican who appeared to spend too much time eating, ambled over to his table. "What will you drink, Señor?"

"Cerveza," said Kilchii. Looking about, he asked, "What do you have to eat?"

"This is a rancho, Señor. We have beef, frijoles, and tor-tillas."

"That will do nicely, ¡gracias."

The bartender returned to the bar, and spoke to the young boy seated near the kitchen doorway, who in turn disappeared through the passage. Moments later, the boy came back through the door and carried a large plate of food. Behind him, the bartender arrived with a beer; they stood expectantly. Kilchii tasted the beans. "This is very good, Señor, gracias." The bartender smiled then left him to enjoy his meal.

Hungrier than he at first thought, Kilchii wolfed down the plate of food and motioned to the bartender for a second helping. The bartender displayed a toothy grin and with a knowing nod, he disappeared into the kitchen. As before, he quickly returned with another plateful of food. "You eat un-til you are full, Señor—another drink?"

Nodding, Kilchii said, "Si ¡gracias."

Slower this time, Kilchii consumed the meal. He sa-
vored the taste of freshly butchered beef, and the spicy-hot
beans flavored with lard. Still, he polished the surface of
his plate with the last tortilla.

Finished, he leaned back in this chair and rubbed his
stomach. The last time he had eaten this much was in
Saint Louis. Lucy's image stepped into his thoughts. Her
smiling face tugged at his heart; he missed her, and he felt
lonely.

Kilchii changed his drink to whiskey and whiled away
the remainder of the afternoon. When the sun waned, it
cast a golden glow over the landscape; saguaro cactus, stood
like sentries silhouetted, in the distance, and patrons entered the cantina.

Kilchii watched them enter. They come in mostly by
pairs, but also in groups of three or four. *They must be reg-
ulars. Without a glance, they drift to their preselected
tables.* No one approached where he sat. Either it was an
open table, or its regular users hadn't yet arrived.

After his fifth drink, he needed to relieve himself. He
saw the bartender and asked, "Which way to the baños?"

The bartender hitched his thumb over his shoulder toward the backdoor. "It is the wall." He laughed, "Follow
your nose, Señor. You cannot miss it."

As Kilchii rose to make his way through the kitchen to
the toilet, two men also stood and went out the front. The
timing of their exit didn't go unnoticed. Kilchii loosened the
Colt in its holster—it couldn't hurt.

When he finished at the wall, he buttoned his fly and
turned. The two men who left the cantina when he had now
stood near the doorway five-feet apart and blocked his way;
they smiled. "Hey, Red, y'all is settin' at our table."

The one talking, based on his clothes, was an ex-
confederate soldier. His partner was a young vaquero; both
appeared down on their luck. "Let me guess. For a service
fee, you'll let me keep the table—right?"

"Y'all is smarter than you look, Red," said the soldier. The young Mexican man hooked his thumbs over this belt, leaned back on his left leg, and extended his right foot. The soldier stood with his feet slightly apart with his hand near his gun.

Two-to-one, they're confident that I won't fight—they're wrong. Kilchii grabbed for his Colt. As he pulled it from its holster, he simultaneously sidestepped to his left. The soldier hesitated before he reached for his revolver. The delay was more than enough time for Kilchii to put two slugs into the man's chest.

The vaquero, caught off guard looked confused as he watched his partner fall. He pulled back his right leg for support and went for his gun, but it was too late—far too late. Kilchii shot him twice just as the vaquero's pistol cleared leather. The pistol dropped from his fingers, and he fell to his knees. He clutched his chest and tore at his clothes.

He stared up at Kilchii; comprehension appeared on his face, he said, "We only wanted a little money." He collapsed.

Kilchii ejected the four spent shell casings from the cylinder and then replaced them with fresh cartridges from his gun belt. By then the cantina patrons were outside staring down at the two men. "There was a dispute about my table," said Kilchii. "Does anyone else take issue with where I sit?"

The bartender raised his hands and stepped forward. "Señor, there is no need for shooting; you sit where you want—it is okay."

The worried expression on the bartender's face was comical; Kilchii smiled. "¡Gracias," said Kilchii, and he holstered his Colt. The crowd parted as he walked back into the cantina and returned to his table. He looked at the Lang leaning against the wall. *I'm getting as paranoid as E.B.* Casually, he picked it up, and thumbed the lever breaking the receiver. The shells were gone. He looked around the room, but all stared elsewhere. From a leather-pouch tied to his gun belt, he removed two cartridges, and thumbed them into the Lang and snapped it closed. After he sat down, he placed the shotgun across his lap. He made a mental note not to leave his weapons unattended.

Both hands filled with a tray; the bartender approached his table. On the tray were a fresh glass of beer and a bottle of tequila with two glasses. Kilchii lifted his brow questioningly. "The beer is from me, Señor, and the tequila is from the hombre who sits near the door." Kilchii glanced to where the bartender indicated, and a hard looking man dressed as a vaquero returned his glance, raised his glass, and knocked back his drink. Kilchii nodded raised his beer and drank a long pull. Killing men made him thirsty.

The man stood and slowly walked over to Kilchii's table. As he got closer to the table, Kilchii saw that he wasn't Mexican. "Can I sit?"

"Okay," said Kilchii. "Your tequila bought you that much."

A smile came to the man's unshaven sun burnt face and he took a seat careful to keep his hands above the table in plain sight. He poured two glasses of tequila and pushed one to Kilchii. "The Johnny[26] was pretty good with a gun. The kid was fast too."

It was Kilchii's turn to smile. "Fast doesn't always mean you'll win."

---

[26] 'Johnny' was applied as a nickname for Confederate soldiers by the Federal soldiers in the American Civil War.

The man raised his left hand—then slowly reached into his shirt pocket and retrieved two shotgun shells. "Not taking things for granted is always a safer bet," said the man as he placed the shells on the table. Then he asked, "You lookin' for work?"

"Depends on what it is," said Kilchii. He glanced at the man's wear. "I've no interest in being a vaquero."

"Don't let the clothes mislead you. Whites and Mexicans alike wear these in this part of Texas. They're functional and plentiful. Check the trading post and you'll see what I mean."

"I'll take your word for it, but you still haven't told me about the work."

The man's smile became a smirk. "We gather cattle in Mexico and sell them to ranches in the U.S. We gather goods, and sometimes people and sell or trade with the Comanche or Mexicans. For the most part, the work isn't hard, but it can be dangerous."

"Dangerous?"

"I don't think it's anything you should worry about. You just killed two of my tougher men; you should do fine."

"What do your men call you?"

"Smith," he said and reached out to shake hands.

Kilchii brought up the shotgun and laid it on the table with the barrels pointed at Smith. He pushed it to his left hand and then shook Smith's offered hand. "They call me Kilchii."

Smith noted the shotgun's position, but didn't flinch. He asked, "Indian?"

"Apache; raised by them."

"They've captured Cochise. The rest are headed for the reservation."

The news saddened Kilchii. He hadn't heard, but he wasn't surprised, his uncle told him, 'It will not be long, Nephew, until the Apache nation is no more.' Kilchii shrugged. "They never really had a chance—"

****

"Join us. Maybe you'll get a chance for revenge."

"Who is we?"

Smith studied Kilchii for a long time. "Listen to me, Red, I ride with the Comancheros. Our leader is a man named Cain and when he gives an order, he expects it obeyed without questions. We can use a good man especially one who can scout and track. Now—are you interested or not?"

Kilchii stared at Smith for several minutes while considering the offer. He thought he'd seen his eyes flinch when he mentioned Cain's name, but then Cain was known.

At length, Kilchii said, "Sure—I'll join. I've got nowhere else to go anyway."

"Good. Our main camp is just across the border. We'll leave in the morning. You point that shotgun in another direction, and I buy you another drink?"

Kilchii asked, "How many men have you got?"

Here he goes again with the questions. Maybe if I answer some of them, he'll quit askin'. "There were ten of us now there're eight. Usually, our strength is close to twenty."

"What happened?"

Aw hell, he'll find out soon enough anyway. "We were headin' north on a raid and south of Langtry we was ambushed by Texas Rangers. Them sons-a-bitches shot us up pretty bad. We lost a trackers and several good men. Cain's been rebuildin' our strength ever since. He'll be glad to have you with us, Red. Just don't ask questions—he don't like it."

"What's he got in mind for his next job?"

Smith knocked back another shot of tequila. "He's not sayin' until it's time."

Kilchii poured him another drink. "If I'm going to scout for the outfit, then I will need to know our objective—right?"

Many tequilas later, Smith was drunk and he knew he should stop drinking, but what the hell, he hadn't been away from camp for nearly a month. "Here's the thing, Red. I'll let you in on our plans, but you can't let on that you know when Cain tells you. Okay?"

Kilchii nodded.

"We're goin' back to Langtry and burn it to the ground. There's no way that Cain can let them get away with ambushin' Comancheros. An example needs to be set—"

****

Glassy eyed, Smith fought his drooping lids as he stared at Kilchii. "Last question," said Kilchii.

"What else?"

"What time do we leave in the morning?"

"Early. You just be ready—understand?" Smith tried to place his elbow on the table, but missed. His head hit the tabletop hard—he passed out. Two of the Comancheros came to the table and took Smith away.

Kilchii asked the bartender to have pen and ink sent to his room. When the boy brought it, Kilchii pulled a sheet of paper from his saddlebag and quickly wrote:

'My Darling wife,

I'm in Texas near the Mexican border where I have found employment. As soon as I earn the money we need to start fresh, I will return home to you and our son, E.B. Surely, his broken arm has healed by now. Tell him to reread my last letter warning him against climbing trees. It is a wonder that he didn't break his neck. If he insists on doing it again, he may well have the same outcome.

I love you both,

Kilchii'

He went over the letter several times. Surely, E.B. and Lucy would understand that he was trying to tell them about Langtry. And that they needed to send word to the Texas Rangers. He put the letter into an envelope and took it to the cantina. He asked the bartender, "Would you have this mailed for me?"

"Si, Señor Kilchii. I will take it to the trading post my-self first thing in the morning."

"Thank you." He nodded and then turned to go back to his room, but stopped when he remembered something E.B. told him about using the locals in your schemes. 'Pay them well,' he said. 'It has to be in their best interest to help you, or they won't.' He returned to the bar, and laid ten silver dollars on the bar. "When I find out that letter got mailed there will be ten more—agreed?"

"Si, Señor Kilchii."

There wasn't anything more that he could do, so he went back to his room to sleep.

The next morning, seated at his, now, 'usual table,' Kil-chii finished the last of his breakfast. To his surprise, Smith came in and joined him. The bartender hurried over with coffee. "Do you wish to eat, Mr. Smith?"

"Nah, just coffee," he said, and waved the man away. To Kilchii, he asked, "You ready to go, Red?"

"I would prefer that you didn't call me 'Red.'"

"Sure, Red," Smith said and then smiled. "I'll make sure no else calls you Red."

It was contrary to his plans, but he was starting to like Smith. Smiling, he said, "You do that." He gulped the last of his coffee and stood, picked up the Lang, and said. "I'm waiting on you, Smitty."

Smith grinned. "Smith's not my real name, so Smitty is okay too."

Outside, four men waited. One held the reins to Smith's horse. They mounted and rode out of town, south for Mex-ico.

They stopped at the Rio Grande. The harsh glare of the noonday sun in the cloudless Texas sky forced everyone to seek the meager shade offered beneath the scrub mesquites that lined the river. Too hot to cook, they talked instead. Kilchii asked Smith, "How long you been with the Comancheros?"

"A while now; Cain found me holed up in Chihuahua about six months ago. He was lookin' for new men after the ranger ambush."

"How many survived?"

"Cain's the only one without a scratch, the other two, Jose and the Comanche were still healin' when I first met them. I didn't think the Comanche was goin' to make it, but he's a tough son-of-bitch."

"What's he called?"

"Cain calls him Comanche. He don't talk much, but they've been together for a long time."

Kilchii studied the two men. Jose was a vaquero turned bandit. His clothes and tack glistened with silver—even his gun belt and holster bore silver Conchos. However, the large rowels on his spurs meant business. They were made of steel and jingled when he walked. His mean dark eyes clashed with his ever-present smile and ready laughter. The knife scar on his cheek was a testament that, since he was still alive, he could kill up close and personal.

Comanche was solemn. His tightly braided thick mane sparsely mingled with grey hung down to his shoulders; a faded red cloth headband held back the sweat from his brow. His gun-belt and bandoliers of cartridges displayed a harsh contrast of cultures worn over the traditional Indian dress of cotton shirt, leather breeches, and moccasins. Around his neck, he wore a gold chain with a gold pendant that held three diamonds. There was something curious to Kilchii about that pendant ....

They most certainly were with Cain when he tortured and killed Father Herberto. They will pay first. Cain will be last, and we shall be alone; he must know the reason for his death at my hands.

"Hey, Red, wake up," Smith said as he nudged Kilchii's leg. "You day-dreamin' about some girl?"

Kilchii, lost in thought, hadn't realized they were ready to move. He couldn't afford to let his guard down like that again—it could cost him his life. "Yeah—a gal I met in San Angela a while back."

"We'll be at the main camp soon, so you'd better keep your wits about you. Cain's a hard man, and he don't allow his men much in the way of mistakes—get my meanin'?"

Kilchii smiled. "Thanks for the advice."

Two hours later, they rode into Cain's main camp. It was a mountain village of sorts—a collection of canvas tents and adobe huts. At the center of the village was a dwelling larger than the rest. Under a covered veranda was a single long table with chairs. As he rode closer, Kilchii saw a large white man with intense blue eyes. He sat at the table's center and watched their arrival. Kilchii remembered seeing the big man the night before Herberto's murder when he scouted the Comanchero's camp. Nearly a year has passed, but Cain looked the same.

Surprised by his placidity, Kilchii smiled and gave a single nod when he made eye contact with Cain. The big man rose from his seat and moved to stand by Smith. "Where are the Reb and the kid?"

"Dead," Smith answered and nodded towards Kilchii. "They braced him lookin' for easy money."

Cain stepped over to where Kilchii still sat his mount. "You took 'em both at the same time?"

"They gave me no choice." No one seemed to notice when Kilchii thumbed the loop off his Colt's hammer, or that leaning with his arm across the saddle horn was merely an excuse to have his hand almost on his pistol's grip.

"Don't kill anymore of my men. They're gettin' harder to find."

Kilchii's jaws clinched and his voice hardened. "It was self defense. Tell your men to stay out of my way and there'll be no trouble."

Cain's eyes squinted as he studied Kilchii. "Have we met before?"

He eased back into his saddle and forced himself to relax. "I can't recall being introduced."

Cain nodded—seeming to have made a decision. "What do they call you?"

"Kilchii and before you ask, yeah it's Indian—they raised me."

"Kilchii," Cain repeated his name. "Where was you before headin' this way?"

Kilchii threw his leg over the saddle horn for comfort. "I was up in the Oklahoma panhandle at Coe's roost. Do you know it?"

"Know of it, but I've never been that far north doin' business. Hole up down here in Mexico is good enough for me."

Smith said, "I've been through there. Coe's price to stay is pretty stiff."

Kilchii said, "Not anymore."

"How come," Smith asked, he seemed genuinely curious.

"He's dead. We tried to hold up a government payroll, but the coach had extra guards. I was the only one that got away."

Cain squinted suspiciously, and moved closer and asked, "How'd you manage that?"

"With this," Kilchii said, and reached back and shucked the .50 Sharps. "I was up high and took out the lead horse from ambush. They rushed out to take the stage and it exploded with gunfire. Must of been at least six men inside the coach, plus the two on top with the regular guard. They didn't have a chance."

"You couldn't help with that?" Cain asked as he pointed to the rifle.

"I made some noise, but it was damn quick. I didn't see any sense in my dying just because they were killed, so I got the hell out of there."

Smith asked, "How far did they trail you?"

Kilchii smirked, "Didn't really. They formed a posse, but hell; they didn't lose the payroll, and they killed Coe and the others, so they just gave up."

Cain seemed to be getting even more suspicious. "If they didn't get a good look at you and there's no body cha-sin' you—why'd you come all the way down here?"

"Men get caught because they keep doing the same crime in the same neck of the woods," said Kilchii. "After they get away with it a couple of times they're too lazy to move on or think of something different. I move on after a job and get far enough away that no one's heard about it— except maybe the local law, but they're just as lazy as the outlaws."

Cain busted out laughing. "You know. He's right. The law is pretty stupid. But you got to watch out for them Rangers. If them bastards get on your trail, you might as well put a bullet in your own skull, cause they'll get you in the end."

Kilchii nodded. "Smith told me about the ambush."

Cain's expression grew dark and angry, he said, "They'll pay. I'm goin' to burn that town to the ground and kill every man, woman, and child; then let's see if another town dares to cooperate with the Rangers." Cain returned to his table to drink and brood.

Smith signaled for Kilchii to follow him, so he fell in behind Smith, who led him further into the village.

Chapter 22

The weeks spent waiting for Cain to recruit more men before they moved on Langtry passed slowly, and for the most part, Kilchii kept to himself. He spied on Cain when he sat at his table beneath the veranda drinking tequila. While he drank, he often fondled an ornately decorated gold watch. Once, Kilchii accompanied Smith when he answered Cain's summons to the adobe to receive orders. Cain casually opened and closed the lid of the pocket watch. Cain saw him looking and held up the timepiece. "It's a beauty. I took this off some dirt farmer on my first raid—killed him and his wife." Cain tossed Kilchii the watch for a closer inspection.

As Kilchii turned the watch over, he found an inscription. It read, 'To my darling John. Love always, Rose.' Then he recalled the pendant on Comanche's necklace—it belonged to his birth mother and this was his father's watch. The one he held as a child in the photograph. His hand trembled and his jaw tightened. "Let go, Red, said Smith. Those words saved his life. He had been about to kill Cain then and there.

Several times after that incident, Smith selected him to accompany him on hunting or scouting duties. He was eager to go; it got him out of the village and away from Cain. The Comanchero leader routinely, without apparent cause, would beat the people. Cain's vicious nature toward the villagers was hard for Kilchii to stomach.

If there had ever been any apprehension about killing Cain, it faded after watching the man in action. Cain ordered a nearby rancho to surrender beef and horses, but the patrón refused. He had four of his Comancheros, including Jose and Comanche, kidnapped the patrón's teenage daughter. Her father relented and complied with Cain's demands and gave him everything he wanted.

Eventually, Cain returned the girl, but only after days of brutal torture and rape. The note Cain pinned to the tattered remains of the girl's clothes read, 'The next time you refuse me your entire family will die.'

Kilchii didn't try to stop Cain. He rationalized his cowardly behavior by telling himself there wasn't anything he could do; surely Cain would have killed him had he tried to prevent the torture and rape, and what good would that do? His desire to kill Cain slowly, up close, and personal overrode everything else. Still, his conscience's voice spoke to him in an unkindly manner for allowing the girl's rape to happen. *How much longer will I be able to wait?*

His answer came two days later when Smith came to Kilchii's single room adobe structure. He stood outside the blanket covering the entrance. "Red, are you in there?"

"Where else would I be?"

"I didn't think it would be healthy to just barge in; I know how touchy you can get."

He smiled at Smith. "You know—one of these days you're going to have to tell me how you ended up down here."

"Maybe, Red, just maybe I will."

Nodding, Kilchii asked, "What's going on?"

"Get your things together. We're headin' out for Langtry in the morning."

Kilchii turned in early, but he couldn't sleep. There were too many problems to consider before allowing sleep to come. How was he going to get away from Smith? He couldn't do anything until he was on his own. Assuming he got away from Smith; how was he going to warn Langtry? He wasn't sure that E.B. had received his letter. *Hell, it might not have even been sent.*

As much as he wanted Cain, he wasn't willing to sacrifice a whole community to get him. And, how was he going to capture Cain? He wanted him separated from the others. Then he could take him—he would tell Cain, who he really was and why he was to hang. Judge, jury, and executioner, he planned to hang Cain for the murder of Father Herberto.

The early-morning temperature of the lower mountains was cold. Foggy breath from the men and beast lingered in the air as they maintained a loose formation. Restrained by their riders, the horses impatiently clopped at the hard soil. Cain emerged from his adobe and mounted his horse. Reining to face then, he said, "Men, it's a three days to Langtry. When we get there, you can take all the plunder you like, but I want the town burnt to the ground, and no one left alive."

Most of the men were solemn, but some, Kilchii notice, seemed excited by the prospect of slaughtering the people of Langtry. His concern about how to warn Langtry that Cain and his Comancheros planned to attack them suddenly seemed over powering. He, considered bolting from the formation, but he held himself in check.

Smith, who had been with their leader in his adobe sided him. "We're to ride point. We'll be out two or three hours ahead of the others." Kilchii nodded without expression, but inside his angst quelled. He would be able to get away and warn Langtry, even if he had to kill Smith to do it.

His mind began to consider his options. If he ducked away from Smith, he could ambush Cain, which would halt the raid. He could kill Smith and riding hard and fast provide the town of Langtry with a six-hour warning, and then help them to set a trap for Cain and the Comancheros.

The trouble with the second option is that he liked Smith and didn't think he could kill him outright. In the end, he decided to capture Smith and leave him tied up while he hightailed it to Langtry. He would do it on the morning of their third day.

As with the night before, they camped with the main body of men. They were out in front of the formation by three-hours or more and less than a day's ride to Langtry. They rode down into a gully formed by a stream to water their horses. Smith dismounted, stretched his back, and then filled his canteen.

Kilchii followed suit. As he stood watching Smith, he thumbed the loop off the hammer of his Colt. When Smith knelt by the water, Kilchii drew the Colt and cocked the hammer. Smith froze when he heard the double click of the cylinder ratcheting in the gun's frame. He slowly raised his arms still holding his canteen. "What's this about, Red?"

"I got two choices Smitty. I can kill you or tie you up and come back later and let you go—you choose."

Smith chuckled, "Well I guess you know my choice, but why are you doing this?"

Kilchii remained silent.

Finally, Smith said, "I got to stand up, Red. My legs are killing me."

Still Kilchii didn't speak.

Red slowly stood and Kilchii noticed that he kept hold of his canteen with his gun hand. "Smith, reach around with your left hand and shuck your iron and toss into the stream."

"Aw, come on, Red. I'd rather see you take it with you than see it rust away in that water. You still ain't told me why you're doin' this?"

"Okay, Smitty, toss the gun back towards me, and re-member I can be very touchy."

Smith nodded and did as instructed. "You goin' to tell me what's goin' on?"

"I'm not who you think, Smitty. I'm a bounty hunter af-ter Cain. I plan to leave you tied and warn the people of Langtry and help them set a trap. Hopefully, I get to see him hang there; if not, then shot dead will have to do."

Smith, his arms still raised, slowly turned around to face Kilchii. "So that's what the letter was about."

Kilchii stared hard trying to read Smith's expression. "Letter?"

"Yeah the letter to Lucy Parker who supposedly has a son who answers to E.B., as in E.B. Parker, the bounty hunter, he's known in Texas."

"You saw my letter?"

"Did you really think the bartender would risk his life for ten dollars? Of course, he showed it me. I read it, it took me a couple of minutes to piece things together, but I did. I told him it was okay and that he could mail it."

"If you figured it out, why did you let him mail it?"

"I'm not who you think I'm either, that's why I talked Cain into letting you ride with me on point. I knew you weren't one of them."

"Okay, so who are you?"

"The name's Clark," he said with a huge grin, "Texas Ranger Tom Clark."

He studied the man's face, and he saw the truth in his eyes. "Well, I'll be damned. I knew there was something about you that I couldn't put my finger on, but never that." He holstered his Colt and stepped forward offering his hand. "Rory McLeod."

Smith—Tom Clark smiled. "Does that mean, I can low-er my hands now—you bein' so jumpy and all?"

Both laughed, and they shook hands.

"Okay, Ranger Clark, what's your plan?"

"Well," he began with a wry smile on his face. "I figured that I would find an isolated place, take you prisoner tie you up, and ride hard to Langtry."

"That's it? You don't have anything better than that? You're a Texas Ranger. You're suppose to—"

Clark interrupted, "The Ranger's have a sayin', 'One riot, one ranger[27].'"

Rory was dumbstruck. Finally, he said, "You mean you're it?"

With a chuckle, Clark nodded.

Rory scowled. "I don't see what you could possibly find funny about all this."

"You would if you could see the shocked expression on your face."

Rory took a long breath and slowly released it to calm himself, and then said, "Listen to me. These men are not some mob out on a Saturday night looking to raise a little hell. Cain has twenty armed men, who know how to kill; some of them enjoy it."

Clark nodded. That's where the men from Langtry come into play. Langtry isn't Saint Louis. It's a Texas town close enough to the Mexican border to have seen plenty of rough men. They're a tough bunch themselves; you'll see."

Rory recognized that further argument was useless, so he asked, "What now?"

"Cain will make camp south of town tonight," said Clark, "and hit them at first light in the morning." He paused and gazed north toward Langtry. "I can't go back to Cain's camp without you—he's too suspicious. But, Kil-chii—I mean, Rory, you could return without me if there was a reason. So why would I stay out all night?"

---

[27] A phrase made famous by Texas Ranger Captain W. J. McDonald in the very early 1900's some thirty years hence.

They were silent for several seconds. Rory smiled and asked, "Does Cain believe that you're not known as Smith in Langtry? I mean would he believe you could go to Langtry without causing them to be suspicious?"

"Yeah—why?"

Rory nodded. "The reason for this raid is revenge for the earlier ambush—correct?"

"Correct."

"What would he say if I told him everything appeared okay, but you that you went into town to check things out?"

"I see," said Clark. "He's sure to be leery after what happened last time, so my goin' into town will help set him at ease. Good idea. I'll get them ready and meet you back at the camp—say after midnight. Can you get him to believe that?"

Near dusk, Rory rode back into the Cain's camp. Cain sat on a log near the fire drinking whiskey. He scowled at Rory, and asked, "Where's Smith?"

Remembering what E.B. taught him, 'To be believable a lie has to contain some truth, and it should speak to what the person wants or already believes.' "We talked about the ambush the last time you were here, so he decided to go in-to town and have a look around. He said he'd be back at camp after midnight."

Cain didn't respond. From the corner of his eye, Rory saw Comanche working his way behind him. Rory thumbed the loop off his Colt and tensed for action. After what seemed like a very long time, Cain said, "That was good thinkin'." He looked to Comanche and said, "Wait at the outskirts of camp and make certain he's not followed. I don't trust those bastards."

Rory released his breath and turned to the fire. "The coffee smells fresh, any left?"

Cain looked at him. "Help yourself and get somethin' to eat too. There'll only be time for coffee in the morning."

Jose, who had also been close by handed him a cup. "You want a little whiskey?"

"Nah—I need something to eat first. I've not had any-thing but jerky since breakfast." He took the cup and found a quiet place to set, watch, and listen.

He had a lot on his agenda for tomorrow, and he still had no plan of how to accomplish it. Under a tree near the horses, he sat on his saddle and leaned against the trunk. The coffee was hot and good. The steaming aroma filled his nostrils and helped clear his thoughts.

Sometime after he finished the coffee, he nodded off. A kick to his boots startled him awake—it was Clark. Rory said, "You're back, so everything must be okay.

Clark winked. "Yep, they don't suspect a thing. One of the guards will wake us around 4:00. Cain wants us out with Comanche scouting to make sure our way into Langtry stays clear."

Rory smiled to himself. *Cain's delivering one of the men I want into my hands.*

He didn't think he could get back to sleep, but when the guard kicked his foot, it surprised him. After he saddled his horse, he went for a last cup of coffee. There was no dis-quiet about his plan to kill Comanche; he made peace with the justice of it many days ago.

Clark sat next to him on a log near the fire, and they sipped their coffee without talk. Comanche squatted across the way and stared at them through the flames, also sip-ping hot coffee. *I wonder,* Rory thought, *if he has any idea that will be his last cup?*

Comanche looked at the sky. The light of the moon was still bright, so they could see where they rode. He stood, and said, "We go."

Clark nodded and rose. Rory stood, but finished the last of his coffee before he followed. At the horses, Clark said, "We'll head out together and separate a mile or so down the road. Comanche, you go north, I'll head northwest, and, Kilchii, you ride to the northeast. At first-light return to the camp and join the attack—agreed?"

As Rory nodded, he looked to Clark and then to Comanche. With meaning in his eyes, Clark allowed a slight nod and mounted his horse.

Comanche led off, with Rory next and Clark following at a distance. Shortly, Rory moved up on Comanche's left and said, "It's still cold. I could have used another cup of the hot coffee." Comanche didn't respond.

Eventually, as the trial widened, Clark moved up on Comanche's right to ride with them. He'd heard Rory's comment. "If I'd known it was goin' to be this chilly—I'd have put a little somethin' in my coffee."

Comanche looked first to Rory and then to Clark. "White men are weak. Comanche like this," he said, and then gestured toward the night sky.

Rory leapt from his saddle. He caught Comanche around the neck, and dragged him from his horse. Clark quickly gathered the reins and moved off to wait for the outcome. It was over when they hit the ground. On impact, Rory heard the sickening crunch as Comanche's neck snapped. They lay very still for several moments, then Rory stood.

"His neck's broke."

"Yeah—I heard it clear over here."

"I didn't mean to break his neck."

Clark sat quiet for a few moments. "It's better this way, Rory. I can swear it was an accident and your conscience is clear."

"I don't give a damn about my conscience. I wanted him to die, but not until he knew why."

"You said you were after Cain. You didn't say anything about Comanche."

"Cain's who I want most. Comanche and Jose helped Cain kill a priest a little over a year ago. Comanche was also with Cain when he killed my white parents." Rory reached down unclasp the gold chain and pulled the necklace free of Comanche's neck. "I mean to see them dead and I want them to know by who and why."

"I understand about your parents, but was this priest a friend of yours or what?"

Rory's anger grew as he remembered the details. "Father Herberto took me in when I left the Apache. He educated me and treated me like a son. Cain and his men shot me and tortured Herberto to death trying to make him tell about the treasure."

"Treasure?" asked Clark. He cocked his head. "Are you foolin' me?"

"It belongs to the church. Father Herberto didn't tell them where it's hidden. When this is over I have to hunt for it and take it to Santa Fe."

"So you know where it is?"

Rory looked sharply at Clark. Hardness shone clearly in his eyes despite the night. "I think I can find it," he said, "and without any help."

Clark held up his hands, "Whoa, Red. I was just bein nosy. I won't bring it up again, and you shouldn't either—if you get my drift."

Rory nodded. "Give me a hand putting Comanche across his horse. You can take him to Langtry with you."

"What are you goin' to do?"

"I'm going back to meet up with them at dawn just as we planned."

Clark pinched his brow, solely confused. "What about the ambush? You could get killed."

"You tell the town not to shoot the redheaded fellow. I'll be alright."

"I think you're plumb loco, Red. There'll be close to forty men waitin'—"

Chapter 23

An orange glow ascended the horizon and warmed the dawn, and the ache Rory felt from chilled muscles began to ease. Squatted on a hilltop that overlooked their camp, he watched for movement. He'd decided to wait for them there rather than return to camp and deal with questions from Cain. The Comanchero leader wasn't overly intelligent, but he was shrewd, and if in doubt, lethal.

When Rory saw their dust, he rose, mounted his horse, and ambled down the hill. As he approached, Cain reined in his horse and waited. "Where are Smith and Comanche?"

Rory shrugged. "Comanche went north and Smith went northwest. I had the shortest trek to Langtry and back. Smith said to join with you when I returned, so here I'm."

Jose asked, "Do we wait for Smith and Comanche?"

"No," said Cain, and then he laughed. "Better if we hit them while they have their pants down sittin' in their outhouses." Cain waved his arm forward, and commanded, "Let's ride."

Rory fell in beside him. They were less than thirty minutes from Langtry. The plan was to cross the Rio Grande southeast of the town. Then circle north, and attack the town with sun at their backs. Clark told Rory, 'There's a ravine that leads out of the river and peters out east of Langtry. We'll be there waitin'. We'll be shootin' down on you so take your hat off, although I can't guarantee that it'll help much. Good luck.' They shook hands and parted.

****

Cain glanced sideways at Kilchii. *There's something about Kilchii ... I wish I could put my finger on it ... somethin' familiar about him ... all that red hair ... reared by Apache.* Then from nowhere the image of a redheaded kid reaching for a rifle rushed to the front of his mind, but he dismissed the idea just as quickly. *I killed him. At least, I think I killed him.* Again, Cain glanced at the Kilchii. *What are the odds, there'd be more than one redheaded child raised by Apache ... I guess it's possible ... but not likely? So, why is he here?*

As they rode down the embankment headed toward the river, Kilchii removed his hat and tied it to his saddle horn. Already suspicious, Cain wondered. *What's that about ... is it a signal ... maybe I should kill him? Nah the gunfire would give us away.* At the river's edge, Cain reined in his horse to the side, so his men could cross ahead of him. He watched Kilchii closely for any sign that he should kill him, but saw none. Kilchii sided Jose, and they led the men across the river. *He was being foolish ... nerves ... he was gettin' too old for this ... maybe he should get a woman and retire someplace deep in Mexico.*

****

When he glanced at Cain, Rory noticed the Comanchero's intense stare. Rory smiled and nodded pleasantly and casually faced forward. From the corner of his eye, he could see that Cain continued to watch him. He was on the wrong side of Cain to draw his Colt and drop him from his saddle, but he tensed, nonetheless; ready for action if Cain moved on him.

When Cain turned away from the front, Rory was almost relieved. It required all the will power he could mus-
ter, but he didn't turn to watch Cain move off. Surely, his
chance would come. For now, he focused on Jose. The river
wasn't deep, but they straggled nonetheless. When they
reached the Texas riverbank, and paired up again, Rory
made sure he sided to Jose's right. Rory straightened in the
saddle and steadied his holstered revolver with his left
hand; his thumb flipped off the leather loop.

They neared the mouth of the ravine, and Rory couldn't
stop himself; he ran his fingers through his hair. He hoped
somehow that his action would draw attention to his hair
color and keep him alive.

The Comancheros, including Cain, crossed the river.
They rode up the ravine that would bring them to the east
side of Langtry. Jose fell into Rory just as the report from
the rifle rang out followed by a salvo the struck the line of
Comancheros. Rory held Jose long enough to confirm he
was dead, and then dropped him to the ground. In quick
succession, Rory took the reins into his left hand, and as he
whirled his horse, he shucked his revolver and searched for
Cain.

Rory saw that Cain survived the fusillade and had tak-
en flight for the river. A few of the other men tried to follow
suit, but most were either dead, or off their horses, and
pinned down fighting for their lives. Though he heard bullets' zing bye, Rory rode undeterred in pursuit of Cain.

From the river's edge, Rory saw Cain, who was nearly
across the water, look back. The half-crazed wide-eyed gape
confirmed that he was fleeing Rory and not the ambush.
Cain pulled iron and sent lead in Rory's direction, but the
shots went wild.

Cain cleared the water and charged up the rocky embankment. His horse slipped and fell throwing its rider. He
regained his footing and tried in vain to remount the horse,
but it wouldn't rise; its leg was broken.

Another Comanchero, who also sought to escape, rode near, and Cain grabbed the horse's reins. When the man refused to surrender his horse, Cain shot the rider out of his saddle. Rory rode out of the river, just as Cain stole a glance back at him. Cain stood his ground, and took careful aim and worked his revolver; it was empty.

Rory bore down on his quarry. Cain mounted and spurred the horse, which leaped forward at a gallop and climbed the rest of the embankment.

Rory followed, but he selected their path, careful not to let his horse lose its footing. At the top, he watched Cain ride hard to increase his distance. Rory loped along until he lost sight of Cain; he halted and inspected the trail. When he noticed the blurred hoof print, he smiled. Cain's horse had a loose shoe and would soon be lame. All he had to do was follow the trail.

An hour later, Rory's rewarded for his patience appeared. Cain's horse was ahead. It limped with its right front shoe partially thrown. Rory reined in his animal and surveyed the landscape for Cain's location. He saw nothing obvious; he dismounted and went to the lame horse and worked free the problem shoe. The horse couldn't carry a rider, but Rory knew he could lead it without injury to a blacksmith to have its shoe replaced.

Back tracking Cain's horse, Rory found where the Comanchero leader abandoned the animal. He found Cain's boot prints in the soft soil. Rory scanned the direction they led, and concluded; *He's gone to higher ground.*

Rory glanced at Cain's horse and saw an empty rifle boot. He loosed the Sharps .50 from his saddle and quickly headed for cover. Just feet away from a small outcropping, the dirt kicked up near his feet followed by the sound of a gunshot—Rory dived behind the rocks.

Rory knew, shooting up or down hill takes a shot or two to adjust for elevation. How many would Cain take? He stole a quick look from behind his cover and received a face full of stone shards for his curiosity; a few of which drew blood; one was all Cain needed. *Okay, I know about where he is, but I'm pinned down ... now what? I'll wait him out ... patience can be a weapon.* His Apache ways served him once again.

To pass the time, Rory watched ants foraging for food. Scouts left the nest. When they found a food source, they returned to the nest for worker-ants that streamed out of the nest following the same invisible path that the scout used to return. Working together, the workers dissected a dead locust, into manageable pieces. It reminded him of his life with the Apache and later with Father Herberto and the monks at San Xavier Mission. Remembering those he lost strengthened his resolve to take revenge on Cain.

After a few hours, Cain sent a few rounds at Rory's cover. He didn't respond, which brought more shots from Cain. He fired wild in frustration. Finally, Cain called out, "What do you want?"

Rory remained silent.

"Listen to me. Whatever it is you want, we can make a deal. Just tell me what you want."

Still no reply; Rory knew that Cain wouldn't give himself up for hanging, so why bother talking.

The morning turned to afternoon as the sun passed overhead and placed Rory's location in the shade of the hilltop Cain occupied. The price for the high ground was to bake in the sun all day long. Water would soon become an issue for Cain. He didn't take anything but his rifle when he climbed the hill, Rory saw Cain's canteen still tied to the saddle.

****

Why does he want to kill me? What did I ever do to him? Cain racked his brain trying to remember the deed that might have brought Kilchii after him. It became hot as the day wore on. He'd lost his hat climbing the hill, and his head felt like it was in an oven.

Then from nowhere, his mind again flashed on an image of a redheaded kid dressed like an Indian reaching for a rifle. *I shot that kid in the head ... saw him fall ... but no one checked ... then my man challenged me ... there was the priest's treasure ... the priest ... that's it.*

Cain fired a couple of shots. "You awake down there?" He paused for a response, but didn't expect to receive one. *Maybe I can get him riled up ... if he'd make a mistake and show himself ....* "It was that fat priest—wasn't it?" Cain set his rifle to his shoulder, he hoped Kilchii would break cover, but he didn't. "Too bad you was unconscious. You should have seen it; he cried like a woman. He begged me to set him loose; he promised to give me anything I wanted. When I set fire to his manhood, he screamed and whimpered like a baby." No matter what Cain said, he couldn't get Kilchii to come from behind the rocks.

Then it occurred to him. Had he actually shot and killed Kilchii, or more likely got him with a ricochet. How was he to know? He had to go down there and see for himself. Should he go now, or after dark? He decided to wait until dark.

****

With each taunt, Rory's blood boiled hotter with rage. His urge to rush Cain's position and kill him with his bare hands could scarcely be contained, but Apache training prevailed; he continued his silence, hunkered down behind the outcropping. He knew if he remained patient, he would get what he wanted; so he waited.

As the day waned, the sun slid down behind the jagged black horizon. An orange-glow radiated beneath purple clouds drawn eastward to meet the darkness; a total blackness void of light, save that from the stars. In the distance, a coyote howled and then stillness overarched.

Then slowly, one by one, the night-noises began; the tiny sentinels of the night on guard.

The horses whinnied. If Rory heard them, so did Cain. *He's got two choices, he comes after me, or he goes for the horses.* Thinking it through, Rory decided that he would stakeout the horses. If Cain came for him, he wouldn't find him behind the rocks, so he would make a run for the horses.

He rolled onto his belly, and crawled toward the sound of the horses. As he closed on their location, he began to whisper a chant his serenade calmed the animals; they stood quietly.

When he reached the horses, Rory gathered the reins of Cain's mount and tied them to the horn of his saddle. Following the smell, he walked them to a sage bush and secured his horse. By feel, he put hobbles on his mare and then found a place to wait.

He didn't have to wait long. Cain was clumsy and moved too fast in the darkness. Stones tumbled, twigs snapped, and he muttered curses when he stubbed his toe or tripped. Rory reached down for a hand full of pebbles and tossed them at the horses, which spooked them, and they tried to pull away. The hobbles held, but they whinnied and jostled and made their location plain. *Even someone as inept as Cain should be able to follow that much noise.*

Though there was no moonlight and only the stars, Rory knew how to see in the darkness. It wasn't seeing as much as not seeing. Looking down at the ground was like standing in dark water, you couldn't see your feet, but watching about you was different. It is the absolute absence of light that made you aware. The horses blotted out the starlight beyond them revealing their images to Rory. There were no details; those were for his brain to provide, but he saw the horses.

The sound of someone dragging their feet through gra-vel and loose stones reached Rory's ears many seconds be-fore he saw Cain's silhouette standing by the horses. As Cain readied to mount, Rory eased from behind his cover, raised the Sharps, and he brought the gun's butt down across the back of Cain's skull. The big man's legs collapsed beneath him as he slumped to the ground.

Sunup was an hour passed, and Rory sat on his haunches with the Sharps across his lap; he sipped coffee from a tin cup. He snapped closed his father's watchcase and slipped it into his shirt pocket. The naked figure staked out on the ground near the fire would soon begin to pay for what he'd taken from Rory.

Cain stirred then groaned as he opened his eyes to look about. They widened when his eyes landed on Rory. When he tried to move, his restraints came taut. He looked down, and saw that Rory had stripped away his clothes. "What are you going to do to me?"

Rory lifted the hair covering the left side of his forehead revealing a white scar. He asked, "Do you remember this?"

"You were with the priest. I should have put two more into you to make sure—I would have too, if it weren't for my man telling me we couldn't harm a priest." His expres-sion changed slightly. "So that's what this is all about—the priest?"

Rory nodded. He stood and finished the last of his coffee and stepped next to Cain splayed figure. Staring down at his captive, he said, "Originally, I planned to hang you, but I've changed my mind. You're going to die the same way Father Herberto died."

"You don't have the stomach for that kind of business. If you're goin' to kill me, then just shoot me."

"You forget. I was raised by the Apache you will find out what I can stomach." Rory stepped on Cain's hand, and he slammed the rifle's steel-plated butt down on his wrist dislocating the bones there and breaking the end of the radius[28]. Cain screamed. Rory went to the fire, returned with his canteen, and gave Cain a drink of water. When the shock of the initial pain subsided, Rory repeated his action on the other wrist.

So the morning transpired; torture then recovery. At first, Cain cried for his freedom, but by noon, he begged for death.

"We're just beginning Cain," said Rory, as he moved about dispassionately from one task to the next. He showed no more emotion than as if he were doing chores at the mission.

Rory cut the skin on Cain's chest like the flap of bib overalls. When he began to peel it downward the pain caused Cain to pass out. When he regained consciousness, Rory stood over him with a wool saddle blanket. He laid it across Cain's chest and slowly dragged it off. Cain's screams resounded for miles.

Delirious with pain, Cain continued to beg for death. "You're tougher than I thought you'd be," said Rory, "I'll give you that. Rest a bit while I stoke the fire. If you're still breathing when that's done I'll think about shooting you."

---

[28] The larger arm bone connecting to the wrist bones, which is cubed shaped.

The hot coals from the fire were next. Rory laid two burning sticks onto the exposed flap of skin on Cain's chest—he howled with renewed pain and passed out. When he came to, Rory cradled his head and gave him water to revive him. "No more—please—just kill me."

"I'll let you rest for a while. I want you to think about Father Herberto and the way he suffered and begged. You said he whimpered and begged like a baby. You're not there yet."

Rory busied himself gathering twigs for a small fire. When Cain became fully awake and aware of Rory's actions, Rory placed the fuel under Cain's manhood and waited. Cain's screams became uncontrollable. "I'm sorry," he begged. He twisted and contorted as he tried to escape the fire. At length the flames sheared his nerves and he no longer felt pain. He wept, "Please just kill and get it over with."

Rory turned to the sound as a horse galloped their way, and he grabbed the Sharps and his spyglass. It was Clark. *What could he want?*

Clark reined in his mount as he approached Rory's camp. He grimaced when he saw what Rory had done to Cain. "I've heard his screams for the last mile or so. The noise carries a far piece."

Rory still held the Sharps. "What brings you out here?"

Clark stared at the Sharps and the way Rory held it. "You didn't come back, so I thought I should come out and see if you was okay."

Cain cried out, "Shoot me please—I'm beggin' you—kill me for God's sake."

Clark moved uneasy in his saddle. "I've seen the Comanche's work, but they ain't ever done anythin' like this. My God, Man—what'd he ever do to deserve this?"

Rory glanced at Cain as if he saw him for the first time he swallowed hard. "I told you. He tortured and killed my friend Father Herberto."

Clark asked, "Would your friend want you doin' this sort of thing in his name?"

Rory hung his head and lowered the Sharps. He walked the campfire, and sat down and leaned his rifle on the nearby rocks. He poured coffee and looked back to Clark, then shook his head. "I guess maybe you're right. Herberto wouldn't want this; he would be angry with me if he knew."

Clark looked at Rory for several seconds. "You don't believe that he does?"

"I made believe for his sake," said Rory, "but, I don't believe in heaven or hell."

"But, you believe his spirit lingers and wants revenge?"

Now Rory stared at Clark, a realization crept in his mind. "I'm not sure—"

"If you believe your friend's spirit is here, then he knows what you've done."

Rory turned away from Clark and the sight of Cain's tortured body to consider the ranger's words.

The gunshot caused Rory to jump and instinctively reach for his rifle. "Don't do it, Rory," said Clark. "I don't want to hurt you."

Rory stood and then relaxed his shoulders. "Why'd you kill him?"

"Look at him, Rory. Whatever he's done—he has to have paid for it by now. You're goin' to have enough trouble livin' with this as it is—maybe my killin' him will help."

Rory looked at the palms of his hands, and then he rubbed his face as if trying to wipe away the image of Cain's tortured body.

Clark asked, "Did doin' this help?"

Rory lowered his hands, and looked at Clark. "Yes, at the beginning, but now I'm not too sure. I went too far. I can see that now, but I don't feel any remorse. I just know I went too far, and that you were right to put an end to it."

"Listen, why don't you take a walk to clear your head, and I take care of this. When I'm done, I'll catch up, and we'll ride back to Langtry. We'll get rip-roarin' drunk and howl to the moon. What'd ya say?"

Three days later, Ranger Tom Clark joined Rory in the saloon for breakfast. "I'm headin' back to headquarters today. They expect me to file a report. I want you to know that you'll be featured highly in that report with the recommendation, should you want the job, that you be recruited as a ranger at the rank of corporal.

Rory smiled. "What's your rank, Tom?"

"Sergeant." They both laughed. "Have a whiskey with me Rory, and then I got to be goin'."

Outside the saloon after their drink, Clark mounted his horse, and he asked, "What are your plans?"

Rory looked up with a cross expression on his face, then let it soften. "I have to finish the trip that Herberto and I started, and when that's done, I'll return to Saint Louis to see if my fiancée will still marry me. I've some money put aside and she owns a business there, so we'll settle down and raise our children."

"Whew, that's a powerful lot of plannin'. Well, I'll be seein' ya." He rode northward not looking back.

Rory called, "If you ever get to Saint Louis, you look me up."

Clark waved without looking back.

Chapter 24

Lucy nearly ran home from the Post Office. She slammed the store's door shut and hung the closed sign. Kate followed her into the kitchen where her father sat with a glass of lemonade. Seemingly unaware of their presence, she dropped into a chair and stared at the envelope. Seconds passed, and her hands trembled as she reverently held the envelope up for inspection. She took a deep breath, and opened Rory's letter and read,

'My Darling Lucy,

I have so missed you, and I long to hold you once again in my arms. When I close my eyes at night before sleep overtakes me, I recall the scent of your hair, which brings you to me while I sleep. I love you so, my dearest.

I'm in Langtry, Texas. Cain is dead. Texas Ranger Tom Clark, who has become my great friend, dispatched him. He is a robust fellow and fearless to his core. His actions have saved my life and most certainly my soul. I realize that things go unexplained, but I hope sincerely, my love, that you will wait until I'm there and I have the comfort of your embrace to tell you of all that has transpired since my departure.

No doubt, my last letter confused you. I trust your father was able to explain its content and meaning. After we're wed, I do so look forward to our making children. If one is a boy, he shall be named after your father.

My mission to find the men who killed Father Herberto is complete. I go now to New Mexico to finish the task that my friend and I set out to do. When that is done, I will come home to you darling.

Lovingly,

Rory'

She hugged the letter to her breast. Near faint, she leaned back and cried with relief and joy. Her father had explained the earlier letter, which, in essence, said he would soon be in harm's way. She worried frantically each day until receiving this letter. How long would it take him to return? She would ask her father, he would know.

Lucy looked up, and to her amazement, there he and Kate stood, they looked expectantly at her. Then she realized that they had been there all along, and that she had been rude. She was too happy to be contrite. "It's done and he's safe," she said. "He has to complete some work that he and the priest began, and then he'll be home." Wiping aware her tears of happiness, she asked her father. "When do you suppose he'll return?"

****

E.B. gloried at his daughter's happiness. It had been a long while since she smiled and laughed as she was doing now. He was reluctant to mislead her, but still, he didn't want to disappoint her either. In the end, he decided to give her his earliest arrival estimation with the intent of extending the date later. "If he rides hard and things go as best they could; I expect he'll be home soon as four months."

Lucy frowned. "That long?"

"I'm sorry, Darling," said E.B., "It could be longer if he's delayed."

"Delayed," she exclaimed and then asked, "What kind of delay?" She was out of her chair and leaned over her father wagging her finger in his face. "You had better tell me exactly what you're talking about, Father."

E.B. swallowed hard and looked to Kate for support, but she had sided with his antagonist, his daughter, and offered no aid; he was on his own. "Lucy, Rory is in south Texas. He has to resupply and ride west into New Mexico near the Arizona border."

He reached for his glass of lemonade to quiche his thirst, the he continued, "From there, he has to locate the campsite where I found him. There is a treasure hidden there, which he has to find from memory, and then deliver it to the Catholic Church in Santa Fe, New Mexico. Once that's finished, he'll head for home. If he's smart, he'll ride the stage line. All that will take four months or more. I love you, daughter, but that's the truth of it."

Lucy relented and turned to Kate, who stood behind her. "But that's so long—" Kate opened her arms, and Lucy rushed into her embrace. E.B. looked on dumbfounded. He thought there was just no way for a man to figure women and their actions. The men who claimed they understood females were either liars or fools.

To get away from the women, E.B. rolled his chair into his room and sat at his desk. It was a bit too early in the day to take a nip under normal circumstances, but today turned out to be anything but normal.

From the left-hand drawer of his desk, E.B. retrieved a flask size bottle of bonded bourbon distilled by a new whiskey maker in Lynchburg, Tennessee. With his teeth, he pulled the cork and spat it onto the desk. After sniffing the nectar's smoky aroma, he put the flask to his mouth and upended the bottle draining its content. The burn took his breath away. It was a few seconds before he could breathe again.

On his desktop sat an expensive walnut-burl-wood writing box. He pushed up the lid and removed pen, ink, and several sheets of the personalized stationery that Lucy purchased to put the box. She had it embossed with his former army rank and name, Captain Eli Baldwin Parker, CSA. He hadn't the heart to tell her he hated the stationery, so he'd tried spilling ink on them, but she had reserves. She said, "Not to worry, Father, there are plenty more where those came from."

Resigned to using the stationery, he wrote,

'To Rory McLeod c/o El Paso International Hotel, El Paso, Texas.

Rory ....'

E.B. folded the paper, and he placed it in his pocket. Then he rolled his chair outside and around the house to the street. One of the neighborhood boys, a sandy-haired youngster, sorely in need a bath, who played in the street, responded to his call and came to him when he waved.

He gave the boy five silver dollars and instructed him to deliver his message to the telegraph office. A dollar was his when he returned with a receipt. The boy darted away on his mission with three of his friends at his side. E.B. chuckled. The money would be spent later to purchase candy from Lucy's store.' He laughed aloud when it dawned on him, that he indirectly paid her to do his errand.

****

From Langtry to El Paso was six-hundred miles in a straight line, but cross-country closer to eight. Rory was five-weeks on the trail when he arrived at the El Paso International Hotel. Trail weary, he entered the lobby. Haley stood behind the sign-in counter. He sorted messages and placed them in the guests' pigeonholes. To his surprise, the manager remembered him. "Ah, Mr. McLeod, how are you, Sir?

"You've an excellent memory, Haley. I'm pleasantly surprised that you are able to recognize me—especially with all this caked on trail dust."

Haley rotated the hotel's register around for him to sign. Almost smiling, he said, "Any friend of Mr. Parker is always remembered at the El Paso International Hotel, Sir. Ahem." Haley raised his hand to cover his mouth and then his pinched business expression returned. "We've been ex-pecting you, Sir. There's a telegram for you. It arrived past two weeks ago."

Another hand full of messages and notes appeared in Haley's hands. Rapidly, he flipped through them, and stopped near the back of the batch. "Ah, here we go." He deftly drew it from the others and held it out to Rory.

It had to be from Lucy or E.B., but which one? He hoped that it was Lucy. The last five-weeks were lonely ones, and she had occupied a great deal of his thoughts, es-pecially at night. He accepted the proffered envelop from Haley and peeled it open,

'Received letter saying you are off to complete promised delivery. Do you think it wise? Trip from the campsite to Santa Fe many days country rugged and dangerous.

I have a friend with Pinkerton Detective Agency. Can arrange for you armed escort.

Wait there telegraph your reply soonest.

E.B.'

Rory looked up at Haley, who held out another envelop. "This one arrived three days ago."

It has to be from Lucy. He snatched it out of Haley's hand and hurriedly ripped it open,

'Dearest, wait at hotel. Will be there in five-days by train[29] have wonderful news.

Love, Lucy.'

"That's tomorrow," he said aloud. "Haley, I need a room for tonight and another tomorrow for my fiancée, who arrives by train."

"That will not be a problem, Sir. And may I offer my congratulation on your pending nuptials?"

"You may, Harley. You, most certainly may." Rory couldn't recall when he had felt more joyous than at this precise moment. Then, he saw his reflection in the huge gilded-framed mirror that hung on the wall of the lobby. Stepping close, he said, "I desperately need a bath and some new clothes. Haley, would you please see to my belongings?" And without waiting for a reply, he bolted from the hotel.

Hours later, he returned bathed, shaven, and wearing a new suit complete with a bowler hat; the store clerk promised it was the latest style. Again, he stood in front of the lobby mirror, and inspected his appearance. He mumbled, "I look like a damn dude, I hope she likes it." Feeling hungry, he sauntered into the attached restaurant for an early meal.

He found a table toward the rear where he could watch the room and its entrances. Tucked in his belt under the back his coat, his Colt clunked against the chair as he sat. Nonchalantly, he slid the revolver from his back and laid it on his lap. When the waiter came, a portly man, who looked more at home behind a bar than taking food orders, Rory said, "I'll have coffee for now. What's good to eat from the menu?"

---

[29] Artistic license, the Southern Pacific Railroad service does not start until May 13, 1881—ten years later.

"Mister, anything Joe cooks is good, chose your pleasure."

"Well then," said Rory as he perused the selections. "I'll have the steak, fancy potatoes, and vegetable."

"Right away, Sir," said the waiter, and he disappeared into the kitchen. Quickly, the portly man returned with a piping hot cup of fresh brewed coffee.

Drawn by the aroma, Rory lifted the cup and sniffed, blew across the surface to cool it, and then took a sip. *This is really good ... haven't had coffee this well brewed since leaving the roost.* As he enjoyed the cup, he caught a movement in the corner of his eye. Someone stood in the shadow of the doorway to the kitchen; his hand dropped to his Colt.

A black gentleman stepped through the door. "Is that y'all, Mr. Kilchii?"

It was Joe from the roost. Rory nearly dropped his Colt when he jumped to his feet to greet his friend. "Joe, how the hell did you get here?"

"Sit back down, Mr. Kilchii, and I tells y'all about it."

"It's Rory, Joe. My real name is Rory McLeod and I'm not an outlaw."

"Back at the roost, I knowed y'all wasn't really bad. What happened to Mr. Coe and them others?"

Rory sobered. "I killed Crow, the Garcia brothers, and Coe. The Wells Fargo guards got the rest.

"I knows it's none of Joe's business, but why did y'all do that?"

Coe was self-defense, but Crow and the Garcia brothers were personal." Rory told Joe about Father Herberto .... Then I headed to South Texas in search of the other men." His expression lightened and he smiled. Now, I'm here waiting for my fiancée to arrive."

"Fiancée—you gettin' hitched, Mr. Kil—I mean, Mr. Rory?"

"Yes I am, Joe. Wait until you meet her. She's the prettiest woman west of the Mississippi—if not the whole United States."

Joe gave Rory a toothy grin. "Is that so, Mr. Rory?"

Rory realized he'd changed the subject to Lucy. "That's enough about me. Now tell me how you got here."

"Well—it was this-a-way. After y'all left, I waited two days and like you says to do, I went down to the canyon and lit out on one of Mr. Coe's horses. I stayed hid for a while, but no one came after me, so I started lookin' for work." He chuckled. "It was just like y'all said. I stopped at a ranch and offered to cook for free and if they liked it they should hires me. They liked it and I stayed for awhile."

"Then what happened?"

Joe stood. "I bees right back, Mr. Rory. Y'all is out of coffee and I wants a cup too." Ducking into the kitchen, Joe returned with a second cup and a china carafe of coffee. After freshening Rory's cup, he poured one for himself; he continued. "They treated me nice and the pay was good, but they kept tellin' me my food was twice as good as what they got in town. So I went to town and gots me a job at the restaurant. Then a fellow there tells me I should come to El Paso and cooks here. So I did. They pays me good, I gots a nice room and I gets Mondays and Tuesdays off." He nodded to the portly man serving tables. "Mr. Johnson, he cooks on them days."

"I couldn't be more pleased for you, Joe."

Joe beamed at Rory's words, and then he wiped a tear from his cheek. "I owes everythin' to y'all, Mr. Rory. If y'all ever needs somethin' just lets Joe knows and I do it—that's a promise."

"I tell you what, Joe. Fix me one of your good meals and we'll call it even."

Joe rose and started for the kitchen. At the doorway, he stopped and turned back showing a generous grin. "Y'all will eats good, Mr. Rory, buts we'll never be even." He stepped through the doorway before Rory could reply.

The next day, Rory waited at the newly constructed train station for the 10:00 train. It blew its whistle a half-mile from the station to signal its arrival. Rory stood and paced the platform; he was nervous about seeing Lucy. It had been nearly a year since he last saw her, and he had changed. Maybe she wouldn't love the man he had turned into; the killer he had become.

The whistle blew one last time as the train chugged into the station. As the train stopped, huge bellows of hissing steam clouded the platform. Finally, the conductor stepped down from the passenger car ready to aid the disembarking travelers.

Drummers with their valises were first to step down. Families, who had loved ones waiting, were next. What seemed a long period passed, and then finally, she appeared. He saw her as she stepped through the coach door and turned toward the platform. She donned the same blue dress she'd worn when they attended the play. She had added some material to make it suitable for daytime attire, but it was the same one; he was sure of it.

"Lucy," he called and waved. She saw him and waved back, but she didn't come down the steps. He moved closer to the train car before he realized that she waited for something or someone. Rory glanced into the car trying to see, but there wasn't anything; then a man stood beside her. A man on crutches they both smiled. It was E.B.

Rory rushed to the steps. Lucy leapt into his arms, and he whirled her around. E.B. called, "Children, you're making a scene." Rory sat her down and stepped back to the coach to aid the conductor, who helped E.B.

"You're walking, E.B. How—when—I mean it's wonderful, but—"

"Let me sit first and I'll tell you all about it." The conductor rolled his wheelchair towards them from the baggage car. E.B. gratefully tipped the man and sat down. "That's better."

Rory looked on, eager to hear of how his friend and mentor could now walk.

"It just happened, Rory. Kate—by the way, Kate and I are married, and—"

"Please, E.B. What about your legs?"

"Oh—yeah. Well, Kate and I were in bed and without warning, a fierce burning pain, it felt like a red-hot needle pieced my back. It was near the bullet wound scar. Then just as sudden, my legs began to tingle. They felt like they were asleep. I could feel them again. Wiggling my toes never felt so good. Kate grabbed a knitting needle and started poking me until I had to tell her to stop; she near drew blood.

"Lucy rushed out and got the doctor. He said, 'It happens that way sometimes. The nerves recover on their own, they don't understand how or why.' The only thing wrong now is my legs are weak, and I need time to strengthen them. I get around pretty good with these crutches, but soon I won't need them."

Seated next to Rory, Lucy held his arm, and quietly listened while her father told his story. She said, "It's been like teaching a baby to walk; only he's bigger." They all laughed at her joke.

"We've been five-days on the train, and my backside is plum afflicted." He chuckled and said, "You'd think all that time in this wheelchair would have toughened it up some."

The crowd, diminished, and left the three of them on the station's platform. "I suspect after all that travel you two want to get to the hotel."

Lucy asked, "Where can I get a bath?"

"You can have a tub brought to your room, but it's expensive, and it takes a while."

E.B. shook his head. "I'll go with you to the bath house, it's quicker."

Later, while they waited for Lucy to make her appearance, Rory and E.B. sat in the hotel's saloon, sipped bourbon, and talked. Rory shared the details of his hunt for the
men who kill Herberto. They wondered what they might do
with the property Rory purchased on the edge of the Territories. With that behind him, he had this last trip to make.

"There will be six Pinkerton men here the day after tomorrow. Will you wait?

"Why should I? I don't expect trouble."

E.B. clinched his jaw and Rory knew what came next
wasn't going to be pleasant. "Father Herberto didn't expect
trouble either and look where that got him. I was the one
who saw what they did before I buried him. I don't want to
take a chance something might happen." He calmed. "Besides, Lucy doesn't want to risk losing you before your wed.
She hardly slept until she received your letter and told her
it was over. I don't want to watch her go through that
again."

"But it's only a trip."

"A trip—it's 800 miles round trip through, renegade
Apaches, Mexican bandits—Cain's wasn't the only band of
Comancheros, you know."

Rory smiled. "If you were after a bounty would you take
six Pinkerton men along with you?"

The old bounty hunter's face flushed red. Rory didn't
know if it was from frustration or anger. E.B. said, "That's
different and you know it."

"I'm a reasonable man and I'll listen to a sensible argument—if you have one."

E.B. looked up and saw Lucy coming across the room.
They stood when she reached the table, and Rory moved
around to hold a chair for her. He leaned down close and
breathed the scent of her hair. He whispered, "No flower
has ever imparted a sweeter scent." His lips nibbled at her
ear, and then he said, "I love you."

Her face burned bright red with her blush. "Hush," she
said quietly. "You mustn't speak to me like that in public."

Still at her ear, he said, "Maybe later in private. I've missed you so, My Darling."

"Rory, stop that and sit down please. You're making a scene."

He stood erect and mockingly looked about. "I don't see any one who is upset with me, except you."

His grin was affable and she relented. "All right, you win. But please sit down so we can all talk—please."

Reseated, his grin intact, he innocently asked, "What shall we talk about?"

Lucy gave him a flinty stare. "You know very well what the subject is—it's your traveling alone to Santa Fe." Her voice and the flush of her cheeks rose simultaneously as she spoke. "I'll not let you go off to risk your life and leave me behind to worry myself to death." Rory's expression was now somber as he looked to E.B. "Rory," she barked. "Are you listening to me?"

He turned back to her, and in a soft but firm tone, he said, "Lucy, I heard every word you said, and I understand that you've been concerned about my safety, but lecturing me and making demands in a loud voice isn't acceptable." He stared at her expectantly and waited.

She flushed again, but this time it seemed from embarrassment. "I'm sorry, Rory. My worry is overpowering at times," she said smiling weakly. "I will calm myself, so we can talk about this rationally."

Rory looked at Lucy. "These last eight months haven't proved that I can take of myself on the trail?" Again, Rory looked to E.B. for support, or at least comment, but E.B. withheld both.

"Yes, Rory," Lucy said, "you're capable. More so than any other man I know, but I still worry. It's so unfair— I lived most of my life wondering when news of my father's death would come. Now, you ask me to live that way again—waiting for news about you. I can't do it. I just can't—"

"What would you have me do?"

"Don't go. The Catholic Church will survive without that treasure. Besides, you don't even know for sure that it remains."

"Lucy, please. Herberto died protecting that treasure for the church. How can I ignore that?"

****

Her eyes welled with tears, and she bowed her head. She had lost ... no amount of argument or pleading would dissuade Rory from undertaking this mission. She glanced at her father, but his expression offered no solace, only a helpless smile.

Turning back to Rory, she saw his pleading face and burst into tears, stood, and ran from the saloon to her room.

In her room, she fell across the bed and sobbed great desperate tears. She would lose Rory to this country—if not now, surely in the future, and she didn't see how she could live with that. To save her sanity, she would give him up and start her life anew. "Lucy, may I come in?" It was her father's voice.

"Yes, father." She rose from the bed and went to the washstand to wipe away tear streaks from her cheeks.

It was still awkward for him to get around with the crutches, but he managed to enter her room and make it to a chair. "Lucy, you must understand that Rory has to do this thing, or he will never be able to move forward with you to build a life together—don't you see?"

"I don't—" She felt herself getting angry again and stopped talking.

"He made this commitment before he met you. His honoring this vow speaks to the kind of man Rory is. I think it would be most important to woman considering marriage."

Finally, a smile came to Lucy's face. "I should have you run the store. You're a better salesman than me. Father, I think I understand, but after you came home, and the worry lifted and then loving Rory—I've been so happy. How can I possibly go back to living that old way of life—just existing?" She felt exhausted and went to her bed. Lying back, she threw her arm over her face. "Father, what can I do?"

E.B. stood without his crutches, and he staggered to the edge of bed. He sat on the bed, took her free hand in his and patted the back, and said, "There, there, dear—I'm sure we can come up with somethin'. Say, I have an idea. Why don't we all make the journey? If we take a wagon, I'll do fine. In fact the exercise will do me good."

Lucy sat up quickly. "Oh, Father, do you really think he will let us go?"

Chuckling, E.B. said, "I don't see how he can stop us. I know where he's goin'. If we have to we'll follow until he sees that we're determined."

She threw her arms around his neck. "Father, I love you."

Chapter 25

"Absolutely not," said Rory. It's too dangerous." Lucy and E.B. sat on the side of Rory's bed and watched him pace the floor. Rory scowled; he noticed Lucy seemed to enjoy their discord. E.B., now reclined, appeared to have only a casual interest.

"Well, now you know how I feel," said Lucy, "I intend to go regardless of what you say. And, if you're afraid for my safety—too bad."

"Damn it, E.B., don't you have anything to say about Lucy's intentions?"

E.B. smiled. "I wonder how much trouble it will be to rig a hammock in the back of the wagon. That way, I can rest when I need to without having to stop." He turned to Lucy and winked, and said, "That's a good idea, don't you think?"

"That's not what I meant, and you damn well know it." Rory saw he was hog-tied, and he fumed.

Lucy rose from the bed, stepped in close to Rory, and pecked a kiss on his cheek. "I'm so glad to have this resolved. It will take a few days to make arrangements, but we'll be ready in time for your planned departure." She exited the room leaving Rory and E.B. to talk.

"This was your idea—don't bother to deny it." The laughter that shone in his friend's eyes infuriated Rory; his scowl at E.B. was dark and angry.

"To the contrary, I thought it was a stroke of genius. You can't stop us from going, and since you love Lucy, you won't let her go without you. Pure genius, I'd say."

"You've boxed me in tight; I'll give you that much. But, E.B., it could be dangerous and anything could happen along the way. If anyone should understand, it's you."

E.B. re-situated the pillow against the head-frame and reclined again. Rory watched as his mentor rubbed his chin in contemplation. He looked up at Rory, his face lit with pleasure. "I have an even better idea. Why don't you marry Lucy, and when we reached Santa Fe you two can take the train to San Francisco for your honeymoon?"

Rory opened his mouth to rebut, but could think of nothing further to say. He paced for a few seconds. "Aw, I'm hungry," he said, "let's get Lucy and have something to eat."

In the hotel dining room, the portly man sat them near the kitchen. Joe came out from the kitchen to meet Lucy and E.B. "Y'all is a lovely girl, Miss Lucy. Ways too purdy for a ugly young man like Mr. Kilchii—I means Rory." He shook his head. "I just ain't use to Mr. Kilchii's new name, buts I'll gets it soon enough, don't y'all worry none, Mr. Rory."

"You're too gracious, Joe." She looked at Rory and smiled. "You're right though. He is ugly—,but I plan to marry him anyway."

Her smile gave Rory a warm feeling. So he took the tease in stride. "A man's looks aren't that important," he said.

Lucy laughed. "Maybe not to other men—"

They drank champagne with their meal, thus they were in good spirits when they retired to their rooms. Rory escorted Lucy to her door. "Your father made a suggestion to me earlier. I've decided it was a good idea. Why don't we get married tomorrow, and from Santa Fe, we'll go to Frisco for our honeymoon?"

"Rory, I hoped for a big wedding at our church back home, and what about our—my friends?"

He gathered her into his arms and lifted her from the floor, and kissed her passionately. He lowered her, and stepped back so he could see her face. "Why can't we do both? I can't imagine why your friends would object."

She hesitated only a second. "I will. Let's wake father and tell him the good news."

The ceremony was a perfunctory affair, with Joe as the best man and witness. When the Justice of the Peace asked Joe for his last name, he didn't respond. "I need your last name as witness to these proceedings. Now tell me your last name."

"Joe ain't gots no last name, Sur."

Rory pulled Joe aside. "Joe, most ex-slaves usually take their former master's last name. Do you remember his name?"

"Yes, I does, Mr. Rory, buts I don't want nothin' to do with that man."

"Fair enough, how have you been called since your escape?"

"Black Joe is how they calls me."

Rory considered, and then smiled. "How about we turn that around."

"Mr. Rory?"

Sticking out his hand, Rory said, "I'm pleased to make your acquaintance Mr. Joseph Black."

At first, he didn't understand, and then Joe grinned; his face beamed with a newfound pride. He stepped back to the desk and said, "Sur, my name is Mr. Joseph Black.

The Justice smiled. "That'll do fine. Can you write—if not you can make your mark and I'll witness it."

Joe took the offered pen and carefully drew the outline of a frying pan with three vertical lines above it. The Justice studied the mark and asked, "What are those lines?"

"That's the smell-good comin' from my skillet—that's what that is. I's a cook, a good cook, too. Can'ts have a fryin' pan without smell goods."

The Justice reared back in his chair and patted his stomach. "I for one can certainly attest to that. I've put on twenty pounds since you started cooking for the hotel." They all chuckled.

It was Lucy's father who reminded everyone why they were there. Twenty-minutes later, Rory and Lucy was wed. They held a small reception party in the hotel. A cake made special by Joe's hands was the centerpiece on the table of food in a room just off the lobby.

When the party began to wind down, Haley approached. He handed Rory a room key. "Mr. Parker has reserved the Bridal Suite for you, and I've taken the liberty of having your belongings moved."

Rory and Lucy turned to E.B., who held his glass high and smiled. After, he wiped a tear from his cheek, he knocked back his drank and threw the glass into the fireplace; the other guests followed suit. The newlyweds retired early ....

When Lucy and Rory came down the next morning, they found E.B. getting around in his chair. Rory suspected the reason, but asked anyway, "Why the chair?"

E.B. moaned as he raised his head to look at Rory. "Too much champagne; that stuff's worse than any whiskey I've ever drunk. Right now, there's doubt if I'll ever walk again, assuming I survive this hangover."

Rory stepped behind the wheelchair, and said, "What you need is breakfast. Joe's cooking will do the trick." E.B. moaned again as Rory whirled the chair and pushed him into the dining room.

By noontime, E.B. was back to on his crutches walking around. He'd purchased a wagon, and a team of mules to pull it. E.B. spent the day at the blacksmith's shop to direct the modification to the wagon for his comfort. Tomorrow morning early, they planned to start their journey to return to the campsite where E.B. first encountered Rory.

Except to come down for food and drink, Rory and Lucy kept to their room until the next morning. A knock sounded at their door, it was E.B. He called through the door, "Come on you two; we're burning daylight."

"Give us a few minutes," said Rory. "We'll be down shortly."

Over an hour later, they came down to find E.B. drinking coffee, obviously having already eaten. "What's been keeping you two?"

Lucy noted the glint of her father's stare, and the impish expression on his face, she blushed.

Rory said, "We had to pack our things. The luggage is being brought down now, and as soon as we eat we'll be ready to leave."

****

That night, the stars sparkled in the clear moonless night. Joe sat on a crate in the alley behind the El Paso International Hotel smoking his corncob pipe. He would miss Mr. Rory and his kin. Good things happened to him when Mr. Rory was around; he now had a real name: Mr. Joseph Black. He chuckled and spoke his thoughts aloud, "Don't that just beat all."

"What are you talkin' about, Joe?"

Startled, Joe slid off the crate and stood to face the voice, but saw only shadows and darkness beyond. Starlight flickered off something shiny. Then, he heard the distinctive click, click of a revolver's cylinder rotating as its hammer cocked. "Who's dat talkin'?"

"Why, Joe. My feelin's are hurt. Don't you remember me?" The man stepped forward into the light of Joe's lantern.

Joe stared, mouth ajar. Finally, he spoke, "Mr. Coe, y'all is supposed to be dead."

A menacing smile crossed Coe's face. "Now tell me, Joe. Who told you I was dead?"

Rory had told him that Coe was dead; killed during the attempted stage holdup. He decided to lie, "I heer'd it from from peoples talkin' abouts the U S Army attackin' the roost, and y'all was kilt dead."

"So you wasn't there when the Army attacked? They dynamited the fortress, burned down all the out-building— even the grass. They stole all my cattle and horses and set explosives to the canyon, blowin' it to hell. I had to skinny up the back-way in to see what they'd done."

Coe stared at Joe, but Joe didn't react. Coe asked, "Joe, who told you to leave afore the Army got there?"

"I don't knows whats y'all is talkin' abouts."

Coe leaned in, and asked, "Was it Rory McLeod?"

Joe's brow lifted as his eyes widened.

"Yes, Joe, I know who he is, and that he just got married."

From the hotel doorway, someone called, "Joe, you out there?"

Coe turned his head slightly to look, and Joe took his chance. He flung his lantern at Coe. It fell at Coe's feet breaking the glass and spilled the coal oil. Flames leaped up and onto the front of Coe's trousers causing him to jump back. He whipped off his hat and beat out the flames before they could take hold.

Joe did not hesitate, he bolted down the alley, away from the hotel, and Coe. He didn't stop until he reached the livery where he kept his horse and saddle. Saddling the black mare, and without water or supplies, he rode fast out of town, westward in pursuit of Mr. Rory.

****

Rory watched Lucy move about the camp. She wore men's trousers for practicality, but he found her attire erotic. He wondered if it was really her clothes, or the fact they were newlyweds.

With coffee brewing and the smell of bacon frying, E.B. finally stirred. He called, "Is breakfast ready?"

"Nearly," said Rory, "you'd better get down here and do your morning business if you don't want to eat it cold."

E.B. left the wagon and hobbled off into the tall grass dragging his crutches behind. He returned to the wagon's water barrel, and splashed cold-water on his face. When he'd settled near the campfire, Lucy offered him a tin cup filled with hot coffee. "Hmm, this smells good," he said with both hands clasped around the tin to warm his hands.

Rory stood, moved to his saddle, grabbed his rifle, and levered a round. He cocked his ear eastward and listened. "Someone's headed this way and they're riding fast."

E.B. rose and used his crutches to get to the wagon quickly. "Lucy, take cover behind the wagon." He yanked his rifle free of its boot and he joined Rory. They waited.

The sound of the horse slowed as it neared the camp. "Mr. Rory, is dat y'all yonder in the camp?"

Rory relaxed and lowered the hammer on his carbine. "Yes, Joe, ride on in."

Joe walked his horse into the camp. Rory and E.B. held their rifles and Miss Lucy stepped from behind the wagon with a pistol in hand. "Whew-whee, I is shore glad I called out afore comin' into camp." He chuckled, "I'd be plum full of holes if I didn't."

Lucy, said, "Joe, you're always welcome. Please come and sit—here's coffee, and I'll fix you a bite to eat."

"Just coffee, Miss Lucy. Ain't no time for nothin' else." He looked around for Rory, who with E.B. was attending to Joe's horse. Joe walked to them, and in a low voice, he said, "Mr. Rory, I gots some troublesome news. Mr. Coe's alive, and he's lookin' to gets you for what you caused to be done at the roost."

"What on earth are you talking about, Joe? I put a fifty-caliber bullet through the center of Coe's chest. If that didn't kill him, I'm positive the guards did."

"I don't knows how, but he's alive. He was at the hotels and meant to kills me, but I gots away afore he could shoot. He knows y'all's real name and that y'all is hitched and everythin'."

"Joe, he said he was out to kill me?"

"Not 'xactly, but that's what he meant—I know it for sure. Y'all gots to believes Joe."

E.B. said, "We do, Joe. Do you have any idea if he's alone or does he have a gang?"

"I didn't sees no one, but Mr. Coe never goes it by his self."

"Rory, you've been around the man, what do you think?"

"I think Joe is correct. Coe's not much on his own, but give him a couple of back-shooters, and he's daring enough." Rory looked at Lucy, concern written on his face. "Here's what we'll do. E.B., you, and Joe lead off with the wagon. I'll hang back and watch our trail. If they come, I'll bring warning and we can get ready."

Lucy asked, "What about at night?"

"We'll take turns on guard," Rory assured her. "They won't catch us unprepared." He paused to consider. "Most everyone in El Paso thinks we're going to Santa Fe to catch the train for San Francisco for our honeymoon. With luck, we'll reach the turn off to Tucson before they catch up. Maybe they'll miss us and give up."

Rory looked at E.B., who subtly shook his head, which confirmed he understood that what he said was for Lucy's sake, and that they needed to stay on guard.

So it began; a routine that transpired over the next eight-days. On the eighth day, they traveled along a dusty trail and around a bend, to arrive at the stage-line's way station.

As they rolled up to the way station, Higgins, the sole occupant, came outside to greet them. "I'll be damned—is that you E.B.?" He looked to Rory and studied him intense- ly. "Why you're the young apprentice. Damn near didn't recognize you without your moccasins. You're all welcome— come in for some grub and snort." As Lucy climbed down from the wagon box, Higgins said loudly, "You're a wom- an—I'll be damn."

Lucy hopped down and turned to face the old-timer. "Thank you for noticing." She offered her hand to Higgins; he rushed to take it, but not before he rubbed his on the leg of his pants. Lucy said, "I'm Mrs. Rory McLeod, but please. Just call me Lucy."

"Yes, Ma'am." Higgins still held her hand, and looked up at E.B. "Say, is this your daughter Lucy that you're al- ways goin' on about?"

"I'm the one," she said. She smiled up to her father.

Coming up the rear, Joe dismounted and walked over to help E.B. down from the wagon. Rory said, "Mr. Higgins, let me introduce you to Mr. Joseph Black, Joe to his friends."

Joe gave Higgins a toothy grin; he nodded to the old man. "Pleased to meets y'all."

Higgins saw E.B. with his crutches. "What have you gone and done to yourself, E.B.?"

"Bush-wacked close to year ago—just recently got back the use of my legs. Let's get inside where I can sit and I'll tell you all the gory details."

"You bet," said Higgins excitement in his voice, and he helped E.B. inside to a chair.

With everyone settled, Rory, with Joe in tow, came to E.B. "Here's what I propose. You and Lucy remain with Higgins. Joe and I will go back to find Coe and deal with him."

"He's goin' to have several men with him; there'll be just the two of you."

"Three, if you count the Sharps. I'll take him at a distance. If any of his gang wants to take issue with me, I'll
give them the same."

E.B. smiled. "I've heard them words spoke before." E.B.
scratched at his beard as he considered their option. "Yeah,
I agree it's the best plan. Lucy will be safe here, beside it's
you and Joe he's after."

"We'll head out after dusk," said Rory. "I'll tell Lucy
we're going out to scout our back trail." With that, Rory
went to be with his bride.

"Shall I give you a tour of the way-station, Mrs.
McLeod?"

Lucy smiled, rose from the table, and they walked outside to be alone.

As the sun's fire dimmed on the horizon, Rory and Joe
mounted up and slowly rode eastward along the road they'd
just traveled. They rode in silence with their long guns
perched on hips ready, to swing into action. Two hours east,
still a moonless sky, Rory smelled the smoke. He signaled
Joe to halt, and swung down from his horse handing the
reins to Joe.

"Joe, you stay with the horses and keep them quiet
while I scouted their camp."

Joe nodded. Rory slipped away into the night—his moc-
casin-covered feet moved soundlessly. As the scent of burning wood grew stronger, Rory heard the hum of conversation and stepped more carefully. Soon, he saw the orange
glow of their campfire. Closer still, he saw Coe setting apart
from six men. They passed a bottle and joked about catch-
ing their prey on the morrow.

Damn, I left the Sharps with Joe. Rory's aim was good
enough to hit Coe with a shot from his Colt, but he wanted
to make sure. He decided to wait—it wasn't long. The men
finished the bottle and one by one stumbled off to their bedrolls for a sound sleep. Only Coe remained awake.

Wrapped with a blanket, Coe seemed dazed as he stared into the fire. Rory circled their camp and positioned himself behind Coe. He slowed his breathing and crept stealthily upon his victim. A few yards distance between them, and Coe leapt to feet and whirled around. Beneath his blanket, he held a double-barreled shotgun, and he pulled both triggers.

Blinded by the flash and deafened by the blast, only Rory's quickness saved his life. As Coe rose, Rory's instinct told him it was a trap, and he dived for the cover of the scrub trees. Even so, buckshots struck his left leg and butt, not life threatening, but painful.

"You're hit," screamed Coe. "I know I got you. Show yourself and I'll make it a clean end." The blanket piled at his feet, Coe hunched forward and squinted at the darkness to find Rory. He broke the shotgun's breech and fumbled with replacement shells. "You coward, stand and fight me."

By the time Coe's men were fully aware of what had happened and prepared to do something, Rory was back at the horses. Joe said, "I thought y'all was a goner, Mr. Rory."

"He nearly got me, Joe, but I ducked in time—let's ride."

Back at the way station, Lucy paced the floor. When the door burst opened and Rory stepped through, she rushed to embrace him, but stopped when she saw blood. "Oh, Rory, you've been hurt." With Joe on one side and her on the other, they helped Rory to the table and chairs.

E.B. assessed his condition. "Lay him face down on the table and skin his trousers off. Lucy started to roll him over, but Joe pushed her aside with a knife in his hand. Carefully, but deftly, he peeled away the back of Rory's trousers exposing his wounded leg and butt. Rory asked, "How bad is it, E.B.?"

"I count three. Judging the size of the holes, it was .0 or .00 buckshot. You're lucky he nearly missed. Your trousers have holes where the pellets punched through. I have to make sure the cloth comes out with the pellet."

"Missed hell—lucky I dived when he stood. It was a trap and like a damned fool, I walked right into it. I should have stayed with my original plan."

E.B. found Rory's medical kit and went to work. The wounds were in the dense muscles of his leg and butt, but none had penetrated deeply. E.B. probed carefully and successfully extracted the shots. He inspected each shot to ensure the cloth remained pasted to the dull-gray balls. Lucy stood fast; she held the lamp and assisted her father as needed.

When the surgery was over, she bound Rory's wounds and helped him dress into fresh clothing. He rested on a pallet before the fire. The warmth soothed his aches; he gave way to exhaustion, and Rory drifted off to a sound sleep—the last thing he heard. "I guess I've been displaced from my hammock." He tried to laugh.

Chapter 26

Lucy sat near Rory and watched him sleep until she was satisfied that he rested comfortably. She was tired, but too keyed-up to rest. E.B. and Higgins played cards, talked, and sipped whiskey, while Joe tended to the horses. Unnoticed, she rose and walked through the station's door, closing it quietly behind her. It was a beautiful night, and she needed fresh air to clear her head.

As she walked away from the cabin, her thoughts focused. Lucy hadn't been to church for many weeks now, and she missed the solace that praying there gave her. Then it occurred to her that God was everywhere, so she knelt by a rock, using it as an altar; she prayed aloud. "God, I know it's wrong, but I'm beginning to hate Father Herberto. He and that treasure have almost gotten Rory killed and now this trip to recover it for the church seems—"

A calloused hand clamped over her mouth and pulled her into the brush. Pushed to the ground on her back, the stranger who pinned her was filthy and smelled of sweat; human and horse. His knife to the side of her throat; her tender skin could sense the blade's razor-sharp edge. "Scream and you're dead—do you understand?"

Lucy stared, her eyes wide with fear. Slowly, she nodded, and he removed his hand—but not the knife. She whispered, "My husband, and my father are inside."

The man smiled. "I know—it's your husband I'm after."

At the mention of Rory, a lump formed in her throat and her eyes searched his face. The man must have seen the change in her expression, and he put pressure on the blade. "They would never hear the scream. You'd die for no-thin'."

Her expression hardened and she raise her upper lip in a cold sneer. "My father is E.B. Parker. If you harm either my husband or me, he'll hunt you down like a rabid dog."

The man chuckled. "Then I'll have to make sure they're both dead." Her resolve waned and she couldn't hide it. The man said, "You talked about a treasure when you was prayin'—tell me about it. Maybe I'll consider a trade."

Her mind began to work. *He wants the treasure, but will he leave Rory alone once he has it? I have to try.* She said, "I don't have all the details, but the treasure is gold and silver ingots, and precious stones placed into Indian jewelry. It's hidden less than two days ride west."

He yanked her to her feet, held her in front of him, and they walked toward the cabin. With the knife firmly held to her throat, he whispered, "Now you can scream." She clinched her jaw; the man could feel her muscles working against his arm. "No matter," he said. I'll do the honors. He called, "Kilchii, it's Coe, and I've got your woman. Come out so we can talk."

Lucy yelled, "No, Rory, it's a trap."

****

Though wounded and exhausted, Rory jerked at the sound of Lucy's voice. When he tried to jump up, his injured left side gave way and he collapsed on the floor. E.B. scrambled for his crutches, and with the help of Higgins, got to his feet. They both helped Rory stand and the three went to the door.

E.B. said, "Wait! Lucy's right—it's a trap. It'll do her no good if we rush out and get killed."

Higgins nodded.

Rory wiped the cold sweat from his face. "How do we handle it?"

"I'll do the talkin'," said E.B., and he hobbled to one of the shuttered windows. Opening it partially, he called, "Coe, this E.B. Parker. Do you know who I am and what I can do?"

"I heard of ya."

"Here's my offer. Release the girl and be on your way and I'll not come after you."

"You take me for a fool, Parker. If I released your daughter, you'd kill me sure."

E.B. gripped the handholds of his crutches, through clinched teeth, he said, "If you harm my daughter in any way— " Fear for Lucy's life tamped his rising anger; he exhaled slowly flexing his finger. At length, he asked, "What do you want?"

"That's better," Coe sneered, "I want the treasure."

E.B. and Rory looked at each other. "Lucy must have told him," said E.B. "Naively thinkin' he'd settle for that."

Rory nodded. "Well, he's welcome to it if he lets Lucy go—unharmed." He glanced around the room. "Where's Joe?"

Higgins and E.B. scanned the room as well. Higgins shrugged and E.B. said, "He must still be out with the horses. If he's not dead, we've got an ace in the hole."

Rory considered, "Joe's careful, and he's capable. If he's dead we'd have heard the noise of the fight."

E.B. turned back to the window, and said, "The treasure's not here. Its hidden two-days ride from here. So, how do you propose we make the exchange?"

Coe hesitated. In Lucy's ear, he whispered, "That true?"

"Yes," she said, "West of here, but I don't know where."

E.B. called, "What's it to be, Coe?"

"Simple, I hold onto the girl and you two go for the treasure. You bring it back here and we make the swap."

Rory shook his head. "I don't trust Coe. One of us has to stay to make sure she remains unharmed."

E.B. nodded. "I don't know where the treasure's hidden, so you'll have to be the one that goes." He looked down at his crutches and added, "Besides, you're the only one fit enough to ride."

"If that what it's got to be," said Rory, "but I know Coe; he won't honor the deal. He'll still kill Lucy and us if he can."

E.B. stroked his chin as he considered their options. He leaned out the window. "Unacceptable," E.B. yelled. "I'll stay here with you and Lucy while Rory goes for the treasure. That way, you'll have two hostages."

Coe paused only briefly. "Agreed," said Coe. "We'll wait till daylight, but nothin' happens till I say. Is that clear? Nothin—"

E.B. brow pinched and he turned to Rory. "What's so important about waitin' til daylight?"

Rory shrugged at first, and then his eye gleamed with understanding. "He's alone. His men were too drunk to ride. They won't come after him until they've had time to sober up."

E.B. smiled at Rory. We've got time to use our ace in the hole." He faced the window, and called, "Alright; we'll do as you say, but if you harm Lucy—"

"Don't worry old man." Coe laughed. "She's too young and too skinny for my tastes."

Rory turned to Higgins, and asked, "Is there another way out of here?"

They saw the sympathy on the old man's face and knew the answer before he spoke. "I'm sorry, Son. That door and them two windows and there's a gun-port over lookin' the coral. We built 'er to hole up in, not sneak out of."

Rory picked up a lamp. "Show me the gun port."

Higgins led him to what appeared to be a storage room. On the wall to the formed part of the coral was a heavy wood panel two-foot tall and six-inches wide—too small to crawl through. Rory removed the panel and passed the lamp back and forth across the opening. "Is that y'all, Mr. Rory?"

"Yes, Joe, it's me. Do you understand what's happened?"

"Yes, Sur, Mr. Rory, I been watching from the coral. Mr. Coe gots hold of Miss Lucy and y'all gots to trade a treasure to gets her back."

"That's correct, Joe."

"Mr. Rory, I don't trusts Mr. Coe. He might not hurts Miss Lucy, but he's goin' to kills y'all if he can."

"I agree, Joe," said Rory; then he paused to collect his thoughts. "Joe, Coe's men were drunk when I went after Coe at his camp. I think he's alone, do you know?"

"Yes, Sur, he's alone—exceptin' for Miss Lucy."

Rory nodded, and held the lamp high so he could see Joe's eyes. "Do you have a weapon out there?"

"No, Sur, I don't. I just come out here to tends to the horses and then all hell broke loose."

Rory turned to E.B., who nodded agreement and said, "Higgins, get my carbine."

The old man hustled away and returned with Parker's .45 Winchester. "Here ya go, Son."

Rory took the rifle levered a round into the chamber, lowered the hammer, and then passed it through the gun port to Joe. "Do you think you can kill Coe?"

Joe averted his eyes from Rory. "I don't rightly knows, Mr. Rory, but I is willin' to try."

"You can't try, Joe," decried Rory. "You've got to kill Coe with your first shot or he'll kill you and maybe Lucy and me. Do you understand, Joe?"

"Yes, Sur, I do. I won't lets nothin' happens to y'all and Miss Lucy. Y'all gots Joe's word."

"Okay, Joe," said Rory, "here's my plan. Coe won't want to shoot me until I've gotten him the treasure, so I'll go out front and draw his attention. When you've got a clear shot—kill him."

Joe swallowed hard. "I ain't never kilts no one afore—God gives me strength."

"It'll be alright, Joe," said Rory trying to sound reassuring. E.B. and Higgins stood behind Rory, and both nodded.

"I needs a little time to gets outs there behind Mr. Coe, so I can gets a clean shot."

"I think I can keep him distracted—" Rory studied his watch, "—for five-minutes. Will that be long enough for you to circle around and get into position?

Joe nodded, his grim expression and set jaw was somehow comforting to Rory. "Okay then, let's do it."

With one of E.B.'s crutches, Rory stood at the door and collected his thoughts. He had to keep Coe occupied for at least five-minutes and somehow get him to expose himself to Joe's rifle. He swung the door open and called. "Coe, I'm coming out and I'm unarmed." He held the lamp high, so that Coe could see him.

"It's not daylight yet and I haven't said you could come out."

"We need to talk," said Rory, his voice firm to dissuade discussion.

"What about?"

Rory could tell by the subtle changes in the way Coe's voice carried that he moved about. "I want to know that Lucy is alright."

"Your woman's fine. I've got her tied up and she's not goin' anywhere until you get me that treasure."

"That's not good enough," said Rory and with the aid of E.B.'s crutch, he began hobbling towards the sound of Coe's voice. "I want to see for myself that you've not hurt her." Rory drifted right towards the coral and clear of the opened doorway. Hidden in the shadows of the cabin, E.B. sat at a table with Rory's carbine—hoping for an unobstructed shot.

"Stop right there. I'd rather have the treasure, but I'll settle for killin' you if you make me."

"I'm unarmed, Coe. Rory slowly turned around with the lamp held high over his head, so Coe could see he was indeed unarmed.

"How stupid do you think I'm? You draw me out from cover and Parker shoots me. You call back and tell 'em to close the doors and windows."

"You heard him, Higgins, close them." Rory didn't look, but he heard the door swing shut and the cross bar dropped into the place. "Are you satisfied now? I want to see my wife."

There was movement to his left; he looked down. Behind a cropping of low rocks laid Coe with a rifle aimed at him. "Move to your left and stay between me and the cabin."

Rory did as instructed. Coe stood, but he kept his rifle aimed at his chest. "Walk toward me, slowly, and keep that lamp held where I can see you."

The light from the lamp shone on Coe's boots. With every step, the light exposed more of Coe. When they stood less than six-feet apart, Coe's face emerged from the shadows.

"I ought to kill you right now for what you done. Why'd you do it?"

"I was after Crow and the Garcia brothers."

"Why? There weren't no bounty on them to speak of."

"It was personal. They killed a priest; he was a friend of mind."

"Okay, but why'd you shoot me?"

Rory chuckled. "So we wouldn't be having this discussion."

"You didn't do the—"

Coe's head suddenly twitched. Nearly at the same instant, they heard the report of the Winchester as it echoed
through the hills. Coe collapsed to the ground. It was as if
someone cut the strings of a marionette. The slug must
have severed his spinal cord. His mouth moved, but no
sound came out and his body went limp. His eyes focused
on Rory, first confusion and then hatred. Joe levered
another round, but no need. Coe's expression became placid
and his eyes vacant.

It was over. Rory dropped the crutch and hopped
passed Coe's body to Lucy. The cabin door swung open; E.B.
stepped out ready to shoot, but when he saw Coe down, he
started toward Rory and Lucy. Only Joe remained at his
position.

****

Eight months later, Rory and Lucy stood on the porch
of the Circle-K horse ranch; the land he'd purchased from
Betty Henighan and her two sons. That's where they decided to live on returning from delivering the treasure to
the dioceses; and going on their honeymoon.

They'd started to rebuild. A fresh coat of White paint
and a roof for the house was their first order of business.
The bunkhouse was demolished and a replacement under
construction. Beyond were the new barn and corrals. It was
the beginning of their dream plan for their lives.

The ranch hand returned from town, along with their
supplies, he brought the mail. Rory passed the letter from
her father,

'Children,
All is well here at the mercantile. Kate keeps the books,
Joe manages the store, and he has turned out to be quite
the salesman. The men respect him, the women adore him,
and the children love him. The room over the carriage shed
is completed and he says he's comfortable there.

I've put my crutches up for sale in the store, as I haven't needed them for some time now. We have refitted the carriage to its original purpose, and Joes uses it for deliveries. Before I forget, he has been spending time with a widow woman, who cooks for Mrs. Jarvis. I wouldn't be surprised to see them wed.

How is married life treating you two? Is there any news regarding grandchildren? Kate is inquiring and I guess I want to know as well.

Your loving father,

E.B.'

Lucy smiled at Rory and tenderly rubbed her swollen belly. She asked, "Should we tell them?"

END

A word from the publisher:

Thank you for reading 'Kilchii'. If you enjoyed this tale of the old west, then do please post a review at your website of purchase, or anywhere online that you may prefer.

Alternately, recommended the book to a friend. New authors and small independent publishers really need the support of readers like you to continue.

Again thank you,

The gang at Gunsmoke Publishing